V.C. Andrews® Books

The Dollanganger Family Series
Flowers in the Attic
Petals on the Wind
If There Be Thorns
Seeds of Yesterday
Garden of Shadows

The Casteel Family Series
Heaven
Dark Angel
Fallen Hearts
Gates of Paradise
Web of Dreams

The Cutler Family Series
Dawn
Secrets of the Morning
Twilight's Child
Midnight Whispers
Darkest Hour

The Landry Family Series
Ruby
Pearl in the Mist
All That Glitters
Hidden Jewel
Tarnished Gold

The Logan Family Series
Melody
Heart Song
Unfinished Symphony
Music in the Night
Olivia

The Orphans Miniseries
Butterfly
Crystal
Brooke
Raven
Runaways (full-length novel)

The Wildflowers Miniseries
Misty
Star
Jade
Cat
Into the Garden (full-length novel)

The Hudson Family Series
Rain
Lightning Strikes
Eye of the Storm
The End of the Rainbow

The Shooting Stars Series
Cinnamon
Ice
Rose
Honey
Falling Stars

The De Beers Family Series
Willow
Wicked Forest
Twisted Roots
Into the Woods
Hidden Leaves

The Broken Wings Series
Broken Wings
Midnight Flight

The Gemini Series
Celeste
Black Cat
Child of Darkness

The Shadows Series
April Shadows
Girl in the Shadows

The Early Spring Series
Broken Flower
Scattered Leaves

The Secret Series
Secrets in the Attic
Secrets in the Shadows

The Delia Series
Delia's Crossing
Delia's Heart
Delia's Gift

The Heavenstone Series
The Heavenstone Secrets
Secret Whispers

The March Family Series
Family Storms
Cloudburst

The Kindred Series
Daughter of Darkness
Daughter of Light

Stand-alone Novels
My Sweet Audrina
Into the Darkness
Capturing Angels

V.C. ANDREWS®

Forbidden Sister

G

GALLERY BOOKS

New York   London   Toronto   Sydney   New Delhi

G

Gallery Books
A Division of Simon & Schuster, Inc.
1230 Avenue of the Americas
New York, NY 10020

Following the death of Virginia Andrews, the Andrews family
worked with a carefully selected writer to organize and complete
Virginia Andrews' stories and to create additional novels,
of which this is one, inspired by her storytelling genius.

First Gallery Books hardcover edition February 2013

V.C. ANDREWS® and VIRGINIA ANDREWS® are registered
trademarks of the Vanda General Partnership

GALLERY BOOKS and colophon are registered trademarks of
Simon & Schuster, Inc.

For information about special discounts for bulk purchases,
please contact Simon & Schuster Special Sales at
1-866-506-1949 or business@simonandschuster.com.

The Simon & Schuster Speakers Bureau can bring authors to
your live event. For more information or to book an event
contact the Simon & Schuster Speakers Bureau at 1-866-248-3049
or visit our website at www.simonspeakers.com.

Designed by Leydiana Rodríguez-Ovalles

Manufactured in the United States of America

Library of Congress Cataloging-in-Publication Data

Andrews, V. C. (Virginia C.)
The Forbidden Sister / V.C. Andrews.—First Gallery Books hardcover
    edition.
        pages cm
    1. Sisters—Fiction. 2. Family secrets—Fiction. 3. Psychological
fiction. I. Title.
PS3551.N454F67 2013
813.54—dc23   2012041927

10 9 8 7 6 5 4 3 2 1

ISBN 978-1-4391-5506-6
ISBN 978-1-4391-8117-1 (ebook)

Prologue

My mother wasn't supposed to have me. She wasn't supposed to get pregnant again.

Nearly nine years before I was born, she gave birth to my sister, Roxy. Her pregnancy with Roxy was very difficult, and when my mother's water broke and she was rushed to the hospital, Roxy resisted coming into the world. My mother says she fought being born. An emergency cesarean was conducted, and my mother nearly died. She fell into a coma for almost three days, and after she regained consciousness, the first thing her doctor told her was to never get pregnant again.

When I first heard and understood this story, I immediately thought that I must have been an accident. Why else would they have had another child after so many years had passed? She and Papa surely had agreed with the doctor that it was dangerous for her to get pregnant again. Mama could see that thought and concern in my face whenever we talked about it, and she always assured me that I wasn't a mistake.

"Your father wanted you even more than I did," she told me, but just thinking about it made me wonder about children who are planned and those who are not. Do parents treat children they didn't plan any differently from the way they treat the planned ones? Do they love them any less?

I know there are single mothers who give away their children immediately because they can't manage them or they don't want to begin a loving relationship they know will not last. Some don't want to set eyes on them. When their children find out that they were given away, do they think about the fact that their mothers really didn't want them to be born? How could they help but think about it? That certainly can't be helpful to their self-confidence.

Despite my mother's assurances, I couldn't help wondering. If I weren't planned, was my soul floating around somewhere minding its own business and then suddenly plucked out of a cloud of souls and ordered to get into my body as it was forming in Mama's womb? Was birth an even bigger surprise for unplanned babies? Maybe that was what really happened in Roxy's case. Maybe she wasn't planned, and that was why she resisted.

Wondering about myself always led me to wonder about Roxy. What sort of a shock was it for her when she first heard she was going to have a sister, after having been an only child all those years? She must have known Mama wasn't supposed to have me. Did she feel very special because of that? Did she see herself as their precious golden child, the only one Mama and Papa could have? And then, when Mama told her about her new pregnancy, did Roxy pout and sulk, thinking she would have to share our parents' attention and love? Share her throne? Was she worried that she would have to help take care of me and that it would cut into her fun time? Although I didn't know how she felt about me for some time, from the little I remember about her, I had the impression that I was at least an inconvenience to her. Maybe my being born was the real reason Roxy became so rebellious.

My mother told me that my father believed her complications in giving birth to Roxy were God's first warning about her. However, despite her difficult birth, there was nothing physically wrong with Roxy. She began exceptionally beautiful and is to this day, but according to Mama, even when Roxy was an infant, she was headstrong and rebellious. She ate when she wanted to eat, no matter what my mother prepared for her or how she tried to get her to eat, and she slept when she wanted to sleep. Rocking her or singing to her didn't work. My mother told me my father would get into a rage about it. Finally, he insisted she take Roxy to the doctor. She did, but the doctor concluded that there was absolutely nothing wrong with Roxy. My father ordered her to find another doctor. The result was the same.

Roxy's tantrums continued until my mother finally gave in and slept when Roxy wanted to sleep. She even ate when Roxy wanted to eat, leaving my father to eat alone often.

"If I didn't eat with her, she wouldn't eat, or she'd

take hours to do so," my mother said. "Your father thought she was being spiteful even when she was an infant."

According to how my mother described all this to me, Roxy's tantrums spread to everything she did and everything that was done with her or for her. My father complained to my mother that he couldn't pick Roxy up or kiss her unless she wanted him to do so at that moment. If he tried to do otherwise, she wailed and flailed about "like a fish out of water." My mother didn't disagree with that description. She said Roxy would even hold her breath and stiffen her body into stone until she got her way. Her face would turn pink and then crimson.

"As red as a polished apple! I had no doubt that she would die before she would give in or get what she wanted."

I was always told that fathers and daughters could have a special relationship, because daughters often see their fathers as perfect, and fathers see their daughters as little princesses. My mother assured me that nothing was farther from the truth when it came to Roxy and my father.

"*Mon dieu.* I swear sometimes your father would look at Roxy with such fire in his eyes that I thought he'd burn down the house," my mother said.

Although she was French, my mother was fluent in English as a child, and after years and years of living in America, she usually reverted to French with my father and me only when she became emotional or wanted to stress something. Of course, I learned to speak French because of her. She knew that teaching it to me when I was young was the best way to get me fluent in the language.

"Your sister would look right back at him defiantly and never flinch. He was always the first to give up, to look away. And if he ever spanked her or slapped her, she would never cry.

"Once, when she was fourteen and came home after two o'clock in the morning when she wasn't even supposed to go out, he took his belt to her," my mother continued. "I had to pull him off her, practically claw his arm to get him to stop. You know how big your father's hands are and how powerful he can be, especially when he's very angry. Roxy didn't cry and never said a word. She simply went to her room as if she had walked right through him.

"She defied him continually, breaking every rule he set down, until he gave up and threw her out of the house. You were just six and really the ideal child in his eyes, *une enfant parfait*. Why waste his time on a hopeless cause, he would say, when he could spend his time and energy on you instead? He was always afraid she'd be a bad influence on you, contaminate you with her nasty and stubborn ways.

"Your sister didn't cry or beg to stay. She packed her bags, took the little savings she had, and went out into the world as if she had never expected to do anything different. She didn't even look to me to intercede on her behalf. I don't think she ever respected me as a woman or as her mother, because I wouldn't stand up to your father the way she would. Sometimes she wouldn't even let me touch her. The moment I put my hand out to stroke her hair or caress her face, she recoiled like a frightened bird.

"Maybe your father hoped she would finally learn a good lesson and return, begging him to let her back into our home and family and promising to behave. But if he did have that expectation, he was very good at keeping it secret. After she left, he avoided mentioning her name to me, and if I talked about her, he would get up and leave the room. If I did so at dinner, he would get up and go out to eat, and if I mentioned her when we were in bed, he would go out to the living room to sleep.

"So I gave up trying to change his mind. Sometimes I went out looking for her, taking you with me, but this is a very big city. Paris is a bigger city, but more people live here in New York. It was probably as difficult as looking for a needle in a haystack."

"Didn't you call the police, try to get her face on milk cartons or something?"

"Your father wouldn't hear of it for the first few months. Later, there were newspaper stories and a magazine article about lost girls, and your sister was featured. Nothing came of it. I used to go to other neighborhoods and walk and walk, hoping to come upon her, especially on her birthday, but it wasn't until five years later that your father revealed that he had seen her. He told me only because he thought it proved he was right to throw her out.

"He was at a dinner meeting with some of his associates at the investment bank. After it had ended, one of them told him he had a special after-dinner date. They walked out together, and a stretch limousine pulled up. The man winked at your father and went to the limousine. The chauffeur opened the door, and your father saw a very attractive and expensively dressed young woman inside the limousine. At first, he didn't recognize her, but after a few moments, he realized it was Roxy. He said she looked years older than she was and that she glared out at him with the same defiance he had seen in her face when she was only five.

"Later, he found out she was a high-priced call girl. She even had a fancy name, Fleur du Coeur, which you know means 'Flower of the Heart.' That's how rich men would ask for her when they called the escort service.

"*Mon dieu, mon dieu!* It broke my heart to hear all of that, but I didn't cry in front of him."

Even now, talking about it brought tears to her eyes, however.

My mother told me more about Roxy after my father had passed away. I was devastated by my father's death, but now that he was no longer there to stop it, I wanted to hear as much as I could about my forbidden sister, the sister whose existence I could never acknowledge.

I had no trouble pretending I was an only child. Since the day Roxy had left, I was living that way anyway. My father had taken all of her pictures off the walls and shelves and dressers. He had burned most of them. Mama was able to hide a few, but anything else Roxy had left behind was dumped down the garbage chute. It was truly as if he thought he could erase all traces of her existence. He never even acknowledged her birthday. Looking at the calendar, he would do little more than blink.

He didn't know it, but I still had a charm bracelet Roxy had given me. It had a wonderful variety of charms that included the Eiffel Tower, a fan, a pair of dancing shoes, and a dream catcher. My mother's brother had given it to her when my parents and she were in France visiting, and she gave it to me. I never wore it in front of my father for fear that he would seize it and throw it away, too.

Of course, I could never mention her name in front of my father when he was alive, and I didn't dare ask him any questions about her. My mother was the one who told me almost all I knew about Roxy after she had left. She said that once my father had seen Roxy in the limousine, he had tried to learn more about her, despite himself. He found out that she lived in a fancy hotel on the East Side, the Hotel Beaux-Arts. I had overheard them talking about it. The Beaux-Arts was small but very expensive. Most of the rooms were suites and some were full apartments. My mother said that my father was impressed with how expensive it was.

"The way he spoke about her back then made me think that he was impressed with how much money she was making. Before I could even think he had softened his attitude about her, he added that she was nothing more than a high-priced prostitute," she said.

She didn't want to tell me all of this, but it was as if it had all been boiling inside her and she finally had the chance to get it out. I knew that she went off afterward to cry in private. I was conflicted about asking her questions because I saw how painful it was for her to tell these things to me. I rarely heard my parents speak about Roxy, and I knew I couldn't ask my mother any questions about her in front of Papa. If I did ask when he wasn't home, my mother would avoid answering or answer quickly, as if she expected the very walls would betray her and whisper to my father.

However, the questions were there like weeds, undaunted, invulnerable, and as defiant as Roxy.

What did she look like now?

What was her life really like?

Was she happy? Did she have everything she wanted?

Was she sad about losing her family?

Mostly, I wanted to know if she ever thought about me. It suddenly occurred to me one day that Roxy might have believed that my father risked my mother's life to have me just so he could ignore her. He was that disgusted with her. Surely, if Roxy thought that, she could have come to hate me.

Did she still hate me?

The answers were out there, just waiting for me. They taunted me and haunted me.

I had no doubt, however, that I would eventually get to know them.

What I wondered was, would I be sorry when I did get to know them?

Would they change my life?

And maybe most important of all, would I hate my sister as much as my father had?

1

My father was always the first to rise in the morning, even on weekends. He was never quiet about it, either. All three bedrooms in our town house just off Madison Avenue on East 81st Street in New York were upstairs. It was a relatively new building in the neighborhood, and Papa often complained about the workmanship and how the builders had cut corners to make more money. He said the older structures on the street were far more solid, even though ours cost more. Our walls were thinner, as were the framing and the floors.

Consequently, I could hear him close drawers, start his shower, close cabinets, and even talk to Mama, especially if their bedroom door was open. The cacophony of sounds he made was his rendition of Army reveille. Of course, being the son of an Army general, he actually had heard it most of his young life. His family had often lived that close to the barracks, depending on where his father had been stationed, especially when they were overseas. When I commented about it once, Mama said the volume of the noise he made after he got up in the morning was a holdover from the days when Roxy lived with us. Her bedroom was on the other side of theirs. She would never wake up for school on her own, so Papa would be sure to make all this noise to get her up much earlier than was necessary. No matter what Mama said, he was stubborn about it. Maybe Roxy had inherited that obstinacy from him. Who could be more inflexible when he had made up his mind than my father?

Even though he basically had defied his own father's wishes and chosen a business career rather than a military one as his older brother, Orman, had, Papa still believed in military discipline. Disobeying an order in our house could lead to the equivalent of being court-martialed. At least, that was how it felt to me, and I'm sure it had felt that way to Roxy, especially when he told her to leave the house. To her it must have been like a dishonorable discharge. Perhaps, despite what Papa said, she had felt some shame. I imagined she would have, even though I couldn't remember her that well anymore. After all, it was now a little more than nine years since I had last seen her or heard her voice.

I often wondered if she had seen me and secretly watched me growing up. During these years, did she hide somewhere nearby and wait for a glimpse of either my mother or me? One of the first things I used to do when I stepped out, and often still do, was to look across the street, searching for someone Roxy's age standing behind a car or off to the side of a building, watching for any sight of us. Even if I didn't see her, I couldn't help but wonder if she followed me to school.

Sometimes I would pretend she was, and I would stop suddenly and turn to catch her. People behind me would look annoyed or frightened. Whenever I walked in the city, whether to school or to the store or just to meet friends, I would scan the faces of any young woman who would be about Roxy's age. I often studied some young woman's face so hard she flashed anger back at me, and I quickly looked away and sped up.

One of the first things my parents had taught me about walking the streets of New York was never to make too much eye contact with strangers. I supposed Roxy would be like a complete stranger to me now. I even had trouble recalling the sound of her voice, but I did sneak looks at the pictures of her that Mama had hidden every chance I had.

I believed that Roxy would be as curious about me as I was about her. Why shouldn't she be? Although I feared it, it was hard for me to accept that she hated Mama and me because of what Papa had done to her. Despite his stern ways, it was also hard for me to believe she hated him. Maybe it was difficult only because I didn't want to believe it. I didn't even want to think that someone with whom I shared so much DNA could be that bad, that immoral. Or did it mean that somewhere deep inside me there was a strain of evil that would someday rise to the surface, too? How would it show itself? What emotions, lusts, and desires did we share?

Having an older sister who had become so infamous to my parents naturally made me worry about myself. When I suggested such a thing to Mama once, she looked at me with pain in her eyes. I know the pain was there, because, like me, she didn't want to believe Roxy was so wicked and sinful or as evil as Papa made her out to be. Then she softened her look and told me to think of Cain and Abel in the Bible. Abel wasn't evil because Cain was. Abel was good.

"Besides, we must not believe that evil is stronger than good, Emmie. You're my perfect daughter, my *fille parfaite, n'est-ce pas?*"

"*Oui*, Mama," I would say whenever she asked me that, but I didn't believe I was as perfect as Mama or Papa thought I was. Who could be?

Yes, I kept my room neat, made my bed, helped Mama with house chores, shopped for her, came home when my parents told me I must, never smoked or drank alcohol with my classmates, not even a beer, and refused to try any drugs or pot any classmate offered. Mama believed in letting me drink wine at dinner, even when I was barely ten, and I drank some vodka to celebrate things occasionally, but that was the way she had been brought up in France, and Papa thought it was just fine.

"The best training ground for most things is your home," he would tell me. My friends at school, especially the ones who knew how strict my father could be, didn't know what to make of that. He sounded so lenient, but I knew that his leniency didn't go any farther than our front door. Sometimes, especially when I left our house, I felt as if I were walking around with an invisible leash and collar around my neck.

Rules rained down around me everywhere I looked, not just in my home. Our school, which was a private school, didn't tolerate sexy clothing or any body piercing, not that I wanted to do that. Our teachers even criticized some girls for wearing too much makeup. It was far more serious for my classmates to violate rules than it was for students in a public school, because, unlike in a public school, they wouldn't simply be suspended. They'd be thrown out, and all of their tuition money would be forfeited. What they did after school the moment they left the property was another thing, however. Buttons were undone, rings were put in noses, and cigarettes came out of hidden places. Students puffed defiantly. Suddenly, their mouths were full of profanity, words they would be afraid even to whisper in the school's hallways. It was as if all of the pent-up nasty behavior was bursting at the seams. They were far from goody-goodies, so why shouldn't I wonder if I was, too?

I probably wouldn't be attending a strict private school if it weren't for Roxy. She had been going to a public school, had been suspended for smoking and for cheating on a test, and, worst of all, was nearly arrested and expelled for smoking a joint in the girls' room. It was one of the better public schools in New York, too, but according to what I gleaned from Mama, Roxy never had better than barely passing grades.

The only thing she excelled at was speaking French, thanks to Mama. But even with that skill, she got in trouble. She would say nasty things in French to her teachers under her breath or even aloud, and when

some of them went to the language teacher for trans-
lations, Roxy ended up in the principal's office, and
Mama would have to come to school. She tried to keep
as much of it as she could hidden from Papa, but often
there was just too much to hide, and whatever he did
learn was way more than enough to rile him and send
him into a rage.

Mama could get away with hiding much of it,
because Papa was dedicated to his work at the investment firm. He was up early to deal with the stock
market and then always working late into the afternoon with financial planning and other meetings.
Mama said that her having to call him at work because
of something Roxy had done was like the president
having to use the famous red phone or something. I
had no doubt that Mama trembled whenever she had
to tell him about something very bad Roxy had done
in school. She said he was so furious that he could
barely speak whenever he had to leave work to attend
a meeting because of something she had done.

"It got so that your sister wouldn't even pretend
to feel remorseful about something she had done. She
would just look at him with that silent defiance, just
as she would when he would rattle the whole house to
get her out of bed in the morning."

Even though Papa got up earlier than I would have
to on weekday mornings, I was used to rising and having breakfast with him and Mama. She was always up
to make his breakfast. I would spend the extra morning time studying for a test or reading. Whenever I did
anything that was the opposite of what Roxy would

have done, such as be at breakfast with him, I could see the satisfaction in Papa's face. I used to think, and still do, that he was letting out an anxious breath, always half expecting that I would somehow turn out to be like Roxy. No matter how well I did in school, how polite I was to his and Mama's friends, or how much I helped Mama, he couldn't help fearing that I would wake up one day and be like my sister.

It was as if he had two different kinds of daughters. One was Dr. Jekyll, and the other was Miss Hyde, only he wasn't sure if Miss Hyde would also emerge in me.

"So what's on for today?" Papa asked. It was the same question he asked me every day at breakfast.

Anyone who thought that he asked it out of habit would be wrong, however. He really wanted to know what I had to do and, especially, what I wanted to do. My route to and from school was to follow Madison Avenue north for five blocks and then turn west for another block. I could do it blindfolded by now. If I had any plans to diverge from the route, especially during nice weather like what we were having this particular fall, and go somewhere after school, I would have to tell him. He even wanted to know when I would take my lunch and eat it with some friends in Central Park. The school let us do that. Even many of our teachers did it, but doing something spontaneously was very difficult.

Maybe because of how angry Papa would get about Roxy if Mama slipped and brought up her name, I tried extra hard to please him. To get him to smile at me, laugh at something I had said or done, and kiss me when he hugged me was very important to me. Although I didn't come out and say it, earning this reaction from him was like telling him that I wasn't and never would be like Roxy. Nothing made me feel warmer and happier than when he used Mama's French to call me his *fille parfaite*. Maybe hearing him say that I was a perfect daughter in French made it even more special.

Sometimes I would imagine that Roxy was standing there beside me in the house, scowling and sneering whenever Papa said that. I knew what sibling rivalry was, how friends of mine competed with their sisters or brothers for their parents' affection and approval. As strange as it might sound, even though my sister was gone from our home and our lives, I still felt sibling rivalry. Perhaps I was competing with a ghost. My visions of her were as vague as that, but I still felt that I was always being measured against her. Was my French as good as hers? Was I as pretty?

Other girls and boys my age might have older brothers or sisters to look up to and try to emulate. I had a sister, a secret sister always to be better than. It wasn't difficult for me to outdo her in every way except misbehavior, but nothing I could do or say really stopped my parents from thinking about her. I knew that was true, regardless of what Papa pretended or how furious and red his face would become at the mere suggestion of her.

Roxy was there; she would always be there, haunting us all. Keeping her bedroom door shut, throwing out her things, removing her pictures from the shelves and the mantel, ignoring her birthday, and forbidding the sound of her name didn't stop her voice from echoing somewhere in the house. Whenever I saw Papa stop what he was doing or look up from what he was reading and stare blankly at a corner or at a chair, I had the feeling he was seeing Roxy. I know Mama did. It got so I recognized those moments when she would pause no matter what she was doing and just stare at something. I would say nothing. Afterward, she often went off to cry in secret.

"If it doesn't rain, we're going to the park for lunch, and then after school, I'm going to Chastity Morgan's house to study for our unit exam in social studies," I told Papa at breakfast. His whole body was at attention, waiting for my response.

"Just you and Chastity?" he asked, his dark brown eyebrows lifted in anticipation of my answer.

Even though Papa was never in the Army, he kept his dark brown hair as short as a soldier's hair and had a soldier's posture, with his shoulders back and his back straight. He had a GI Joe shave every morning and wore spit-polished shoes. He was a little taller than six feet and tried to keep himself physically fit. He would walk as much as he could and avoid taxicabs whenever possible, but his job was sedentary. Despite his efforts, he had slowly gained weight over the years, until his doctor warned him about his blood pressure and cholesterol. He tried to watch his diet, but Mama was French and cooked with sauces he loved. It did him no good to try to pass the blame onto her, either, because she was ready to point out how the French were thinner and healthier because they didn't ask for seconds as he would often do.

Except for that and the topic of my sister, my parents rarely argued. If anyone complained, it was Mama about herself. I thought it was an odd complaint.

"I'm too devoted to that man," she would mutter. "But I can't help it."

I wondered if that was true. Could you love someone too much? What was too much? From what I saw in the lives of my classmates, especially when I visited them at their homes, their parents could use love inoculations, affection booster shots. Chastity Morgan's parents were like that. Eating dinner in their dining room was like eating at a restaurant. Their conversation was mostly directed to their maid. I was there when Chastity's father sent food back to be cooked longer or complained about being given food that was too cool. I half expected him to leave a tip at his plate before he left the table.

Most of the time at these dinners, her mother would talk to Chastity and me without saying more than two words to Chastity's father. Her father often read a paper at the dinner table, too. My father would have him face a firing squad for doing something like that.

When Chastity came to my house for dinner, the contrast was so great it almost brought tears to her eyes. Both of my parents made her feel like part of our family. Papa directed a great deal of conversation her way. However, I wished he wouldn't, because his conversation was mostly interrogation. Maybe Chastity

wasn't aware of it as much as I was, but he was looking to see if she would be a bad influence on me, even
though we had been best friends for two years, and
she was the only one at school who knew I had an
older sister. I had even told her where Roxy lived and
what Roxy did.

I didn't do that because I was proud of Roxy. I did
it because I wanted company when I eventually went
to spy on Roxy, and I knew this would excite Chastity. She and I had been talking about it for weeks,
and I had decided that I was finally ready to do it.
She understood that it required lots of planning. I just
couldn't go hanging around the hotel for hours and
hours. My parents, especially my father, would want
to know where I had been and what I had been doing.
I needed a solid alibi, and telling my father that I was
going to Chastity's house to study would suffice.

I was sure I could get away with it, but lying to
my father wasn't something I liked to do or did often.
My reason for that wasn't simply fear of being caught.
I couldn't help feeling that my father would see even
the smallest, most insignificant untruth as a serious
betrayal and, more important, evidence that I was
heading toward becoming another Roxy. With such
disappointment, his love for me would suffer a nearly
fatal wound.

If and when that happened, I was sure I would
be able to see it in his face immediately. It would certainly be there if he found out my secret plan to spy
on Roxy. Why would I want to know anything about
such a sister? What did this say about me? Would he

now definitely believe that I was more like her than he had hoped or expected? And how would my mother react? Would she blame me for bringing such unhappiness back into our small family? I would no longer be their *fille parfaite*. Why would I risk all of this just to spy on Roxy? What was the attraction, the fascination? Why didn't I despise her for doing what she had done to both of them?

However, no matter what they pretended, deep in my heart, I knew that even they, even my father, wanted to know more about her. No matter what you said or did, you really couldn't wash your hands completely of your child. Blood was too strong. I was convinced that she lived in Papa's dreams and even his nightmares. In his heart of hearts, he didn't want to see bad things happen to her and wished that there was some way to bring her back.

"Maybe Kelli Fisher will study with us," I told Papa, hoping to make my alibi more credible. "She's a good student, too. Her twin brother, Carson, might come along," I added nonchalantly, just to make it all seem more truthful.

He nodded but kept his eyes so fixed on me that even if I weren't lying, I'd inevitably act as if I were. However, he was thinking about something else.

"You like this boy?"

"He's all right," I said, which was a girl's code for "Ugh!" Papa didn't know that, of course.

"What's 'all right' mean?"

"No second look," I said. "And barely a first."

Mama laughed, but Papa kept his military-serious

expression. "I hope your mother has done a good job of explaining the minefields out there when it comes to sex, Emmie."

"Oh, Norton," Mama said.

"You know, I don't go for this false modesty when it comes to training your children, Vivian. We just have to look to your sister, Manon, for a good example of what result that can have," he said sharply. Like his father and his father's father, he could swing words like a machete.

Because Papa avoided mentioning Roxy and therefore using her as the example of what not to be, he relied heavily on the story of Mama's sister, Manon, who got pregnant at sixteen and married a much older man, a friend of her young uncle. Mama would counter with the fact that they were still married and had a nice family.

"Only you French can pretend not to see what's on your right and left flanks," Papa told her. "Yves or Leaves or whatever he calls himself is surely out there pollinating other *jeunes filles*. It takes only one foolish time," Papa warned me. "You go a little bit farther and farther out on this weak branch until it snaps and drops you in one pool of muck. That's what teenagers frolicking in sex do, swim in muck."

Although he didn't add them, I could hear the words, *Just ask your sister.*

"Norton, *s'il vous plaît*," Mama pleaded.

He gave me one more look of warning and returned to his breakfast.

I had yet to bring a boy home to meet my parents,

because I was terrified of how Papa would make him feel. It would surely be like a CIA interrogation. I once told Chastity that my father would probably water-board any boy I had been out with more than once, let alone twice.

And all because of Roxy!

Under these circumstances, who wouldn't expect me to be more and more interested in whom and what she had turned out to be? I had every reason to hate her. Look how she was affecting my life. She was like someone who had died but wouldn't stay buried. She could be thousands of miles away, not only blocks away, but it wouldn't matter. Papa would always look past whatever I had done to see if Roxy had a hand in it, if her influence was in my blood. There were many nights when I raged to myself about it. I wouldn't dare rage at Papa, but I could mutter and think my protest aloud when I was alone.

"If you're going to forget her, Papa, forget her. Don't keep looking in me to find her! And don't deny that you do!"

I even imagined his guilty, remorseful face, but none of this fantasizing helped to make it easier.

I would look out my bedroom window at the street below whenever I had these thoughts. I could see the corner from where I stood. I knew Roxy was just a little north of us.

"Why didn't you go farther away?" I whispered. "Did you stay here just to spite Papa? Or did you stay close because you were sorry and really do miss us?

"I'm going to know the answers to all of my questions about you, Roxy. I swear. I'm going to force you to look at me. And I'm going to make you do what I have done too often because of you.

"I'm going to make you cry."

2

"We're going to do it today," I told Chastity as soon as I met her in the school hallway.

As usual, she was walking with her head down, not expecting anyone else to say hi. When she heard me, she looked up quickly and twisted her thin lips so hard I thought either the upper or the lower would snap like a rubber band. Her facial features were too small for her round, chubby face. She had nice mocha-brown eyes, but her lazy lids were habitually narrowed, giving the impression that she was falling asleep, even while walking. She had naturally curly light brown hair, which in her case was a disadvantage, because it almost always looked like a nest made by a drunken rat.

"Yeah, right," she said. I couldn't blame her for her skepticism. Three times this week alone, I had said so but backed out before the school day ended.

"I'm really serious this time. I told my father I was going to your house to study after school. I even told him Kelli and her brother were joining us."

"Really?" she said, permitting more credibility to slip in. She knew how I felt about lying to my father.

"Yes, so if he ever asks you about it, you know what to say, okay?"

"Absolutely," she said, her eyelids fluttering like the wings of a bird waking up. Her whole face lit up with excitement. It was as if someone had turned on Christmas-tree lights. Actually, that annoyed me.

Sometimes I thought Chastity was more interested in my sister than I was. Never a day passed when she wouldn't ask me about her. I knew she was more concerned about sex and boys, because she couldn't go an hour when we were alone without bringing up some boy or talking about some sex scene she had seen in a movie. She would get upset with me if I didn't show as much enthusiasm. It wasn't that I didn't have the same thoughts and feelings; it was just that I was reluctant to talk about it. She had no clue as to why I would have these inhibitions. She just thought I was very shy and needed her prodding to pry me out of my shell. In fact, whenever she got very graphic about sex, she thought she was doing me a big favor. If I made a face, she would get irritated.

"Like you don't fantasize and masturbate," she would say, and wait for me to admit that I did.

"We can study for our test while we wait around across from the hotel," I said.

"While we wait around? Really, Emmie," she said, taking on that superior *I'm more sophisticated* look, "I don't think we'll be studying much in the street."

"As long as it's something," I said.

"You just want your lie to seem like less," she muttered, and shook her head, holding on to that arrogant
look of superiority.

However, if I were pressed to answer, I would have
to admit she was right. I knew anyone would think it
was crazy to be so nervous about going a little more
uptown and watching the entrance of a hotel to catch
a glimpse of my notorious sister. I wasn't going off to
some friend's house to smoke pot or something, and I
wasn't going off to have sex with a boy. Anyone else
would laugh at my anxiety, but once I had made up
my mind and committed to going, I could barely listen
to my teachers in my classes or even to the other girls
when we broke for lunch.

I could feel Chastity's eyes on me all day. She was
anticipating me changing my mind, and I knew how
much of a disappointment it would be. Every chance
she got when we were alone, she brought up my sister.
I had to admit that some of the questions she asked I
often asked myself, like how do you make love with
any man just because he pays you? How do you get
past the ugly, smelly ones?

"Does she close her eyes and imagine she's with
someone else? Does she have to pretend she likes
them, enjoys them, even appreciates them? How does
she prevent diseases, and does she ever worry a man
will hurt her? How can she like herself after doing all
this? Could she ever fall in love and have a family? Just
have a real romance? Or has this life made it impossible?"

On the other hand, both of us admitted to believing

that there was something exotic about being in an escort service.

"Does she really make a lot of money? Where does she go? Do they take her on expensive trips all over the world? Who buys her clothes and pays for her apartment? How often does she have to work, if you can call that work?"

These and other questions circled my head like gnats. Sometimes I wanted to put my hands over my ears and shout, "Stop!"

When we were in school, we'd whisper these questions to each other. Usually, we'd even whisper them when we were talking on the telephone. It was as if we believed my father had our phones tapped.

At least Chastity had been true to her word and not told anyone else about Roxy, and if we were talking about her in the girls' room or outside the school and someone else came near us, she would clam up. I didn't think it was just because she was being loyal and faithful to me. I think she would be jealous of anyone else sharing our secret. It gave her a sense of superiority over some of the girls who looked down on her. She knew about someone who was really into sex, so she had a way of knowing things the other girls would never know.

Many of the things she said and the questions she asked often embarrassed me, however. She had a copy of the Kama Sutra that she had gotten down in the Village. It had all sorts of drawings and photographs in it. If Papa ever knew I even looked at it, he would be as enraged at me as he had been with Roxy. Every time

Chastity showed me something, she asked if Roxy would do this or that.

"I have no idea," I told her. "How would I? You know as much about her now as I do."

"I tried practicing this," she would tell me, pointing to a sexual position. "Your sister probably knows all about this."

I always changed the subject when she became that graphic, but today I was determined that Roxy would be the subject no matter what. I could feel the determination harden up in me. No more excuses, no more procrastination. *Today is really the day,* I thought.

As soon as the final bell rang, we looked at each other with anticipation and then walked out of the building. I tried to appear as natural and as normal as ever, even though my heart threatened to pound a hole out of my chest. Some of the girls wanted us to join them in the park and then maybe walk down to Bergdorf Goodman to annoy saleswomen with our questions about new styles and clothes we weren't ever going to buy. I had my excuses ready. Chastity and I were going to my house to study and help my mother prepare a French dish for dinner, Terrine de Saumon aux Epinards-Riz. I could pronounce it perfectly, of course, which gave my fib authority. The story was that my mother was teaching us how to cook French food and make French pastries.

"What for? I'm having a maid and a cook when I get married," Carol Lee Benson said. She had a way of widening her nostrils when she wanted to show us how special she thought she was.

"Ditto that," Dawn Miller added. Dawn had a perpetually bored look on her face, no matter what we discussed, but that was her way of appearing cool and superior.

"It's very educational, and besides, it's fun," Chastity piped up.

"Fun? French food should be a controlled substance for you. If you don't lose twenty pounds, you'll be hired as a blimp to advertise dog food," Cathy Starling said, and they all laughed. Cathy loved being sarcastic.

When Chastity's face blanched, her lips nearly disappeared.

Dawn grabbed my arm and pulled me closer to whisper. "If you don't stop hanging out with Chubs there, you'll never have a boyfriend in this school," she said. "She's like a male repellent."

I pulled my arm out of her grasp. "We've got to go," I said as sharply as Papa could, and we marched out of the building to the background of their laughter.

"They so immature," Chastity offered in her own defense.

I knew how sensitive she was about her weight, but I also knew that she wasn't doing much about it, and her parents weren't helping by ignoring the situation. Only her younger sister, Faye, ever said anything, usually only when they had an argument.

We walked faster.

"I'm going on a diet soon," Chastity finally added. She looked to me, and I nodded. "You probably thought they were right. You don't have to pretend you don't."

"Stop it, Chas. Of course you should lose some weight. You'll feel better about yourself. But there's no reason for them to be so damn nasty just because we're not doing what they want us to do when they want us to do it."

"Right," Chastity said. She looked relieved. However, when we passed the pastry shop, I saw the napoleons and tarts draw her attention like eye magnets.

"Keep walking," I said. She laughed, but disappointment dripped from her lips.

When we reached the corner where the Hotel Beaux-Arts was, I stopped. I had gone by the hotel twice before but without pausing. I was practically in a run each time, not sure what terrified me more, the prospect of seeing Roxy or my father somehow finding out. I had time, however, to scout the area across from the hotel's front entrance and knew that we could safely hang out by the bus stop.

I began to feel foolish almost as soon as we stopped there and focused on the front of Roxy's hotel.

"I don't know why I wanted us to do this. It's dumb. It's like waiting to catch a glimpse of a rock star."

"Relax. We haven't even been here a minute," Chastity said.

"Even if we're lucky and see her come out or go in, I can't guarantee I'll recognize her."

"You will," she said confidently.

I looked at her. Now that we were there and actually

doing it, I wondered how this could be of any real excitement to her. Roxy wasn't *her* long-lost sister. What did she really hope to get out of it? Did she fantasize, as I often had, that Roxy would see us standing there and call us to her? Would she take us to her apartment and tell us all about her escort experiences, revealing sexual exploits beyond anything either of us could imagine? Would she tell us things no mother or school nurse would ever tell us about our own bodies? Would she, as Chastity hoped, explain some of the things Chastity had shown me in her copy of the Kama Sutra? I'm sure Chastity was dreaming that we would both become sophisticated women overnight, and there would be such an air of maturity about us that our girlfriends would gape at us with surprise and envy. No one would ever criticize her for being heavy again. Boys would see all of this in us and be very attracted.

And what about the men Roxy met? Were some of them famous and powerful? Would she have all sorts of inside stories to tell us? Did Chastity envision Roxy giving us some secret information or clever advice about men, something that would suddenly make us more attractive and interesting to the boys at school, especially the older boys?

Was this what excited her? All of this fantasy? Was I a victim of my imagination, too?

I opened my social-studies textbook.

"You're not really going to start asking me questions about that social-studies stuff, are you?" Chastity asked, tweaking her nose as if the textbook stank.

"We'll get bored quickly if we don't do something else," I warned.

"Not me. Besides, that stuff bores me. Wait. A taxi's stopping in front of the hotel."

I held my breath and watched the driver get out and go to the trunk of the car. The doorman rushed forward to greet whoever was stepping out of the cab. It turned out to be an elderly man with a cane. He wore a black suit and had thin gray hair growing in puffs along the sides of his head. I thought he must have been at Theodore Roosevelt's inauguration. He looked that old. The taxi driver handed his luggage to the doorman.

Both of us felt deflated.

"At least we know it's a real hotel," Chastity said.

"Of course it's a real hotel. Why? What else did you think it might be?"

She shrugged, but I realized that Chastity didn't really believe my sister was some elegant and sophisticated escort. She was thinking like my father. She was thinking we would find nothing much more than a prostitute. Maybe we wouldn't find someone who would hang out on one of the avenues hawking herself for business under the supervision of some pimp, but we would find a prostitute nevertheless.

I realized it was purely the kinky sexual aspect of all this that interested and fascinated Chastity after all. Learning how my sister became an escort and what her life was really like wasn't important. She wanted to hear or see something purely pornographic. I suppose I couldn't blame her. What else did she expect from me? Who else would have admitted to having a sister like mine and admit that she had been thrown out of our home and our family?

"Why did you finally decide to come up here today?" Chastity asked. "Why is today so special? Is it her birthday or something?"

"No. No special reason. I just did."

She pulled in the right corner of her mouth so hard that it ballooned her cheek.

"I mean, what makes you think she would be going out this time of the day, anyway? Do you know something about her schedule or something? Did you find out something you never told me?"

I shook my head. What was I going to say? I had no reason for us to be there at that particular time except for the fact that it was when I could find a way to do it, a way to fool my father.

"You're right," she said after another few seconds. "This is dumb. We should come here at night sometime or maybe just before she would go out to dinner or something, don't you think?"

"I don't know. I guess this is silly. She could walk right by us without me knowing."

"You don't even have a relatively recent picture of her?"

"Nothing after she was fifteen or sixteen. Pictures of her when she was younger are buried in boxes in a closet."

She nodded and thought. "Your sister must have done something awfully terrible to have her own parents throw her out when she was that young. What did she do, exactly? Did she get pregnant? Get caught stealing?"

"From what I know, it wasn't just one thing but an accumulation of things."

"Yeah," Chastity said, but with disappointment. I knew she was hoping for some juicy story.

We both came to attention when a black limousine pulled up. The woman who stepped out was young and attractive, but she wasn't Roxy.

"Not my sister," I quickly said when Chastity looked at me.

"You sure? You just said you might not be able to recognize her."

"I'm sure."

We watched the woman enter the hotel. The door-man nearly fell over himself getting the door opened for her. Even from where we were standing, we could see how he lit up.

"Okay," Chastity said after another ten minutes, during which I read some more of my social-studies unit. "This is very stupid. Let's go."

I had expected her to say that eventually, but not this quickly. The novelty of what we were doing was rapidly losing its hold on her attention, and I suspected that she had not stopped thinking about those napo-leons and tarts we'd passed in the bakery window.

There was no weather threat to drive us away, either. The day itself had actually grown warmer as the afternoon grew older. I had heard there was an unusual warm front on the way. More people were out on the streets. Some of the men had taken off their jackets and walked with them folded over their arms. Women wore light clothing, many with no jackets and definitely no sweaters. Most of the small restaurants and cafés had their windows open. Those that could had tables and chairs out on the sidewalk.

"Another fifteen minutes, maybe," I said.

"You want to stay longer?"

"I don't know. I guess we can wait a little longer, since we came here anyway."

Her face brightened with an idea. "Why can't you just go in there and ask for her?"

"Are you nuts?"

"She won't tell your father you were here, right? From what you've said, they haven't spoken for years, so what's the difference? C'mon. We're wasting time, and at least we'll know if she's here now or not."

"No, I can't do that, Chastity."

"Why not?"

"I guess we'll just leave," I said. I closed my book and put it into my book bag.

"What a drag this was," she muttered. "I can't believe how you wasted our time."

Just as we started away, however, I saw Roxy come out of the hotel. I didn't speak, but Chastity realized I had stopped short, and when she looked at me, she saw the expression on my face. She gazed at Roxy, too.

"Her?"

"Yes," I said, my heart thumping. Would she see me? She didn't even look our way. She turned and started down the avenue. She wore a dark blue beret and had her shoulder-length hair pinned on the sides but falling straight down the back of her neck. She was dressed in an elegant dark blue designer suit, the skirt about mid-calf and tight at her hips.

Although it had been so long since I had seen her and my recollections of her were understandably vague, studying her pictures in the closet whenever I could sneak in and the resemblance she had to Mama made it easy for me to recognize her instantly. Both of us had Mama's petite facial features and Mama's color hair. Her posture and her walk also reminded me of Mama. She was taller than I had expected her to be, but Papa was a tall man.

"Wow. She is beautiful," Chastity said softly.

I almost didn't hear her. Amazingly, I felt pride. For the moment, at least, I didn't think of Roxy as being a woman for hire. She was instead this stunning young woman who walked with great self-confidence, looking forward and seemingly unaware of all the men who turned her way or passed her on the sidewalk but left their eyes behind.

"Let's follow her," Chastity suggested.

I paused. "Follow her?"

"Let's see where she's going. Maybe she's going to meet a man. C'mon," she said, speeding ahead.

"Wait."

She stopped, her hands on her hips. "What? This is what we came here to do, isn't it?"

"Yes, but . . . let's stay far enough behind. I don't want her to see me following her," I said.

She looked after Roxy. "We're far enough now. C'mon."

I joined her, and we crossed the street. Roxy was a good half-block ahead of us, but I was walking too slowly for Chastity.

"We'll lose her if she turns or something," she said.

I sped up, and a few minutes later, we saw Roxy cross the street and go into a boutique. I wanted to keep walking. Maybe this was enough for today, I thought, but Chastity stepped off the sidewalk and started across before I could say anything. I hurriedly followed her, and we approached the shop.

"We'll just walk by and glance in," Chastity said. She was really enjoying this. I almost didn't matter. Again, before I could respond, she charged forward. I stepped up alongside her, realizing that I could use her body to block myself from view. When we reached the shop, even though I was very nervous about it, I looked in and saw that Roxy was looking over a dress the saleslady had handed her. We hesitated and saw Roxy go into a dressing room.

"I bet this place is very expensive," Chastity said, remaining at the door.

"Let's go before she sees us spying on her."

"Wait. I want to see what she looks like in the dress."

"But . . ."

"Stop worrying so much. She won't see us. She certainly doesn't expect you to be here, right?"

"Yes."

"So let's pretend we're interested in what they have in the window. C'mon," she urged when I hesitated.

I joined her, and we were able to look past the

mannequins and see Roxy come out of the dressing room wearing a beautiful low-cut black evening dress. It seemed made for her, and when I looked closer in the window, I saw that the clothes in the shop were indeed fitted and made to order. I nodded at the sign to point it out to Chastity.

"Wow. That dress must cost thousands."

"Maybe," I said. "Probably."

Roxy looked happy with it and went in to change back into her other clothes.

"Let's cross the street before she comes out," I said.

Chastity nodded, gazed longingly at a dress on one of the mannequins, and followed me. She was looking down all the way. I could feel her depression.

"You could lose weight and get into one of those dresses someday, Chas," I said.

"Yeah, sure," she said, but looked helpless.

"What?"

"It's like there's someone else inside me making me eat all the wrong things," she said. "Your sister is really very beautiful. If I could be that beautiful, I wouldn't care if I was an escort or whatever she's called. I bet she's having a good time."

"I don't know. Maybe she's like someone's slave or something."

"You've got to talk to her, Emmie. I'm sure there is lots you can learn from her. It's stupid. Your father is just being a pighead. Don't listen to him."

"I can't do that," I said. "If he found out, he'd disown me, too."

"Just for that? I doubt it."

"You don't know my father. I told you, we can't even mention her name."

She stopped walking and leaned against the side of the building at the corner just below the boutique and looked thoughtful.

"Okay," she said. "Then you have no choice but to keep spying on her and following her. How else will you learn anything about her? Someday she might move away from New York, and the chance for you ever to get to know her will be lost forever and ever."

"I know."

She was telling me something I thought often.

"She's out of the shop," Chastity announced with renewed excitement, and stepped forward. Roxy was headed our way.

"Let's go," I said, panicking. "She's sure to see me standing here."

"No, quick," Chastity said, seizing my hand to pull me a little way down the side street. "You look the other way," she ordered. "I'll watch for her."

I had no choice but to do what she said.

After a moment, she said, "Okay, she went by. C'mon," she urged, taking my hand again.

I put up some resistance, but the truth was, I wanted to go and learn as much as I could about my forbidden sister.

3

After another block and a half, Roxy stopped at a restaurant. Less than a minute later, she and another young woman were led out to a table on the sidewalk. Again, I pulled back into a storefront entrance quickly. Chastity did the same.

"Do you know who she's with?"

"How would I possibly know that, Chastity?" Was she just thick, or did she really believe I wasn't telling her everything I knew?

"She's very pretty, too. I bet she's also an escort. Do you think she's an escort, too?"

"I don't know. I told you, you know as much about my sister now as I do."

"Who else would she hang out with? She must be another escort. They're probably comparing notes. I wonder if they work for the same service. How do you get into such a thing? How much money do they make?" She rattled off all her questions in one breath and then turned to me, expecting answers.

"Don't you hear me? I don't know any more about

any of this than you do, Chastity." I was no longer hiding my annoyance with her.

She nodded, disappointed. From the way she was looking at my sister and her friend, I could see how much she longed to be as attractive as they were.

"I bet they have interesting lives," she muttered. "Just as I said, I bet they even know celebrities and go to exotic places. Just think of it. Lots of movie stars don't want to be followed and have their picture taken every time they go out. What's better than an escort service? She must know lots of famous people."

What a strange thing was happening, I thought. I didn't bring Chastity along to get her to idolize my sister. I needed company. If anything, I had expected she would get bored and want to do something else. Now it looked as if I would have trouble getting her to leave. Before I could suggest that we do leave, someone else arrived at my sister's table.

He was an elegant-looking man, probably about fifty, dressed in a dark blue velvet sports jacket and a blue tie. Even from where we were standing, we could clearly see that he was tan and handsome. A diamond pinkie ring caught the late-afternoon sun. Both my sister and her friend rose to greet him and be kissed on both cheeks.

"Is he French?" Chastity asked.

"How would I know?"

"Stop saying that," she snapped.

"Well, how would I? I can't hear him, can you?"

"But isn't that the way French people kiss?"

"Lots of people do that now."

He sat at their table, and the waitress arrived to take his order. They were all having coffee.

"I know. I bet he's their boss or something, or maybe he's tonight's gentleman for one of them. Or . . ." Her eyes widened. "Or they're both going to be with him. It's a something *trois*."

"*Ménage à trois*," I said.

She looked at me, excited, and nodded. "Yes, that's it. They're having a *ménage à trois*." She squinted. "What exactly is that anyway? C'mon," she urged. "Don't tell me you don't know. You're part French."

I almost laughed. "You don't have to be French to have a *ménage à trois*, Chastity. It's just a French expression."

"For what, exactly?"

"Why did you say it if you didn't know what it was?"

"I know a little," she said.

"It's sex with three willing people. Men like two women; women like two men."

"I mean . . . how do they do that? One watches?"

"That's as much as I know," I said firmly. "I think we should go soon. They could be there a long time."

"Wait. I have an idea. Your sister doesn't know me. I could walk by and maybe pick up a few words they're saying."

I started to shake my head.

"You just head down this street and around the block. I'll meet you a block down and tell you what I heard."

"Don't let them think you're listening in, Chastity," I warned.

She hesitated. "You don't think that guy's dangerous or something, do you?"

"I don't know. Maybe forget it."

She considered and then shook her head. "No. I'll do it. Go on," she said, and headed to the corner to cross.

I watched her for a moment and then hurried down the side street. By the time I came around to head back to Madison Avenue, Chastity was waiting at the corner. She looked as if she would burst with excitement.

"What?"

"I was right. He was French. Your sister was speaking French to him, and English, and then they all laughed. I pretended I had something in my shoe so I could listen more, and I heard her say she had a full weekend. I wanted to stay longer, but I think the other woman was looking at me, so I walked away. You think that man was after her, wanted a date?"

I shook my head.

"Why not?" she asked petulantly. I knew she wanted to be the one to make discoveries, and she was the one who had eavesdropped on their conversation. Why would I disagree?

"It's not the way an escort service works," I said. I didn't want to tell her, or anyone, for that matter, that I had read up on them. "Their schedules are kept, and the clients are screened. They don't go out on dates."

She looked angry now. "So you really do know more about your sister than you're saying."

"No. That's just general stuff. I don't know anything specific about her."

"So I could be right," she said, satisfied with herself. "Maybe that man is her favorite or something. Maybe he's in love with her and wants her to be his and only his." Her imagination was in a stampede. "He's going to rescue her from this life and . . . and take her away. Maybe he has an estate in Europe or lives in an old castle or . . ."

"He looked a lot older, didn't he?"

"So?"

"Men don't usually fall in love with girls who sleep with other men for money," I said.

That threw her for an instant, and then she brightened with another idea. "Maybe he doesn't care. Maybe he's so in love with her that he would forgive her for anything. Besides, he's French."

"First, he's not necessarily French because he speaks French, Chastity. My father speaks French very well."

"Well, I think he's French."

"And second, that's a stereotype. Just because someone's French, it doesn't mean he or she has fewer morals."

She shrugged. "My father thinks so, and he's a lawyer."

"Well, he's wrong. Besides, what does that say about my mother?"

"I think he only meant French men."

I looked at my watch. "I think I'd better head home," I said. None of this was making me feel any better.

"When do you want to do this again? I think we should go there in the evening. I know how," she added before I could object. "You get permission to stay over my house, and we can go up there whenever we want, stay late and everything. Okay? Maybe this weekend. I heard her say she had a full weekend. We'll see something important."

"I'll see," I said.

Suddenly, I felt terrible about this, and not only because I was doing what would surely disappoint my father. It was like some girl's younger brother bringing a friend to spy on his older sister when she was getting undressed, taking a bath, or making love with her boyfriend. I hadn't even spoken to Roxy for years, but suddenly, she was the one I was betraying. It was wrong of me to let someone like Chastity Morgan exploit my sister and use her for her lustful fantasies.

We started down the avenue.

"Why don't you ask your father more about her and find out what she did, exactly? There had to be one big thing that broke the camel's back, right?"

"My father won't talk about Roxy and won't even permit her name to be mentioned. I told you that. Why don't you listen to what I tell you?"

"I wonder how he explains it to people who know."

"People don't know about what she does."

"But you said that's how you and your mother found out about her. Someone your father works with."

"My father never told him she was his daughter."

"Oh. Wow. That must really drive him crazy. Maybe someday, when you talk to your sister again, you can talk her out of doing what she's doing."

"I doubt it. Look," I said, stopping, "I'm depending on you to keep this to yourself. If you don't, I swear I'll tell people some of the secret things you told me about yourself and what you do."

"Of course I won't talk about it. I promised, didn't I?"

"Okay," I said. We reached the corner where we would separate. "You had better study for tomorrow's test," I reminded her.

"Ugh. Don't forget to get permission to come over Friday."

I nodded and walked away. I didn't feel at all the way I had expected. Chastity's excitement and imaginings dominated the entire experience. I had barely looked at Roxy. Chastity saw her up closer than I had, and what's more, she heard Roxy's voice, her laughter. Rather than fill me with any excitement and pleasure, the entire event depressed me. I made up my mind to come up with some excuse for why I couldn't go to her house on Friday.

In the meantime, I thought I might find a way to return to Roxy's hotel by myself. It might mean more lying, I thought, but I couldn't help it. Now that I had bitten the apple, I wanted the whole thing. I wanted to know more about her, and even though I wouldn't admit it, I wanted her to know more about me.

I had been hoping to get home before my father

arrived. Most weekdays, he didn't get home from work until just before dinner, but today he was already there. I was frightened because his presence was unexpected, and I thought maybe, just maybe, he had thought to have me followed after school or something. Maybe he didn't believe anything I had said at breakfast. I could barely breathe when he looked at me, but I knew I had better do all I could not to look guilty about anything.

"Why do you look so disturbed?" he asked me immediately, however. Papa was great at reading faces, especially mine.

"I wasted my time studying with them," I said. "All they wanted to do was gossip. Now I have to work harder tonight for tomorrow."

Papa's eyebrows rose, and then he laughed. "She's a chip off my old block, all right."

I breathed with relief, but I was still nervous. I hadn't lied this much to either of my parents until now.

"I'll just put my things away and come down to help you with dinner, Mama," I said.

"No need. It's all done, Emmie. We'll call you when it's time to eat."

I nodded and hurried up to my room. I did try to study, but my mind kept wandering back to Roxy. I had always struggled with memories, trying to conjure up anything that would remind me of her. Because I was so young when she left, it took me a while to understand that she was no longer there. I remembered asking about her, but Papa wouldn't respond, and Mama always told me to do something else or pay attention to something else. I vaguely recalled going into her room to look for her. After a while, she seemed to drift out of my young mind like a passing dream.

She was still dreamlike to me, even after seeing her as much as I had today. How could she look so beautiful and vibrant if she were all that Papa said she was? Maybe most of it wasn't true. Maybe she was just living on her own with her own friends and had a good job. After all, I thought, how would Papa know? He didn't want to know anything about her.

Or did he?

Was he secretly keeping an eye on her?

What if I went back to the hotel and he was doing what I was doing? What if he were somewhere nearby watching for her and he saw me? He'd be very angry, but he wouldn't want me to know he was there, too.

He was more cheerful than usual at dinner. His financial moves had gone well for him today at his investment-banking firm, and he was talking again about an early retirement and our moving out of the city.

"We'll be in lots better shape than my brother. That's for sure," he said.

My uncle was almost as unmentionable as Roxy these days. From what I understood, Uncle Orman sided with my grandfather and was highly critical of Papa for not pursuing an Army career as their father and their grandfather and great-grandfather had. Papa could have been a candidate for West Point.

In my father's family, when you broke a tradition,

it was like breaking an egg. There was no way to put it back together.

I guess I should have expected that Chastity would call me in the evening. Her imagination was taking her in all sorts of directions. First, she saw us as amateur detectives.

"We've got to find out more about the escort service. I thought of a way. We need to bring someone else in on this, too."

"What? Why? Who?"

"A boy. We need a boy's voice."

"A boy's voice? Why?"

"Well, I was thinking, what if we do find out the name of the service and the telephone number? We could get this boy to call and pretend he wants a date with your sister. You told me her French name. If he's told she's booked that night, we'll know, and we can watch to see who picks her up, get the license number or something."

"Chastity, you're running away with yourself. We're not detectives. We couldn't find out anything if we knew someone's license number. What's the point?"

"I think I can. My uncle Tommy is a city policeman, isn't he?"

She made my heart flutter. "Forget that," I said. "You're thinking of things that will make this all worse for me. We don't tell anyone, especially some boy from our school, about my sister, understand? And if you went to your uncle . . . he might call both our parents. Promise me you won't even think of such a thing again," I demanded. "Promise, or I'll never do anything with you again."

"Oh . . ."

I was silent.

"Okay, okay. Don't bust a blood vessel." She took a breath and went right on to a new fantasy. "I wonder if there is such a thing for girls our age."

"What? What thing?"

"An escort service. I don't mean young girls for older men," she added quickly. "But how about an escort service for high school boys? We might be able to organize it. I bet we could make a lot of money."

"That's even more ridiculous, Chastity."

"No, it isn't. There are plenty of boys today who are pretty awkward when it comes to dating and things. They'd love to pay to have everything arranged. And don't say it's illegal. If it was illegal, your sister would be in jail, right?"

I suddenly realized I might have created a monster. "I don't know, Chastity. And don't ask your father!" I added.

"I won't, but I think it's a very exciting idea."

"You should just study for the test tomorrow, Chastity. You're getting crazy. Let's forget about my sister for a while."

"What do you mean? We're going back up there, aren't we? I heard her say she had a full weekend."

"No," I said. "I decided it's not a good idea."

"What?"

"I want to think more about it first."

"Well, that's not fair. You got me into this, and now you just want to stop?"

"We'll talk about it tomorrow," I said quickly. "I really want to study."

"That's not fair," she repeated, and hung up.

I was actually shaking. *She's going to cause some sort of trouble,* I thought. *I have to find a way to keep her satisfied.* Papa was always fond of saying, "Two can keep a secret if one is dead." Now I was afraid I had trusted someone too much. Chastity and I had been drawn together out of a common need for a best friend. My life was so restricted, so controlled, most of the girls in my class considered me a waste of time. Chastity was usually ignored or forgotten whenever it came to parties or get-togethers. We just seemed to gravitate toward each other.

We both felt safe talking and fantasizing about boys and men we knew we would never really speak to, much less have any sort of intimate relationship with. Romance for us was still something kept at a distance, a dream. Other girls our age whom we knew weren't much more sophisticated, and most of them were virgins, but for some reason, our virginity had a capital *V*. I could feel it in the way boys and other girls looked at us, especially me.

What would happen if they suddenly found out I had a sister who worked for a high-priced escort service? Would it make me seem odder and forbidden, like someone who could spread a disease, or would it suddenly make me interesting to them? There were a few boys I found attractive and interesting. I wished one especially, Evan Styles, a sophomore, would give me a second glance, but that had yet to happen.

Evan was one of the more popular boys. His father was a mayoral assistant, an attorney, and he and Evan's mother were often in New York magazines, photographed at charity events or government events. The question wasn't whether there were any girls interested in Evan. The question was who wasn't? Besides being bright and very good-looking, he had a winning personality. I knew our teachers were fond of him.

What would get him to look seriously at me?

I thought about Roxy. She was so well put together— her hair, her makeup, and the way her clothes fit. But it was that air of self-confidence that surprised me the most, the way she walked and held herself. Where did she learn how to do that if she had been thrown out onto the streets? Wouldn't that make it far more difficult to have any self-confidence?

I looked at myself in the mirror. My hair was neat but dull, I thought. I wore nothing but a little lipstick, and that usually wore off or looked bland. I rarely wore earrings to school, and I was never excited about my clothes. Whenever Mama took me shopping for something new to wear, she always wondered aloud if my father would approve. I might as well be wearing a uniform. *I'm in Papa's private family army,* I thought.

I need to buy something more attractive to wear. I've got to do something else with my hair, and I should wear more makeup to school.

Just a short look at Roxy had stirred all of these thoughts in my mind.

What would happen if I ever did speak to her and spent any time with her?

Maybe I shouldn't think of the two of us as being like Cain and Abel in the Bible.

Maybe I should think of myself as Eve.

And of Roxy . . . as the snake.

4

"I need something new to wear to school," I announced at breakfast the next morning.

"Why? What's the special occasion?" Papa asked me.

"It's nothing special. I look so drab and boring."

"You're going to school, not a gala ball," he said.

"Now, Norton, a woman has to feel good about herself to do well in anything. Clothes are more important to us."

"To you French, you mean," Papa said, sipping his coffee. "She has nice enough clothes."

"Nice but not what's really in fashion," I ventured.

He put his cup down and began to stir it again, which I knew was an indication that he was wrestling with two contradictory thoughts. While he did, he fixed his gaze on me with those searchlight eyes like some detective looking for a clue. Of course, I wondered the same thing I often did whenever I asked for something. Did Roxy ask for similar things? Did my asking set off new alarm bells in Papa? My heart was starting to thump.

"Fashion? Don't become one of those clones, dressing like everyone else, thinking like everyone else," Papa finally said.

"She's not," Mama said. "Look at the grades she gets and how well behaved she is. Her teachers have nothing but good things to say about her." Mama looked at me and smiled. "I know exactly what she's feeling. She's a beautiful flower put in a pot and hidden in a closet. You can't keep her a little girl forever, Norton."

Papa grunted, which was something he would call a strategic retreat.

"I'll take you shopping after school today," Mama promised.

"I don't want her wearing anything ridiculous," Papa warned, "like those shirts that leave their middles naked."

"You know they don't let the girls look like that in her school, Norton."

"They're too lax in her school already. I've seen some of the girls there."

"When?" Mama asked.

"Well, maybe not exactly there, but . . ."

"Norton, could you let this girl breathe, *s'il vous plaît*?"

He glanced at her and then at me.

"You're the one who told me when we first met that if you hold a bird too tightly, you'll crush its wings," Mama added.

Papa stopped stirring his coffee. "Is that what you think happened?" he asked.

I knew exactly what he meant. He was referring to Roxy.

Mama blanched. I immediately regretted asking for anything.

She sucked in her breath and then stiffened. "We're not going to make this into something more than it is," she said. "It's time your daughter had some new things to wear. I might buy myself a new dress, too," she added. "You go to work, and let us enjoy being women, *n'est-ce pas?*"

Papa stared at her a moment. His eyes softened, and then he nodded. "Okay, okay. You're right," he said, holding up his hand.

He looked at me, and for a moment, I thought he wasn't looking at me with any anger. He was looking at me with fear.

"I won't get anything that would make you ashamed of me, Papa," I said.

His eyes brightened, and he smiled. "I know. You're my *fille parfaite*. Besides, what chance do I have with two French women?"

Mama rattled off some French expressions so quickly I couldn't keep up, but Papa laughed.

The tension evaporated.

What would happen when I changed my hair and wore more makeup?

All day, I was excited about going shopping with Mama. When Chastity heard, she asked if she could come with us.

"Okay," I said, "but we're going right after school."

"I'll call my mother. I have her credit card. She'll

say yes, I'm sure. I haven't bought anything new for a long time." I didn't say it, but I knew that was because she was hoping to lose weight.

Mama didn't mind Chastity coming along with us. She was always hoping that I would have more of a social life at school and encouraged me to have friends.

I saw how she was eyeing the other girls around my age while she waited for us, checking out what they wore. I really didn't have any stylish jeans or knit tops. The one-piece, drab-colored dresses I wore practically made me invisible. We went directly to the juniors section at Saks, and I began by trying on jeans. When I put on a pair with a tie-dye blue-and-white tunic in the dressing room and stepped out to show her, I saw the pride in Mama's face.

"I didn't realize what a beautiful figure you have already, Emmie," she said. "You have a better figure at your age than your—"

She clamped her lips, her eyes watering with both pride and sorrow now. I realized that for the longest time, I had held back on being an active teenager, not because of any shyness but because I sensed that everything I would do and would want to do would stir up unpleasant memories of my sister for both my mother and my father. I knew that if Papa could keep me his little girl forever and ever, he would. Mama was caught between wanting me to do everything any girl my age could and should do, things she had done, and her sensitivity to Papa's fears and emotions.

But whether or not it really was a result of my seeing Roxy beautiful and seemingly happy, I was suddenly experiencing a surge of feminine appetite. I, too, wanted to be beautiful, attractive, sexy, and buoyed by the same self-confidence I thought I had seen in Roxy.

Yes, I wanted clothing that would flatter my figure, a figure I had been keeping a secret, even from myself. Yes, I wanted my face to light up, use makeup to highlight my eyes and my lips. Yes, I wanted boys to notice me, really notice me, and not see me as part of the wallpaper or something. I wanted to be invited to parties, to go to friends' houses to gossip and listen to music. In short, I wanted to be like most of the other girls my age and be more carefree after school and on weekends. I had never gone to a movie with a boy, held hands while we were walking, teased and excited each other with looks, caresses, and stolen kisses. The truth was, I was ready to explode, and I was afraid that being kept so tightly under lock and key, I would reach too fast, try too hard, and, despite my caution, be more like Roxy than I intended.

"You should get three or four pairs of jeans," Mama said. "And at least as many tops. We should do something with your shoes now, too, and then we'll look at some dresses."

Chastity, who had been fingering and sifting through a variety of garments, decided to try on a pair of jeans, but the saleslady said she had nothing in her size in the juniors section. She told her to go to the women's section. I thought she would burst into tears, but instead, she chose a knit tank dress. I knew the girls at school would pounce on her and ask her if Omar the Tent Maker had made her new dress.

"That color doesn't flatter you," Mama told her, and got up to help her choose something that did more to flatter her figure.

I tried on a boat-neck knit dress with bat-wing sleeves. I knew I looked hot in it, but the hem was too high. Papa wouldn't let me out of the house. Mama saw the pain of disappointment in my face.

"It will be our secret," she said. "You look too beautiful in it to deny it."

"Are you sure, Mama?"

"I'm sure," she said.

Although Chastity was happy about the choices Mama helped her make, the envy in her face when she saw me modeling different things had an odd effect on me. I was no longer feeling sorry for her. I was angry. *Why should I deny myself just to keep her happy?* I thought. *Let her lose weight.*

I asked Mama to help me with some new makeup. Despite the way she dressed and lived now, I knew from old photographs that she had been a typical young French woman who cherished anything haute couture. Her clothing in all of the old photographs was stylish and sexy. She had been and still was a beautiful woman.

She knew just what I needed and promised to spend time showing me how to do my makeup so it wasn't overpowering.

"As someone in Paris once told me," she said, smiling at a memory, "your makeup shouldn't create a new face but highlight the beauty that is in it already.

And you have much beauty to highlight, *ma chère*," she said.

Chastity listened and watched as Mama chose lipsticks, rouge, and some eye shadow for me. Chastity then bought everything I did. Mama helped her make the right choices, too.

When we were done, Mama said she would make an appointment with her hairdresser for me. "It's time we had you looking your age," she said with a firmness I knew she would have when Papa questioned her about anything. Chastity said she would be going to her mother's hairdresser, too.

We took the taxi home, dropping Chastity off on her corner. I hugged my bags and boxes. For me, the afternoon was ten birthdays and Christmases all wrapped into one. When Papa came home, Mama told him about my jeans and blouses. She didn't mention the dress or much about the makeup.

"We have to wean him into your maturity," she whispered. "It will be all right."

Papa looked at me with both pleased surprise and concern the next morning. I had my hair pinned up and wore a pair of blue crystal earrings Mama had loaned me. They were the first thing Papa questioned.

"Where did you get those?" he demanded. "You didn't mention you bought her any jewelry yesterday," he told Mama.

She shook her head. "I'm very disappointed in you, Norton. You bought me those earrings in France seven years ago for my birthday."

"I did? Oh. Yes," he said. His failure to remember put him on the defensive. He said nothing about the makeup I had on, nor did he complain about my jeans being too tight. "Well, okay," he said just before he left for work. "You look very nice, Emmie. Be careful."

Who else's father would tell her to be careful because she looked nice? He did give me a kiss and a hug, which was something he didn't do that often in the morning before he left for work. When I glanced at him, I thought I saw great sadness in his eyes quickly replacing his moment of joy. It nearly brought tears to mine.

After he walked out, I turned to Mama. She had seen his teary eyes, too. She smiled. "He's losing his little girl," she said.

And he's already lost one, I thought, but I couldn't wait to get to school to see the reactions to my clothes and makeup. Some of the girls were surprised and happy for me, but there were others who looked so envious that they seemed angry. It was as if I had violated some unwritten assumption: *Emmie Wilcox will always look uninteresting, bland, and drab. She will never be competition for me.*

I so overshadowed Chastity that no one noticed her new clothes, shoes, and makeup. Right before lunch, what I had dreamed might happen, did happen. Evan Styles stepped up beside me in the hallway. I was in such a daze from the compliments I had received that I didn't notice he was there until I heard him say, *"Parlez-vous français?"*

I turned and for a moment was so surprised, I didn't speak. He shrugged.

"I thought you were part French and spoke it at home," he said.

"Oh. *Oui. Je parle français. Pourquoi demandez-vous?*"

"*Demandez-vous,*" he muttered. "Oh. Why do I ask?"

"*Oui. Pourquoi?*"

"I'm in first year French. I mean, *moi les premiers francais d'année,*" he replied, pointing at himself.

I laughed. "*Je prends français premier-ans.*"

"Oh. *Je prends. Oui.* I thought," he said, looking around and then leaning toward me as if he were going to tell me a great secret, "if I could talk to you every day, I'd get way ahead of anyone else in the class. I mean, my parents know French people, but I don't see myself talking with them much except, you know, simple stuff when they come to dinner, like *comment allez-vous? Je suis bien.* Or *Quelle heure est-il?* Like they don't have a watch."

"*Bien. Quand voulez-vous que nous parlions?*"

"When do I want . . . oh, how about right now? At lunch."

"*Mais oui,*" I said, and we walked on to the cafeteria.

I saw Chastity waiting for me near the food line. Her eyes widened when she saw me enter with Evan. I smiled at her and shifted my eyes toward him, but she didn't react.

"Why don't you take that table in the corner for us?" Evan said. "What do you want for lunch? Burger?"

"Just a salad and a cranberry juice," I said.

"*Très* sage," he replied.

I started for the table when he started for the line.

Chastity hurried over to me. "Where are you going?"

"Evan wants to practice his French with me. I said yes. He's getting me my lunch."

She looked back, and then her whole face seemed to begin to slide off her skull. She muttered a soft "Oh" and started away.

"I'll tell you about it later," I offered. She didn't turn back.

I could feel most of the other girls and some of the boys looking our way when Evan brought me my lunch and set his down beside mine.

"So? Your mother is French?"

"*Oui. Ma mère est née à Paris.*"

"Let's see. Your mother was something in Paris."

"Born."

"Oh, right. That makes her French."

"Yes, it does," I said, laughing.

"But you were born here in America, right?" he asked, as if that were a real concern.

"Yes. I can run for president."

He smiled. *What a sweet smile he has,* I thought. It seemed to begin in his eyes and then ripple through his face to soften those perfect lips. I realized he had a much darker complexion than most of the students.

"You're out in the sun a lot?"

"We took a long weekend in Puerto Rico. My father had some business to do for the mayor."

"*Vous êtes-vous amusés bien?*"

"Huh?"

"Did you have a good time?"

"Oh. Yes. I mean, *oui*. I was on the beach most of the time."

"*La plage.* That's beach."

"*La plage,*" he repeated. "Were you brought up speaking French?"

"*Non. Anglais,* but my mother, *ma mère,* spoke French to me, too. She still does."

"You really can't learn a language in a classroom," Evan said.

"Yes. You can learn to read it well, but holding a conversation is different. Maybe you'll spend a summer in France."

"Yeah, I think so."

"*En français.*"

"*Oui, je—*"

"*Pensez.* Think. *Ainsi.*"

"So?"

"*Oui.*"

"I knew it," he said. "You're just going to have to cancel all of your dates for the next few weeks and spend your weekends with me."

"Is that so?"

"*Absolument,*" he said, and we both laughed.

Was this really happening? I felt like Cinderella. I didn't even notice any of the other students in the cafeteria. Their chatter seemed to die away. I was too intent on hearing every syllable when Evan spoke. I wanted to memorize the movements in his face when he smiled, laughed, and thought seriously about something. I was never as disappointed as when the bell rang to end lunch period.

"So, what about Friday night? I was thinking we would go to this French movie at Lincoln Plaza. I mean, it has subtitles, but I think I could learn a lot with you beside me."

"*Peut-être.*"

"Maybe. You mean maybe you'll go, or maybe I'll learn a lot?"

"*Tous les deux.*"

"Huh?"

"Both," I said.

"Man, this is great. I'll walk you home after school today, okay? That way, I'll know where to go to pick you up Friday."

"If my parents say yes," I said.

"Just tell them it's a school project," he said. "See you later."

"*Plus tard,*" I called to him as he started away.

He turned back to smile. To me, it looked as if his face actually radiated. I stood there watching him walk off and didn't even realize that Chastity had come up beside me. She had followed us out of the cafeteria.

"He didn't ask you out or anything, did he?" she demanded. "We have something to do Friday night."

"We'll do it on the weekend," I said. "I promise."

"He asked you out?"

I nodded, hoping she would be happy for me, but

she turned away in a sulk and walked faster toward the classroom.

I felt sorry for her, but if this was the price I had to pay, then so be it.

I had never been as grateful for my mother having been born in Paris. *Vive la France,* I thought, and hurried after Chastity.

Some way, somehow, I'd get her to be happy for me, I thought, but when she discovered that Evan was walking me home from school, she was even more put out. It was as if we were still in grade school and she saw my wanting to be with a boy as something of a betrayal.

"Do you want to walk part of the way with us?" I asked her when Evan caught up with us at the end of the day.

"No. I have to do something first," she said, and quickly walked off.

"She sounded upset," he said.

"She'll get over it," I said.

He smiled. "I wrote out my cell number for you to call later, I hope with a *oui, oui.*"

I took the card and put it in my jeans pocket.

"I'm sure that with you, I'll eat and sleep French," he said.

"Sleep French?"

"I meant dream in French. Do you?"

"No," I said, laughing.

"Let's walk. *Marchons?* I just looked it up. How's my pronunciation so far?"

I just smiled.

"Well, I won't mind if it takes me longer than I had thought, as long as you're my tutor."

I held my smile, and we started for my home.

It occurred to me as we walked that I hadn't thought about Roxy all day.

Was that good or bad?

I had a feeling that it wouldn't be long before I found out.

5

I wasn't confident that Papa would approve of my date, but I was hopeful. After all, Evan's father was an important mayoral assistant. I was sure Papa probably knew who he was. He kept up with politics almost as much as he did with business. I told Mama before I asked Papa, of course. She had become my negotiator. I was glad she said she would present it to him at dinner.

When we had all sat at the table, Papa looked at us suspiciously. "Why do I feel there's something you two want to tell me?"

"Because there is," Mama said.

He sat back, folding his arms across his chest. "Go on."

"Emmie has been asked out on her first real date," she began.

He unfolded his arms and sat forward quickly. "Date? When?"

"When was she asked out, or when is the date?"

"Both," he said, the corners of his eyes tightening with impatience. Having been brought up in the military world, Papa had that snap to everything he said most of the time, especially anything he asked, but lately, all Mama had to do was look at him with her soft, loving eyes, and he usually began to soften.

"She was asked today for this Friday night."

"What sort of date?"

"To go to the movies."

"And you approve?"

"I wasn't much older than she is now when I went on my first date," she said.

"You're French," Papa said, as if that explained any behavior he would disapprove of.

"It was all right for me to be French when you asked me out on a date. Do you remember our first date?" she followed quickly, which was a very good question strategically.

"Of course. We went to dinner at a restaurant on the Left Bank in Paris."

"No," she said. "That was our second date. The first date was a walk."

"Oh, I don't call that a date."

"To me, it was a very nice date. I wouldn't have gone out with you again if it wasn't. That's how much you know about going on dates."

"All right, all right." He looked at me. "Who asked you on a date?"

"Evan Styles."

"Styles? Why do I know that name?"

"His father is Martin Styles. He works for the mayor."

"Oh, right." He thought for a moment and then looked at Mama. "So, all of this happened so suddenly. Was it because of the new clothes she wore to school?"

"No," I said, even though I thought my new look might have attracted his attention. "He is taking French and wanted me to help him."

Papa shook his head. "You know that's just an excuse, right? I'm sure he's not just interested in French."

"I know, Papa, but I have to let him think I believe him," I replied, and Mama laughed.

"What's so funny?"

"She's right about that. You always have to let a man think you believe him."

"Very funny, Vivian."

"You don't have to worry about this girl. *Très bon,* Emmie."

"Yes, well, just don't get ahead of yourself, young lady," Papa said. "You don't know all that much about men yet. I want you back before eleven."

"Oh, Papa. What if the movie gets out later? We might want to stop for a soda or something. It's been so nice out. Maybe we'll walk. There's no school the next day."

"She's old enough to stay out to midnight, Norton, *non?*"

I waited anxiously for his reply. I could see the memories flashing past him. How had Roxy gotten so out of hand? What mistakes had they made? Could he have done more in the beginning to prevent it? Was he making a mistake with me?

"I would call you if anything would prevent me from coming home on time, Papa. Always."

He voiced that familiar grunt that was his reluctant approval. "I'll tell you this," he said quickly, however. "I don't care how much importance you women put on your clothes. If he noticed you only because of your new clothes, he's pretty shallow."

"Let her make her own opinions and discoveries about the young men she meets, Norton. And besides, who are you to talk about noticing someone's clothes? Your appearance is very important to you. Who else works so hard on his shoes and his clothes in your office?"

"That's different."

"*Pourquoi?*"

"Because someone in my business position has to appear well put together. Attention to detail gives my clients confidence in me."

Mama just smiled at him.

"It's true," he emphasized.

Mama nodded. "Well, maybe the young man is just shy and finally got around to asking her," she offered.

"Shy? That'll be refreshing to see in a teenager these days," he muttered.

I smiled to myself. I knew that Evan Styles could be called anything but shy. As soon as we finished dinner and I helped Mama clean up, I called Evan to tell him my parents had said okay.

"That's great. We can make the eight-twenty show if you want to have a bite to eat before we go. I can come by at six-thirty. We'll catch a taxi. I know a nice little restaurant near the movie theater. Okay?"

"*Oui,* but leave ten minutes to say hello to my parents."

"Really? Should I wear a tie?"

His little note of sarcasm took me by surprise, and for a moment, I didn't know what to say.

"I'm kidding," he said quickly. "But you know what? I will wear a tie. It will impress my parents, too."

I thought I would wear my new dress. If I put on my light trench coat, Papa would not see how short the hem was. I would need a wrap for later anyway. The days were still unseasonably warm, but the night temperatures dropped quickly.

"Okay," I said. "*Je laverai mon visage.*"

"What's that mean?"

"I'll wash my face."

He laughed. "I see being with you is going to be fun."

"*Peut-être.*"

"No maybes about it. Impressed that I knew the word?"

"No comment."

"Actually, Mr. Denning is constantly saying that in class whenever anyone asks him a question. He wants us to find our own answers. See you in school tomorrow," he said.

I expected that Chastity would call me to question me more about Evan, but she didn't. I couldn't wait to go to sleep, anyway. It felt as if I were a little girl again, looking forward to Christmas morning or my birthday. As much as I wanted the night to pass quickly, I had trouble falling asleep. All sorts of questions and worries rumbled through my mind. Was Papa right? Was it just my new look that interested Evan? Once he learned more about me, would he lose interest quickly? Would his friends question him about why he wanted to go out with me in the first place? How would other girls, jealous girls, treat me? Would they all be as sullen as Chastity?

Somehow, I finally exhausted my brain and fell asleep, but I was up even before Papa the next morning. He was very surprised to see me in the kitchen when he came down.

"Something's put a fire under your shoes," he commented.

Mama just smiled. I thought he did, too, but he kept it hidden under his hand. I don't think I ever got to school as quickly. I practically ran up the avenue. I wondered when I would see Evan. His classes were on a different side of the building, but to my delight, he was waiting for me near my locker when I arrived. Usually, Chastity was there, but she was either late that day or not coming to school at all. I had little time to think about her. Evan was ready to practice French.

"*Bonjour. Comment allez-vous?*"

"*Bien, et toi?*"

"*Toi?* That's the informal, right?"

"*Absolument*, Monsieur Styles."

I exchanged my books in my locker. He stood by my side and talked, and then, as he walked with me to my homeroom, he told me more about his family and where they lived. He told me about his older sister, Tami, who was in college, the time they went on a family vacation in southern France in Beulieu-sur-Mer and stayed at a very famous expensive hotel, La Réserve. He met many people, including people his age, who could speak not only two languages but three. He said that was when he decided he would learn to speak French. He spoke very quickly, as if he had to get it all said before we parted to go to our morning classes.

Chastity showed up late for homeroom. The first thing she did when she sat across from me was ask me if I was still going on a date.

"Yes, why not?"

"I thought you might have changed your mind," she said sullenly.

"Hello? Like, why?"

"I thought you might have realized he was toying with you," she said. I imagined she had spent a good part of her night thinking of reasons to discourage me.

"Why would he be doing that?"

"The boys here are like that," she said when the bell rang. "I heard they make bets about how much they can tease and take advantage of a girl."

"When did you hear this?" I asked. She had never said anything like this before, and I certainly hadn't heard anything of the kind, especially something that made it sound like a male conspiracy.

"I heard," she said, shrugging. "Some of the girls were talking about it in the girls' room."

"When?"

"Oh, I don't know, exactly. I heard it."

"Well, why didn't you ever tell me this before?"

"You weren't being taken advantage of before," she said.

"And I'm not now," I snapped back at her, and hurried to our first class.

She realized how angry she had made me and at the end of class told me she was just trying to be helpful. I grunted like Papa but didn't go out of my way to be talkative or friendly. At lunch, I was with Evan again anyway. He got my lunch, and we sat alone at the same table.

"I'm sorry I talked so much about myself this morning," he said.

"That's all right. I enjoyed hearing it all, especially your experiences in France and your trip to Monte Carlo. My parents always talk about the Café de Paris there, too."

"I'm sure. Tell me about your family now," he said.

I told him about Papa and his military family and Mama and her French family, but of course, I didn't mention my sister, Roxy.

"I'm surprised you don't have any brothers or sisters," he said. "If I had a daughter as pretty as you are, I'd want to try for another."

I smiled but kept my eyes down. Truth is comfortable in your eyes, but falsehood looks for ways to escape and clearly shows itself in the way you look at the person to whom you are lying. Papa taught me that. He said it was something his father, who knew about enemy prisoner interrogations, taught him.

"My mother had a difficult birth," I said. It was half true anyway.

"Oh. Well," he said, eager to change the subject, "since your father was brought up on Army bases and your grandfather was a general, maybe I should get a haircut before meeting your father." He looked serious.

"No," I said emphatically. He had beautiful hair that had been cut in a layered style. Papa would criticize the way his hair fell over his eyes, but he wouldn't say anything to him. He'd mumble about it to me, I was sure.

Evan laughed. "I was just joking, but I do want to make a good impression."

"Just salute," I said.

"Really?"

"No." It was my turn to tease him.

He realized it and laughed. "I'm glad you have a sense of humor, too," he said. "Most of the girls at this school take themselves too seriously."

"Oh?"

Out of the corners of my eyes, I could see the way the other students were looking our way and talking about us. Chastity was with some of the girls we usually hung with, but she looked as if she was sulking.

"I haven't dated too many from here," he continued.

I didn't want to ask him any more about his love life. I recalled Mama once telling me in French that when a woman is with a man she likes, she shouldn't talk about other women or ask about old girlfriends.

"Even a flicker of a memory about another girl he liked is static on your radio," she said. "Keep him tuned in to you."

She had been reading one of her favorite French romance writers, and when I asked her about the story, she told me that. I wondered if she had ever discussed such things with Roxy. If she had, did Roxy appreciate the advice or resent it? Was Roxy arrogant about men? Was this part of why she didn't respect Mama enough, because Mama had fallen in love too soon for her liking? It was so hard to understand it all by only being able to read between the lines and guess and assume.

Evan couldn't walk me home after school. He said he had things to do at home, things he had promised his father he would do. He didn't go into any detail, but I had the impression that it had to do with the mess his room was in.

"I don't want to get grounded tonight," he added, and then, without any warning, he kissed me good-bye and told me in French that he would see me later.

I watched him walk off.

Apparently, I wasn't the only one. Moments later, Chastity was at my side. "Don't think just because he kissed you that he really likes you," she warned.

"Why are you so down on him? Whenever we talked about him before, you were complimentary. I think you even said he was dreamy or something."

"I'm not saying he's not good-looking."

"And popular," I reminded her.

"And popular. But how come he's so interested in you all of a sudden?"

"Maybe he is taking advantage of me," I said.

"You think so?" Her eyes lit up with hope.

"Yes, to learn French and do better in class."

"What?" She shook her head. She couldn't see the small smile on my lips. "He's not interested in your French. I heard some of the girls in his class talking about him today. He has a reputation for dating a girl for only one thing. If he can't get it, he drops her fast." I knew she was either lying or exaggerating. Her eyes were moving like pinballs, looking at everything but me.

"Well, you're the one who's always telling me we should be as sexually liberated as the boys are."

For a few moments, her mouth opened and closed without making a sound. "You mean, you would . . . you would do it with him, maybe on the first date?"

"I don't know. Weren't you the one who said that you read it's usually impossible to plan these things? Don't worry, you'll be the first to know," I said.

She was stunned enough to be quiet for the rest of the way until she had to cut off to go home. "I'm really worried about you," she said.

I patted her hand. "Don't worry. I'll call you tomorrow to tell you how it went. I'll tell you everything in detail," I promised, actually offered as a peace token. She seemed happy enough about that.

"If it doesn't go well, or even if it does, you probably won't see him again Saturday night. You can come over then, and we can go up to your sister's hotel and—"

"I'll let you know tomorrow," I said quickly, and walked on. I was really beginning to regret ever having let Chastity know about Roxy. With no real social life or excitement, it had become her own single most precious thing. As I drew closer to home, I pushed her out of my mind and concentrated on preparing for my date with Evan.

I could see that Mama was sincerely happy for me. She would never say it, but she was very worried that the situation with Roxy would have so heavy and negative an impact on me that I would have a horrible young life. Papa was like a dark cloud hovering above anything I would do that could draw me closer to being the kind of daughter Roxy had been. I was sure Mama felt she had failed terribly with Roxy and was afraid that she would do something to cause a repeated disaster involving me. It took great courage for her to stand up to Papa and insist that I have more fashionable clothing and be more of a teenager now. He didn't know it, but Evan was very important in my life. He was my first real date, and if he was a disaster, or if anything Chastity said was even slightly true, I could have a very big setback. Actually, both Mama and I could.

Thinking these things, I almost decided against putting on the new dress, but when I did, I looked so good in it that I was determined to challenge Papa if he should disapprove. I waited as long as I could before going downstairs, and I did put on my trench coat first. Papa had been sure to get home from work in time to meet Evan. He was sitting in the living room reading the *Wall Street Journal* when I came down. Mama was in the kitchen. If Evan was on time, I thought, he would be there within five minutes. *Please be on time,* I prayed.

"Oh, you look so nice," Mama said, hurrying to see me.

"How can you tell? She's wearing that coat," Papa said.

Mama could see I was wearing the new dress and quickly figured out why I was being so cautious. "I mean her hair, her face, Norton. Can't you give your beautiful daughter a compliment?" she asked, putting him on the defensive immediately. I knew Mama's strategy. "Young girls are very sensitive and need some confidence building."

"What? No. I mean, of course. Yes, you're beautiful, Emmie. I didn't mean . . ."

The doorbell rang. I sighed with relief.

"That must be your young man," Mama said. She went to the door quickly. Papa looked at the hallway in anticipation.

"*Bonsoir,* I'm Evan Styles," Evan said to my mother.

"*Bonsoir. Bienvenu,*" Mama said.

Evan stepped in and saw me. "*Bonsoir,* Emmie. *Comment allez-vous?*"

Impatient, Papa rose and came to the living-room doorway. "So, this is the young man trying to learn French?" he asked.

"Yes, sir," Evan said. "I'm pleased to meet you, Mr. Wilcox." Evan extended his hand and then looked at me. "Or should I say, *enchanté?*"

Papa relaxed his shoulders and shook Evan's hand. I should have warned Evan about his handshake. It was extra firm, almost to the point of causing a little pain. Evan didn't blink, however.

He was wearing the tie he promised he'd wear. He looked very handsome and sweet.

Papa put his hands on his hips, taking on that drill-sergeant demeanor. "I don't want her out past midnight," he said.

"Zero hundred hours, sir. I understand."

Papa didn't smile. He glanced at me and then at Mama. "We don't go by military time, son," he said. "Midnight is just midnight."

"I understand," Evan said. For a moment, I held my breath. He looked as if he might salute, and I knew Papa wouldn't find that at all funny. Thankfully, he didn't.

"Well you two have a wonderful time," Mama said.

"*Un merveilleux temps,*" Evan said, his eyes twinkling when he looked at me.

"*Très bon,*" Mama said. "Yes, have a wonderful time."

Papa still hadn't cracked a smile. "Be careful," he told me, and returned to his chair and his paper.

Mama gave me a kiss, and I walked out with Evan.

"Wow," he said. "You're not on military time, but I bet your father's on guard duty tonight. I hope you remember the password to get back in."

"I do. It's 'I'm home,'" I said, and he laughed.

We hurried to the corner, where he flagged a taxi. I took a deep breath when he opened the door for me.

I'm on my first date, I thought, and then I suddenly wondered if Roxy had ever had a formal first date or if she simply met boys places without telling Papa and Mama. I had no idea why that would make a difference to me now, but it did.

It was almost as if I wanted to be very sure that I didn't do anything she had done.

That way, Papa would go on loving me forever, and I'd never end up without a family, living in a hotel, whether I was pampered and beautiful or not.

Loneliness, after all, hunts especially for the hearts of orphans.

6

I had no way to judge my first date with a boy, but to me, it seemed as if every moment that passed was better than the previous one. When I took off my trench coat in the restaurant, Evan's eyes widened, and a big smile rippled across his face.

"Wow," he said. "That's a beautiful dress, but it's only beautiful because you're wearing it," he quickly followed.

I blushed so deeply it made me tremble. "Thank you."

I slipped into the booth quickly. For a moment, he just stood there looking at me.

"What's that line they use in the movies?" he asked as he sat across from me. "Where have you been all my life?"

He was so good at these compliments that I began to worry that maybe Chastity was right. If there was one thing I didn't want to be, it was gullible. Girls had to navigate a fine line, I thought. It was wonderful to have these nice things said about you, but how deep did sincerity go in them? Should they sound warnings? Should I graciously accept them or flick them off as if they were so much sparkle? I didn't want to offend him, but I didn't want to appear naïve, either.

"I was always just down the hall, Evan."

"Yeah. Well, it serves me right for not looking in more than one direction."

The waitress brought us menus, and we ordered soft drinks.

"I have a confession to make," he said as he read the menu.

"So soon?"

He laughed. "Not that sort of confession. You know Buzzy Gibson? He's a junior."

"I don't really know him."

"Well, he was the one who told me to check you out. He's going with Missy Wagner, otherwise you might be sitting here across from him tonight."

"I don't think so," I said. "I don't know him, but I know who he is. I mean . . ."

"He's not your type? Girls make that decision quickly, I hear. At least, they do when it comes to who is definitely not their type."

"Maybe. I don't think I can speak for all girls, even most. I can only speak for myself."

He widened his eyes. What I said obviously impressed him.

The waitress brought our drinks.

"I think I'll have the chicken salad," I told her.

"*La même chose,*" Evan said.

"Pardon?"

"He means the same thing," I told her. She shrugged and wrote it down. "You pronounced that very well," I said.

"Another confession," he said.

"Oh?"

"I spent most of the afternoon memorizing some common French expressions just to impress you. It can't hurt my grade in class, either, I guess."

"If you learn everything yourself, I won't be able to help," I teased.

"Oh, don't worry about that. I'll need your help for years."

I smiled and sipped my soda. The waitress brought us some bread and butter. I finally looked around the restaurant. It wasn't very big or expensive-looking, but it wasn't a fast-food place, either.

"Have you been here often?"

"I suppose," he said. "My father likes places like this. He calls them unassuming and places where you can talk to real people, whoever they are."

"Maybe he just means people who aren't phonies."

"You mean like plastic socialites?"

I shrugged. "Is your father going to run for some office?" I asked.

"Probably. Actually," he said, "it's supposed to be a secret, but the mayor is working on getting him the nomination for congressman, but if he's elected, we're not moving to Washington, D.C. New York is close enough."

"Now it's no longer a secret," I said.

"Somehow, I feel I can trust you."

"Why?" I asked, really curious.

"It's in your eyes. You're the type of person who hates telling lies or hurting someone else's feelings. Am I wrong?"

I shook my head, but I wanted to tell him it wasn't wise to believe in someone's goodness too soon. Did older boys, especially boys like him who came from wealthy, famous families, appreciate advice from someone like me? If he was too arrogant to accept good advice no matter what the source of it, he wasn't for me, I thought. *Not my type*, I told myself. I couldn't help the small smile on my lips, but he didn't seem to notice.

The waitress brought our platters, and we started to eat. He talked more about his family, especially his sister. He was very proud of her. She had been her high school's valedictorian and was on the dean's list at college. He said her plan was to go to Harvard Law School and become editor of the *Law Review*.

"I guess I have some impressive footsteps to follow," he said.

I admired the relationship he apparently had with his sister. I think he saw that in my face when he finished talking about her.

"What's it like being an only child?" he asked. "Are you spoiled?"

"Hardly," I said, and described my responsibilities at home, my father's military style, and my efforts always to please him. "I mean, I love him dearly," I said. "But as you know, he is the son of an Army general."

Evan smiled. "I'm glad my suspicions about you were correct," he said.

"What were they?"

"Simply that you'd be great to talk to, someone who was sincere, honest, and sweet."

More wonderful compliments, I thought. They made me nervous. Again, I wondered if most girls would be grateful and leave it at that. Was it good or bad that I had such distrust? Roxy surely knew how to handle men. Wouldn't it have been great to have had a relationship with an older, more experienced sister? There was only so much I felt comfortable asking my mother. I couldn't simply shake off all of my father's warnings. Was it really that dangerous simply to put all your trust in your own feelings?

"Shouldn't we get going for the movie?" I asked. His compliments were beginning to make me feel a little uncomfortable, anyway, especially since I wasn't being completely honest, letting him believe I was an only child.

"Right." He signaled for the waitress. "I hope that was all right," he said, referring to the restaurant, when we left.

"Oh, it was perfect. Thank you."

He held my hand, and we hurried up the street and then crossed to the movie theater.

It was a very interesting French movie, entitled *Illusion*. It was about a young woman who thought she had fallen in love with a ghost, because when he disappeared and she went looking for him, she was told he had been killed in an automobile accident years before she had met him. Later, she discovered she had been having a romance with his twin brother, whom no one knew existed.

"How was the translation, the subtitles?" Evan asked when we were leaving.

"Just okay," I said. "There were quite a few places where I thought non-French-speaking people were not given enough or exactly the right expression."

"It must be something to be able to speak and read two languages like you do."

"My mother can speak English, French, Italian, and Spanish."

"Just like many of those people I met when we were in France," he said. He checked his watch. "We can try walking back. We have close to an hour and ten minutes."

"Okay," I said. He took my hand. "Do you think your parents would let you come over to my house for dinner tomorrow night? My parents would send a car for you."

"Send a car?"

"Yeah, sure," he said, making it sound like nothing.

"I don't know. I'll have to ask."

"Well, maybe if I get you home before midnight, your father would let you off the base again, give you another liberty pass or something."

"He's not that bad," I said, laughing.

Suddenly, he stopped walking. We had not gone very far, so I thought he had decided to hail a taxi, but instead, he turned to me and brought his lips to mine.

It wasn't a long kiss, but his lips were so warm and soft I felt myself stirring.

"I thought I would do that now," he said.

"What? Why?"

We were still in a very busy section, and many people hurrying along paused to look at us.

"So that later, when we're at your front door, it won't be such a big deal to kiss you good night."

"Well, I hope it's still a big deal," I said.

"No, I don't mean that. All the little tension won't be there now."

"I didn't expect it to be there later, either."

He laughed. "Man, I do like you, Emmie. As my father would say, you're as full of surprises as a box of Cracker Jacks."

We walked on, talking about the school, our friends, and things we would both like to do. When I had first agreed to go on the date with him, I was afraid we would have very little to talk about, since we had such different backgrounds and he was older, but it didn't take long for me to feel as if we had known each other a long time. If there really was something called positive energy, I was feeling it now. I think we were both disappointed when we reached my block. Both of us slowed down. He looked at his watch.

"We still have fifteen minutes," he said. "I think it would be sinful to give up any one of them by bringing you home early."

"On the other hand, my father will be impressed."

"I suppose," he said reluctantly.

It was very quiet on the street, with only a pedestrian

here and there and little car traffic. Evan paused and kissed me again. He held on to me, keeping his face close.

"I really like you, Emmie," he said. "I've never had as good a time on a first date or anything."

"I like you, too," I said, and we kissed again.

Neither of us spoke until we reached my front door. He looked at his watch. "Seven more minutes."

"You can be sure my father's watching the clock," I said.

He nodded, gave me another kiss, and started away. "I'll call you in the morning, hoping you can come to dinner," he said.

"Okay." I waved and stood there for a moment, watching him hurry to the corner to flag down a taxi. Then I went inside. Papa was waiting up in the living room. He was watching a late news show.

"Cutting it close," he said, nodding at the miniature grandfather clock on the mantel.

"We decided to walk back. It's so nice out, Papa."

"Well, I'm glad he's not lazy."

"Oh, no. He was the one who suggested it."

"Where did he take you to eat?" he asked, his voice softening.

I told him and described the restaurant.

"Sounds sensible."

"He said his father likes to go there."

"That so?" He flipped off the television and stood. "Sounds like you had a good time, then."

"Yes, I did. He asked me to dinner at his house

tomorrow night. He said his parents would send a car for me."

"Really?" He looked thoughtful.

"Can I say yes?"

"Let me sleep on it," he said. Then he did something he had never done. He smiled and said, "Your sister never asked permission for anything. She just did what she wanted."

I held my breath. Would he say anything more, tell me anything more about her?

"Did you tell him about her?"

"No, Papa. No one at school but Chastity knows about her, remember?"

"Just wanted to be sure," he said. "Let's go to sleep. Your mother went to sleep an hour ago. I thought mothers were supposed to be the ones waiting up. That's the French for you," he added, smiling again. He put his arm around me, and we walked upstairs together. At my bedroom door, he kissed me good night and said, "Maybe we'll sleep in a little tomorrow morning. I could use more sleep these days."

"Aren't you feeling well?"

"Yes, sure. I'm just at it a little too much these days. I'll slow down," he said, sounding like someone trying to convince himself.

I watched him walk to his and Mama's bedroom. His habitually perfect posture wasn't there. He was slouching as if he suddenly had a great weight on his shoulders. I don't know why such a small thing bothered me, but it did. I even felt tears coming into my eyes.

I guess getting older meant realizing your parents wouldn't be young forever. We were all in such a rush to be older. We never really gave much thought to what that meant for our parents. Papa had told me once that even though his father and he didn't get along all that well, and even though his father never forgave him for not making a career in the Army, one of the saddest days of his life was the day his father retired.

"My old man was an old man," he had said. "All that spit and polish that had kept the wear and tear hidden was gone. He looked a lot smaller to me, too, when he was out of uniform. I congratulated him just like everyone else, but I didn't want to. I didn't want to celebrate the beginning of the end for him, and I knew how empty his life was going to be without his precious Army duties.

"But that's the way it is," he'd quickly concluded, maybe because he realized he was being a little too sentimental for a tough guy.

I hadn't said anything. I just hugged him. He kissed me on the forehead and held me longer than he ever had. And I held on to him, because even at that young age, I knew there would be a time when he would no longer be there to hold me. I mean, I always knew that. It just wasn't something young children permit in their world of thoughts. Everyone else's parents could die, but not yours.

My memories of my night with Evan quickly overcame my moment of sadness. I was eager to get to bed just so I could lie there and recall every second, especially every kiss, every touch. When I closed my eyes, I saw his eyes vividly. He was there under my eyelids. I tried to remember every word he said, too. It was as if I had a video recording and could play the whole evening back by just pressing my eyelids closed. It turned out to be one of the most contented nights of sleep I ever had.

Mama was really surprised at breakfast when the first thing Papa said to me was, "Okay, you can go."

"Go where?"

"She was asked to the Styleses' house for dinner tonight," he said, sounding proud that he knew before she did. "They're sending a car for her."

"Really? Well, I guess I don't have to ask how your date was, then," she said. She even sounded a little jealous that Papa knew more than she did.

"I had a good time, Mama."

She stood there, smiling at me. "*Merveilleux,* Emmie. I'm so happy for you."

She glanced at Papa. I think he knew as well as I did that Mama was always afraid that I wouldn't have a happy time as a teenager or when I was a young woman off on my own. For a moment, at least, it was truly as if the clouds had parted on our ceilings, and we could feel the rays of hope and happiness again.

I practically lunged at my phone when it rang later on in the morning. I couldn't wait to tell Evan that I could come to his house, but it wasn't Evan.

"So, how was your date?" Chastity asked as soon as I said hello.

"Oh. Very nice. The movie was very interesting. You should try to see it."

"Why would I want to see a French movie by myself?" she countered. "Unless you would go again."

"Oh, I would," I said.

"Oh. Well, are you coming over tonight?"

I sucked in my breath. She wasn't going to like this. "No, I can't. I was invited to Evan's house for dinner."

"What? His parents invited you?"

"Yes. It wouldn't be nice to say no, right?"

She was silent.

"I mean, my parents approved, and you know my father."

"Right," she said. "Maybe you could come over on Sunday, then. Tell your father we're studying again. We could still see your sister, I bet. And you can tell me all about your fancy dinner."

"I didn't say it was going to be fancy."

"Sure."

"Actually, Evan took me to a very simple, inexpensive place last night. He's not stuck-up."

"Whoop-de-do. Are you going to come on Sunday or not?"

"I'll call you in the morning," I said.

"Right. Call me," she said sharply, and hung up without saying good-bye.

I felt sorry for her again, but I was determined not to let that spoil my happiness.

Twenty minutes later, Evan called.

"That's great," he said when I told him my father had said yes. "I guess it was smart bringing you home a little early, huh?"

"*Absolument. Très intelligent.*"

"Hey, I have a great idea. I'll have the car pick you up an hour earlier, so you and I can practice a short French dialogue to impress my parents, okay?"

"*Je consens.*"

"Um . . . I . . . consent?"

"Agree, consent. Or you could just say *d'accord.* See, it's not as hard as you think."

"How's five sound?"

"*En français.*"

"Five, five . . . *cinq,*" he said.

"*Bien. Cinq.* Oh, how formal is this dinner?" I asked, thinking about what Chastity had said.

"My father wears a jacket and tie. For a Saturday-night dinner, we do dress, but it's not black-tie."

"Okay," I said, a little unsure. Now I wished I had saved my dress for that night.

I hung up but was immediately overcome with worry.

"I just made you an appointment today for your hair," Mama said, stepping into my room. "Two o'clock. I thought it would be a good excuse to do it, no?"

"Yes. They dress a little formally, Mama. I don't know if I have anything nice enough."

She thought a moment and then ripped off her apron. "We're off to shop."

"Really? But you just bought me new clothes, Mama."

"That was a start. I've got a lot of making up to do, for myself as well as for you," she said. "*Allons.*"

Papa didn't put up a syllable of resistance. It was as if we all wanted this incoming tide of new happiness to keep washing onto our family shores.

But there is a lot out there in the sea, and the shore has little to say about what washes onto it.

7

This time, Mama and I knew we couldn't get past Papa's scrutiny so easily, but she wanted me to have a more conservative look anyway, so we bought a black dress, but it was calf-length. She bought me a purse to go with it and then another pair of shoes. Afterward, she bought herself a new dress and a pair of shoes, too. I felt this was a different sort of shopping spree, very different from when she was buying me new school clothes. It was as if my going on a date and being invited to a boy's home for dinner had opened up a new world to us both, a world I thought she had missed with Roxy.

I could feel how she was looking at me differently, too, talking to me more like one grown woman to another. I sensed that there was a moment in time, perhaps, when your mother becomes more like your sister. We giggled over some of the clothes we both tried on, complimented each other when something looked good on us, and then went to celebrate our successes at lunch. Mama talked more about herself as a young girl, some of the boys she had dated and thought she had loved. There were revelations about her family that I had never heard. According to what she told me, her mother was almost as strict as Papa. In some ways, what her sister Manon had done had put her in a place very similar to the place I was in because of Roxy.

"My mother was always worried that I would have the same fate as Manon," she said. "I could see it on her face whenever I went with a boy or a boy came to our home. Fortunately, she was very fond of your father. She saw he was a no-nonsense man right away. I think she liked him more than I did in the beginning. Suddenly, everything he said and wanted was sensible, and everything I said was questionable.

"But my love life was far from perfect. I had many disappointments, especially when I was your age or a little older. Affections were more fleeting. We were all so eager to have a romance, to be involved with someone, but it didn't take long to realize that it wasn't wise to put too much faith in someone so quickly. After all, we were both just exploring our own feelings, going into what your father calls 'uncharted territory.' Just as you're doing now, we were exploring, testing ourselves." She smiled, and I could see that she was smiling at some memory.

"Was there one special boy before Papa?"

"Oh, there was, but it wasn't as deeply felt. There wasn't that sense of commitment, what my father described as an investment of life in someone else. He was a bit of a romantic, my father. No one but me knew it, but he loved reading Daphne du Maurier. He'd see one of my mother's or sister's romance novels and say he was going to read it to see what the big deal was."

She laughed, and then she looked at me intently, deeply, and said, "I envy you for the journey you are about to begin."

"Are you sorry about anything you did when you were younger, Mama?"

"No. I'm with Edith Piaf. *Je regrette rien.*"

I hoped I would regret nothing, too. She hugged me, and we finished our lunch.

Hearing my mother talk about her past like this, revealing more of her intimate memories and her feelings, drew us closer to each other than ever. It was always difficult to imagine your parents when they were your age, even when you saw pictures of them back then, but her willingness to share with me enabled me to have at least a glimpse of her as a young girl.

Papa thought we had drunk too much wine or something when he saw us afterward. We were still giggling and making jokes about the people we had seen and the things we had done.

"Who's the teenager here?" he cried, pretending to be upset.

Afterward, Mama talked him into taking a walk with her in the park. "For a little while," she said, "we'll be like we first were."

I watched them go off together. All these years, I had viewed them only as my loving guardians, here to provide for me and guide me. Although there were certainly many flashes of affection between them, they were always quite aware of my presence. They loved each other very much. That was obvious, and despite the tragedy of Roxy, we were still a strong family, but when they walked off together holding hands, I could see my mother's reminiscences with me still in full bloom on her face, especially in her eyes, and I realized that my father was obviously touched. The love he'd had for her at the very beginning, that passion, had been resurrected. For a while, at least, he would act more like a young man again. In fact, the way they held on to each other, stayed close as they walked off, made them look like two teenage lovers.

Was this a side of them that Roxy had never known? If she saw them now as I did, would she regret even more what she had done and lost, if she regretted it at all? I sensed how important it had become for me to know this, but I didn't want to go searching for her with Chastity again. Having Chastity there ruined it for me. She was just a voyeur looking for some titillation. I was looking for answers that were critical to who I was and who I would become.

Later, when the Styleses' family driver called to say that he was waiting outside, Papa and Mama came out, too, to see what sort of car they had sent. It was a black Town Car, and the driver was in a chauffeur's uniform.

"I hope that's not on the public's dime," Papa muttered.

"Don't spoil her night," Mama warned him.

When I had come down in my new dress and shoes, Papa had looked speechless for a moment. Just as you would suddenly enter a new world with your mother, you would with your father, I realized. Fathers, I decided, were far more comfortable seeing their daughters as little girls, while mothers couldn't wait for them to grow up and get into dresses and hairdos and makeup. When the realization came to fathers that their little girls were on the threshold of being women, they first recoiled. There was safety and comfort when your daughter was a child. She moved in that bubble-gum-and-lollipop world, with little or no idea of what eventually would awaken inside her and make everything she did and everything she said suddenly far more complicated.

Except for the danger of pedophiles, of course, boys and men didn't hear any sexual suggestions in what a little girl said or see any passionate interest in a little girl's smile or the look in her eyes. Little girls were really only cute; women were pretty. Little girls could sit on their fathers' laps with no one raising eyebrows. That would more likely raise smiles. Young women couldn't. You could hug and kiss your father at any age, of course, but there was always that awareness that you were a woman now. The affection had to be more sophisticated.

Maybe Papa had seen this happening too quickly in Roxy. Maybe he had tried, as they say, to put the toothpaste back into the tube, and that was impossible. She had crossed over, and the little girl was not coming back. He wasn't prepared for it, not that he ever would be, but it was just too soon, not only for him but for Mama, too.

The chauffeur stepped out quickly when he saw us and came around to open the door for me.

"I hope that turns into a pumpkin at midnight," Papa called to him.

The chauffeur smiled and tipped his hat. "No worries, sir," he said. He had an Australian accent to go along with the expression.

When I looked back as we drove off, I saw Mama put her arm through Papa's and watch the limousine disappear. They were watching me do a very grown-up thing. They knew I was moving on. It made me sad, and I thought, why couldn't parents return to their youth when their children were old enough to be on their own or when their children were wives and husbands, mothers and fathers? Why couldn't they become carefree and adventurous again? They had completed their obligations and fulfilled their responsibilities. Wouldn't a nice long drink from the Fountain of Youth be a wonderful way to go on?

Of course, all grandmothers and grandfathers might protest. That was something special, too.

Evan's family lived on a cul-de-sac on one of the most expensive streets on the East Side. He was waiting at the entrance when we pulled up and rushed to open my door before the chauffeur could do so.

"You look beautiful," he said when I stepped out.

"Thank you."

There was a doorman and a man behind a desk in the lobby manning security cameras. The lobby was all gold and black tile, and there was a large chandelier illuminating the statuary and the artwork. There were small tables and chairs that looked as if they had never been used. I saw that someone had to have a special card to use the elevator.

"This is like a museum," I said, gazing at the pictures.

"Sometimes it feels like it," Evan said. "I have to warn you," he continued when we stepped into the elevator, "my mother can come off snobby sometimes. She's a stickler for perfection when it comes to her dinners. Another couple is coming, the Vincents. Mark Vincent works with my father in the mayor's office. He's okay, but his wife, Millicent, outdoes my mother when it comes to snobbery."

The elevator door opened right to their apartment entryway. When I commented, Evan told me that every apartment in the building was that way. I thought the place was more difficult for a burglar to break into than Fort Knox. The Styleses' apartment looked twice as large as ours. It was on the twelfth floor. I could see that the living-room windows and the dining-room windows faced the East River and provided magnificent views.

Evan's father was the first to greet us. It was easy to see that Evan got some of his handsome features from him. He wore a black sports jacket and a black tie and looked to be about six feet one. He had a tan face and was slim and athletic-looking.

"You did pretty well for yourself, Evan," he said when he saw me. "Welcome, Emmie, or should I say *bonsoir*?"

"Whatever you wish, Mr. Styles," I replied, and he laughed.

Evan's mother then appeared. She looked as if she had just walked off a photo shoot for *Vogue*. A more elegant and beautifully put-together woman I had never seen. She wore a black dress, too, and a wide diamond bracelet and diamond teardrop earrings. Evan had her beautiful eyes, I thought.

"Mother, this is Emmie Wilcox," Evan said.

"Welcome, Emmie. You look very nice," she said. I saw the way she had been inspecting me from the moment she saw me.

"Thank you."

"You must have done something special to impress my son," she continued. "He rarely, if ever, asks to invite any of his friends, especially a young lady, to one of our dinners. Adults are too boring."

"It's easy to see what she did to him," Evan's father said.

"Yes, whatever," his mother said. She sounded as if she had expected a real answer and was disappointed. "The Vincents are here."

"Already?" Evan said, glancing at me.

"You could sound a little happier about it, Evan. We'll have dinner in fifteen minutes. You can introduce her to the Vincents and then show her the apartment, if you like. I have a few other things to tell Martha before she begins to serve."

"Will do, Mom," Evan said, and either for my benefit or just as a joke, he saluted. He glanced at me, and I shook my head.

Evan's father led us into the beautiful living room. There was a black-and-white marble bar with cushion seats. The Vincents were sitting there having cocktails.

"Hi, Evan," Mr. Vincent said quickly.

His wife just smiled. Her eyes were all over me. I thought she wore twice as much makeup as Evan's mother. Whoever had done the work on her nose and lips was probably in hiding. Her features had that exaggerated look that worked as a flashing billboard announcing, *I had plastic surgery.*

"Hi. This is Emmie Wilcox," Evan said. "Mr. and Mrs. Vincent."

"Hello," I said.

"We heard you speak French," Mr. Vincent said. "Were you born there?"

"No, but my mother is French and was brought up there," I said.

"Do you get there often?" Mrs. Vincent asked. "Paris, perhaps?"

"Not for a long time," I said. "We might go again soon."

I didn't know why I said that. It just seemed like something Mrs. Vincent expected to hear. My mother often talked about another trip to France, but Papa still hadn't committed to any.

"I love shopping on the Champs-Élysées," Mrs. Vincent said.

"You love shopping anywhere," Evan's father told her, and Mr. Vincent laughed.

"Well, that's what people do, especially in Paris. When in Rome, do as the Romans," she said. "That's a very pretty dress," she told me. "Where did you get it?"

"Don't tell her," Mr. Vincent said quickly. "She'll be there tomorrow."

"Saks," I replied.

She looked disappointed. "Oh. Well, they do have some nice things from time to time, but next time you look for something new, I have a great boutique that caters to junior fashions."

"We have two daughters about your age," Mr. Vincent said as a means of explanation.

"Oh, do they go to our school?" I asked Evan.

Before he could reply, Mrs. Vincent said, "No. They go to a very upscale private boarding school in Connecticut."

"I'm going to show Emmie around before dinner," Evan said quickly. He spoke with the desperation of someone who needed to escape.

Everyone smiled. Evan's mother returned as we left.

"About ten minutes, Evan," she said.

He nodded.

"Maybe this wasn't such a good idea after all," Evan said when we were far enough away for no one to hear.

"Why?"

"I don't know," he said. "I guess it wasn't fair to put you on display so quickly."

"I'm not on display. If anything, I think they are."

That struck him as funny.

Both his mother and his father had home offices. His father's really looked like an office, with machinery, shelves of books, and a desk with papers in neat piles, but his mother's looked more like the showcase for an office you might see in a furniture window. There was more art on the walls, nicer furniture, but a smaller desk with nothing on it.

"My mother is very concerned about my parents' social life. Her file cabinet is full of guest lists. There are drawers for the A list, the B list, and the C list," he said. "And then there is the never-ever-invite list." I looked at him and he laughed. "Just kidding. Come on."

He showed me an entertainment center with a nearly wall-size television screen.

"My dad gets screeners from Hollywood producers, so we get to see first-run movies here," Evan explained.

He opened the door to his sister's bedroom. It had a beautiful canopy bed and very pretty matching furniture that included a vanity table with a large oval mirror. The frame picked up the theme of doves embossed on her bed's headboard.

"It's beautiful."

"Yeah. I know she misses it."

We just glanced in through the doorway of the master bedroom. It was, I decided, almost as large as our entire downstairs. There were separate his-and-her en suite bathrooms.

"That's a customized bed," Evan said. "My mother has the sheets and pillowcases customized, too."

"A family of four could sleep on it," I commented.

"Yeah, well, my sister and I were always discouraged from crawling into bed with our parents. My mother claims she needs the space because my father is too restless a sleeper. *Voilà,*" he said when we continued down the hallway and stopped at his doorway. "My *pied-à-terre.*"

I laughed.

"Isn't that a good French expression for it?"

"Not really. A *pied-à-terre* is usually a second residence, part-time, in a big city away from your primary residence."

"Sort of a hideaway?"

"In a way, maybe."

"Well, that fits. I hide out here," he said, and we walked into his room.

"Is it always this neat?" I asked immediately.

"No," he said, laughing. "I'm supposed to impress you, right?"

I looked at his posters of old movies. He was obviously a *Scarface* fan. He had two of those. There was a little nook for his computer and desk, with windows that looked out toward the East River. Right then, the lights were dazzling.

"I don't know how you work here. I'd be staring out the window."

"You get used to it, I guess."

"Evan!" we heard.

"Dinner bell's ringing," he said.

"I hope I don't use the wrong fork or something."

"Oh, don't worry. If you do, you'll be tossed out the window."

As soon as we sat at the long and beautiful dining-room table, two men in jackets and ties, both wearing white gloves, began to bring out salads and open bottles of wine. The red was poured into a decanter. I could feel Evan's father's eyes on me as everything was being done.

"Being French, you might know about wine," he said with a smile.

"She's only a young girl, Martin," Evan's mother said sharply.

"I know a little," I said modestly. "The decanter is used to aerate the wine. Aerating it softens the tannins and makes it a more enjoyable experience."

No one spoke for a moment.

"Well, maybe we should let Emmie taste the wine first."

"We're not serving wine to someone her age, Martin," Evan's mother said.

"Do you drink wine with your meals at home?" Evan's father asked.

"Quite often," I said. "It's not unusual for people my age and even younger to drink wine in their homes in France."

"The French," Mrs. Vincent said, as if that explained everything.

"If she drinks it at home, she can certainly taste it here," Evan's father insisted. He nodded at one of the servers, who poured a little into my glass.

"Well?" Mr. Vincent asked, smiling at me.

"Do you really want me to do it?" I asked.

"Of course," Evan's father said.

Mrs. Vincent rolled her eyes at Evan's mother.

I looked at the wine. "You should use three senses

to judge wine properly," I began. I lifted the glass so I could see the color. "Tilt the glass away from you to reveal the width and hue of the wine's rim."

Mr. Vincent's face brightened, but his wife's expression didn't change.

"There's good clarity," I said.

"What's that mean?" Evan asked.

"You don't want the wine to be hazy. The color should be rich and full. What year is the wine, Mr. Styles?"

"Oh, my God!" his mother exclaimed. "I can't believe you're letting her do this."

"I believe we have a 1997," Evan's father said, ignoring his wife. He looked up at one of the servers. Both were standing there and looking fascinated with me.

"Yes, sir," the server closer to me said.

"Well, it's not very young. We should see a ruby, sort of brownish-red. We do."

Next, I swirled the wine in the glass by holding the glass's stem. Then I smelled it.

"What are you looking for now?" Evan asked. He was obviously enjoying how I had taken on the challenge and how it seemed to irk his mother.

"The smell of a wine is called its nose. Smelling is important to tasting. Most of what we taste is what we smell," I said. I was reciting it the way Mama had explained it to me and didn't mean to sound like a wine lecturer, but I could see that Mrs. Vincent and Evan's mother were reacting to me as if I were.

"It's a bit fruity," I said, "which is fine."

I sipped the wine but didn't swallow. Instead, I worked it around in my mouth for a few seconds.

"What are you doing?" Evan asked.

"We call it chewing. You get more of the flavor this way, and then you should sip it and suck a little air in to continue aerating."

I held up the glass. There was just a little remaining.

"It's very good, Mr. Styles."

"Well, thank God for that," Evan's mother said, shaking her head.

"Remember, a child shall lead them," Mr. Vincent said.

"How much wine do you drink a week?" Mrs. Vincent asked me.

"Oh, not much. A glass or so when it's appropriate," I said.

Under the table, Evan felt for my hand and squeezed it. I looked at the big smile on his face.

The adults took over the remaining conversation and direction of the dinner. Occasionally, Mr. Styles would ask me a question. He knew the firm Papa worked for, and I was able to tell them a little about Papa's life as the son of an Army general. After that, their conversations went from places they had been to politics and then the real-estate situation in the city. We were almost forgotten.

As soon as he could ask for us to be excused, Evan did so.

"You don't have another bottle of wine hidden in your room, do you?" Mr. Vincent kidded.

"Nothing that good," Evan replied.

His father laughed, but his mother didn't.

As soon as we stepped into his room, Evan closed the door, and then he kissed me.

"You were terrific," he said.

He had his iPod in a speaker base and turned it on. Then he sat on his bed, flipped off his shoes, and lay back with his hands behind his head.

"Take a load off," he told me.

I sat on the bed.

"So, are you impressed with everything?"

"*Mais oui.*"

He sat up and swung around so he was lying beside me, looking up at me. He touched my hand and then tightened his grip and pulled me down slowly. We kissed again, his hands moving up to my shoulders and then around to my breasts.

I started to sit up again, looking toward the door.

"Don't worry about them," he said. "They're too into their own stuff to remember we're even here."

"Have you ever brought anyone else up here, Evan?"

"By anyone else, you mean female?"

"Yes."

He shrugged. "It's happened," he said. "Not for dinner, but then again, none of them knew squat about how to taste wine," he added, smiling, and reached for me again. We kissed, and he moved his hands around my shoulders and down to the back of my dress. I felt him working on the catch and the zipper. He kissed me on the neck, and as he started to undo my dress, he moved over me. Were we going too fast? How old was Roxy when she first did this with a boy? How old was Mama? As Evan moved his lips softly over my shoulders and then onto my chest, pulling on my dress to lower it, I felt myself tighten. How could we be doing this with his parents and their friends out there? What were they thinking we were doing?

"Relax. Don't worry," Evan said, but as soon as he lowered my dress and began to undo my bra, I pushed back.

"We're going too fast," I said. It came out like a gasp.

"Too fast? I really like you," he said, "and I thought you really liked me."

"I do, but . . ."

"But what? No one's going to bother us. Stop worrying about it."

Despite what he was saying, I couldn't help but think that if it were my father out there, he'd be worrying about it.

Evan moved toward me again, and I moved a little farther from him.

He smiled. "Okay, okay. We'll go slowly. I promise," he said, holding up his hands.

Just then, we heard his mother calling.

"What?" he shouted back.

"Your father has something to tell you, and he is showing those new pictures of the 9/11 memorial. Maybe your friend wants to see them. They haven't been released on television yet."

"Her name is Emmie," he shouted back.

"Emmie," she said.

"What's he got to tell me?"

"I don't intend to stand here and talk through a door, Evan. Come to the entertainment center," she said.

"Okay, Mom. We'll be there in a minute," Evan called back.

We heard her walking away. I was working on getting my dress zipped up again and quickly fixing my hair.

He smiled at me and kissed me on the neck. "Saved by the bell," he whispered.

I thought he wasn't wrong as we left his room to go to the entertainment center.

8

Everyone else was already in the entertainment room. Evan's father looked up at us when we entered. The way the others looked at us made me feel they knew we weren't only talking in Evan's room and that now I had my dress on crooked or something.

"What's up?" Evan asked.

"You can sit," his mother said, and we did.

"You know," his father began, "that there has been some talk about my running for Congress."

"Yeah, sure," Evan said, glancing at me.

"Well, I just received a phone call from the nomination committee. They unanimously decided that they want me to run. Part of the reason for this dinner tonight was to wait to hear their decision. Mark is going to be my campaign manager."

"That's great, Dad."

"You know how it is with people running for national office, especially these days," Evan's father continued.

"Expensive?"

"Yes," he said, laughing. "That's true, but what's also true is we're going to be under a magnifying glass held by the press and the opposition."

"Magnifying glass?"

"What your father is saying," his mother continued, "is that all of our actions and words take on more meaning now. That includes you."

"Evan's never done anything to embarrass you guys, and I'm sure he won't now," Mark Vincent said. "But your mother's right. It's squeaky-clean time, okay?"

"I'll be clean, but I won't squeak," Evan said, and that broke the serious mood.

"We've opened a bottle of champagne," his father said, rising. He handed glasses to both Evan and me. "We voted on you and Emmie participating in the toast."

"Especially since she knows so much about wine," Mrs. Vincent added. "And isn't champagne wine?"

"Yes," I said. "Legally, only that coming from the Champagne region in France can be labeled champagne. That's why you see so many called sparkling wine."

No one spoke for a moment.

"My God," Mrs. Vincent finally said, "this girl is a walking encyclopedia on alcoholic beverages."

"I know only a little about wine," I said. "No other alcoholic beverage."

"Do your parents generally approve of your drinking wine anywhere else but your home?" Evan's mother asked.

"No, they don't, but they won't be upset about tonight and this," I said, looking at the bottle of champagne Mr. Styles was holding.

"Just a little," Evan's mother warned his father.

His father looked at her and then poured us both a good half-glass.

"To the next congressman from New York," Mark Vincent said, standing. "Good luck, Marty."

"Yes, *bon chance*," Evan said, and looked at me. "Right?"

"*Oui*," I said.

We all drank.

"Well, now, let me show you guys these pictures," Evan's father said, and turned down the lights.

Afterward, Evan decided to ride back to my house with me in the Town Car.

"I'm sorry everything turned out to be so formal and serious," he told me almost as soon as we got into the vehicle.

"I'm glad I was there, Evan. It turned out to be a very special night for you and your parents."

"I guess. But I wish I had spent more time with you. Alone! It was supposed to be my special night. I mean ours."

"I hope we'll have others."

"Will we?"

"Yes," I promised, and he kissed me. He wanted to do more, but I was very nervous with the chauffeur glancing in the rearview mirror.

When we arrived at my house, Evan got out with me and walked me to the door.

"Maybe we can do something tomorrow. We could go to the park or something."

"I have a ton of homework that I put off," I said.

"We'll go late in the morning. I'll take you to a fancy lunch, say a hot dog in the park," he added, smiling. "I'll come by about eleven-thirty," he said before I could protest any further. "Okay?"

"Okay," I said, "but I want to be home by four at the latest."

"Deal," Evan said, and he kissed me a little more passionately than before. He held me for a moment afterward and just stared into my eyes.

"What?"

"You're a real discovery and a wonderful surprise in every way," he said, and then returned to his Town Car. I watched it drive off. He waved before it disappeared around a turn.

I couldn't help feeling wonderful, even though I knew Evan was somewhat disappointed. I thought I had handled myself like a lady, a mature lady. It was as if I had passed some test I had created for myself. Roxy wouldn't have been as successful at the dinner when she was my age, I thought. Was it wrong for me to feel so confident now? So superior? Would I suffer for it somehow?

I looked up at the lights on the buildings and the skyline and smiled. *I can't help it,* I thought. *I'm pleased with myself.*

Both Mama and Papa were up and waiting when I entered. I was in such a dazed state for a few moments that I didn't see them sitting there.

"Emmie?" Mama said.

"Oh."

"So?" Mama asked. "How was your evening?"

"I don't know where to begin," I said, and then just did. I described the apartment, the views, and the formal dinner. I told them I was asked to taste the wine and then related the way I explained how to do it, the way Mama had taught me. I said nothing about going into Evan's room, of course, but I finished by telling them about the reason for the champagne toast.

Papa wanted to know all about that, but Mama was impatient to hear more about the apartment and how the women were dressed.

"You don't sound as if you like his mother and her friend that much," she said when I finished my description of Evan's mother and Mrs. Vincent. I thought my mother could sense everything going on in my body and my mind, no matter how small or insignificant the change was. She was attuned to every little gesture or inflection in my voice. Sometimes I thought she could pick up my thoughts even before I thought them.

"Well, Evan warned me they were snobby," I said.

"Congress, huh?" Papa said as if he had heard nothing else. "Well, this is the best year to run against an incumbent. He might win."

"Evan's father knew about your company, Papa."

"Oh? Well, why shouldn't he? We're pretty big and growing bigger every day," he said proudly.

I thought this was a good time to mention Evan's coming around to take me to lunch and a walk in Central Park.

"Now, don't go neglecting your schoolwork over some school romance," Papa warned.

"I don't think you have to warn her about her schoolwork," Mama said.

He gave his usual grunt. "Let's go to sleep," he said, standing.

That was easier said than done, at least for me. I lay there for hours reviewing the night and my feelings for Evan. I don't think anyone had to be a fortune teller to see that our feelings for each other were going to get intense. A part of me had wanted to give in to his advances in his room, but the rest of me had held back. That resistance was bound to grow weaker as time went by and we spent more and more of it only with each other. Was that a bad thing or just what should naturally happen? It excited me to think about it.

But it was exactly when I thought these thoughts, titillating myself with the sexual possibilities, that Roxy came to mind. She would always loom there beside and above me. Could I end up becoming like her? Could I be fast and loose with myself and maybe more sexually active than other girls my age? I had an older sister whom my father called nothing more than a glorified prostitute.

I had no doubts about many of the girls I knew. For them, virginity was always a burden. It was as if once you got over it, you were free in more ways than one. You broke the ties that chained you to your childhood, the ties that kept you from being taken seriously as a young woman. In their way of thinking, if you didn't do this, you had no right to speak. You hadn't paid your dues, and you weren't in the club. I could see this in the way the more sexually experienced girls talked and looked at the less experienced.

Would I guard my virginity because I thought that was right to do or because I was afraid of what would come afterward, afraid of what sort of woman I would become? Was it wrong to think of myself as someone special, and was it naive to believe that if Evan thought so, too, he would respect me and not want me to be just another girl in the pack? How long could our relationship last?

Of course, there were high school sweethearts who went on to get married. I didn't know anything about statistics, but it seemed to me that most of those relationships didn't last. One or the other was always wondering if he or she had missed out. I imagined one might even come to resent the other for trapping him or her.

I had no illusions about myself and Evan. It was very possible that we could have a high school romance that would last for years, but when he left high school, he would meet other girls, and I would meet other boys. Was it possible in today's young persons' world to have a romance that wasn't completely intimate? Now that I thought about it, would a boy, especially a boy like Evan who was so good-looking and popular, tolerate that? I liked him. I really liked him, but deep inside, I knew that he probably wouldn't be that tolerant. I knew that if we didn't become intimate, he would move on, and other girls would look at me as being the dumb one, not him. That was just the way it was.

Whatever I eventually did, however, I wouldn't do it simply to please others and fit in. I really didn't care about their opinions of me. Girls who worried about belonging and being accepted were very insecure, I thought. They were girls like Chastity, and in the end, they would be very unhappy no matter what they decided or did. I was sure of that, but all of my brilliant thinking didn't keep me from falling asleep with confusion. I was almost as afraid of tomorrow as I was excited about it.

I tried to do as much of my schoolwork as I could in the morning, but at around ten, Chastity called to ask me how my dinner was. She sounded different—calmer and more accepting of my relationship with Evan. She even sounded excited for me and very interested in all I described.

"You never explained how to drink wine when I was at your house for dinner," she whined when I told her about that, however. "As I remember, your father didn't let your mother serve us."

"He wasn't sure your parents would approve."

"Well, we could do it ourselves, drink wine, and you could show me, okay?" she asked.

"It's best enjoyed with food, Chas. Tell you what. One of these nights when my parents are going out, you'll come over to have dinner with me, and we'll drink a good wine."

"Just you and me?"

"Probably," I said. I knew what she was hinting at.

"Probably," she repeated. Then she told me about some of the gossip she had picked up from Carol Lee.

Nothing passed through the school as quickly as news about a new romance, and with Evan's popularity, ours went right to the front page. From what she was telling me, it sounded as if most of the girls were just plain jealous.

"I don't care what they say," I told her. "You don't have to bother telling me any more you hear them say, either."

"Whatever. So what are you doing today? I can come over later, and we can take a walk up to you know where."

I told her about Evan coming to take me to lunch and going to the park. She was very quiet and then suddenly burst out, "See you someday. 'Bye."

Less than an hour later, Evan was at the front door. Papa put his newspaper down and got up quickly to greet him.

"Good morning, Mr. Wilcox. How are you?" Evan asked. "I mean, *comment allez-vous?*" He smiled at me.

"*Bien,*" Papa said. "So, I understand your father is going to run for Congress."

"Yes, sir."

Mama came into the entryway, and Evan greeted her completely in French.

"You're learning well," she told him.

"I have the perfect tutor," he said, nodding at me.

"When is your father going to announce his candidacy formally?" Papa asked him.

"Very soon."

"You have to be right on everything now, son. Nowadays, when someone runs for a political office, the whole family runs."

"Yes, sir," Evan said. "We already discussed that, sir."

I didn't think that Papa could see how Evan was pretending to be military in his posture and his voice, but I knew that if Papa sensed he was being mocked, he would be very, very angry.

"We're going. I want to get back to finish my homework and study for a math quiz," I said, more to impress Papa than anything else.

"Have fun," Mama said, and we left.

"It's funny," Evan said as we started walking toward the park, "but I can't help feeling like I should salute your father."

"He has that effect on people," I admitted.

"He doesn't blow a bugle in the morning, does he?"

"Practically," I said, and he laughed.

"I like him. I like both your parents, and you know why?" he asked, taking my hand.

"Why?"

"They made you," he said, and leaned over to kiss my cheek.

Would I ever be happier with someone than I was with Evan at this moment? Maybe all of those risks and dangers I was envisioning last night were foolish after all. Maybe I could be intimate with him and not regret it ever because this was very special. I was so pensive that he asked if I was all right.

"Yes, I'm fine. I'm just enjoying the day."

"I hope because you're with me," he said.

"What do you think?"

He widened his smile. We entered Central Park. The city was still experiencing a bit of Indian summer, so the park was crowded with women pushing carriages and talking, couples like us just walking and enjoying the weather, and younger kids on skateboards. There were many people from foreign countries there, too. Papa had explained that because of the currency-exchange advantage that foreigners had with the American dollar, places like New York were experiencing greater tourism. Evan asked me what the languages were whenever we heard people talking. I was able to recognize Italian, Spanish, and German easily, but some of the Slavic languages were difficult. I wasn't sure about the Asian languages. I suspected some Vietnamese.

We sat on a bench, and he put his arm around me. For a while, we did what many people do in the park, people watching. The sun felt warm and soothing on my face. I lowered my head to his shoulder, and he kissed my hair and sucked in his breath.

"You smell fresh and sweet," he said.

"Mama gets our shampoos and perfumes from my aunt in France."

"Tell me more about your family in France," he said.

I explained that I didn't know that much, because I had been so young when we were there, but I told him as much as I could remember. I was very tempted to tell him about Roxy. At one point, it was on the tip of my tongue, but before I could do it, he decided we should get something to eat.

We did, and then we walked to the zoo and fed some of the animals. On the way back, he told me he had never been as happy or as comfortable with any girl as he was with me. We made all sorts of plans for the week and the next weekend. At my front door, he kissed me as passionately as he had the night before and then stood there looking as though he might burst into tears because he had to be away from me until the morning.

"I'll call you later," he said. "Before you go to sleep."

"You'd better," I told him. He gave me another quick kiss and walked off. I watched him disappear around the corner.

While I was still standing there, I had the sense that I was being watched, too. I looked around slowly but saw no one in particular looking my way. Even so, the feeling persisted. It even made my heart beat faster.

Roxy, I thought, *are you out there? Have you always been?*

Finally, I gave up searching the block, studying every corner and alleyway, and went in to do my schoolwork, but I couldn't help peering out my windows occasionally to see if anyone resembling Roxy was out there watching our house. When I told myself that my forbidden sister was haunting me, I guessed I meant it in more ways than one. I was sure Papa would be furious if he knew how much I thought about her.

He was very talkative at dinner. I was pleased to

hear how much he liked Evan. He said he was surprised that there still were young boys who could be
as refined and polite. He said it restored his faith in the
future. Mama and I exchanged looks, both of us hiding
smiles. We were like two teenagers who couldn't wait
to be alone to giggle.

Evan called in the evening as he had promised. He
told me he had rarely had a day like the day we had.

"I can't remember when I spent so much time in
Central Park. None of my friends thinks it's all that
cool a thing to do. Their girlfriends want more excitement."

"I would have gone someplace else if you wanted
to," I said, afraid he was saying these things just to
please me.

"Oh, no. They think like that because they don't
have you," he said.

It made me feel wonderful to hear him say it. I
wondered if he could sense it through the phone, hear
it in the softness of my voice. It really took a specially
trained person to hide his or her feelings completely, I
thought. Whether you intended to or not, your voice,
your eyes, or little gestures you made betrayed you.
Maybe that was why Roxy never cried or spoke when
Papa yelled at her or punished her. She kept herself
well locked up inside. She wouldn't give him the satisfaction of knowing how she really felt. How it must
have frustrated him to be unable to get her to react.
How strong she must have been to resist someone as
strong as Papa. Surely, it was that strength that enabled
her to survive on her own.

The older I became, the more interested I was in Roxy. Every time I had a new experience, I wondered how she would have reacted to it. But wasn't that only natural? Surely, everyone who had a brother or a sister measured himself or herself against them at one time or another. Children were always crying something like "She did it, too!" or "You let him do it!" It was easier to defend yourself by implying they favored one of you over the other. An only child didn't have that same advantage, and like it or not, I was an only child now.

I tried to put these thoughts aside and concentrate on what Evan was saying. He went on to talk about the commotion now in his house because of his father's decision to run for Congress. He told me how excited his sister was about it. He said it was her secret ambition to run for a political office someday, too, and their father's success would help her in the future. Finally, he sounded excited about it himself. I told him so, even though I knew he had been trying to be aloof and cool about it.

"It's impossible not to be," he admitted. "You heard them. It's going to take over our lives for months and months. That's why I'm glad I have you to help me keep my feet on the ground," he added.

I told him I was happy about that, too, and then he said, *"Bon nuit."* He added before we hung up, "I've been practicing this in the mirror."

"What?"

"Je t'aime."

I didn't speak.

"Why is it," he asked, "that 'I love you' sounds better in French?"

"It sounds wonderful in any language," I said. I wanted to add many things, but I didn't. I didn't tell him I loved him. Maybe I would come to say it. Right now, I liked him a lot, and he made me feel good, but I believed people shouldn't say *Je t'aime* so easily or quickly. What made things special in this world was how rare and precious they were. Maybe I was like my French grandfather, whom I had never met. Maybe I was a true romantic at heart. Love was too deeply felt and too large an emotion to be tossed about loosely. Save it, hold it in your heart, and cherish the day you really believe it, I thought.

But I did go to sleep thinking and dreaming about Evan. Perhaps I was on the doorstep of real love. Could it really happen this quickly? I wanted to believe it, but I had the feeling that if Roxy were there with me and I had told her all of this, she would smirk and say, "Relax, sis. This is just your first romance. You haven't experienced anything like it, so you don't know exactly how to act and think."

"Does it get better?" I would ask her.

"Better? Sure. It's like anything else you enjoy. The more you do it, the better it becomes."

"But didn't you ever love anyone more than anyone else, Roxy?"

She just would look at me. And then she would slowly disappear with the question still ringing in her ears.

I fell asleep before she could return, and once again, I was up before Papa in the morning. He looked surprised but also still groggy, which was unusual for him. I had the feeling my enthusiasm was a little too much for him this time.

"Watch yourself," he told me, as if he believed I was already so lovesick I might be careless crossing the street.

It was true that there was more of a bounce in my steps as I hurried to school. I anticipated that Evan would be waiting for me near my locker. I know I was at school earlier than necessary, but I was hoping he would have the same enthusiasm and be there, too.

He wasn't. Students began arriving in large groups, their voices loud, their gestures overly dramatic. I had my books and was slowly making my way to homeroom, looking everywhere as I walked, hoping to see Evan. I lingered as long as I could and then thought that maybe the excitement about his father running for Congress had overflowed. Maybe he had to be somewhere to take pictures with his mother and father. All sorts of possibilities streamed through my brain.

I saw Chastity arrive. She was almost late. I waved to her, but she either didn't see me or ignored me and joined Carol Lee Benson and Dawn Miller as they rushed to their lockers to get their things before the warning bell rang. A sudden cloud of dark disappointment rushed over me. It was like a blanket being thrown over a fire to smother it. I had my head down as I approached the doorway to my homeroom. Just before I entered, I felt a hand on my right elbow and turned to see Evan. He was like Superman swooping down to pull me up out of a pool of depression.

"I thought you weren't coming to school or something," I said, rushing my words, realizing the bell was going to ring any moment. "I thought there was some sort of family political thing you forgot to mention."

"No, nothing like that yet," he said, but he didn't smile.

"What's wrong? You look like you just lost your best friend or something."

"Maybe I did. Don't go to the cafeteria for lunch. Meet me at the west entrance. We need to talk," he said, and the bell rang.

"But why—"

Before I could add another word, he turned and hurried to his corridor. Chastity, Carol Lee, and Dawn came up behind me.

"See that look on Evan's face? What did you do, tell him you're pregnant?" Dawn asked, and to my surprise, Chastity joined in the laughter.

I gave her a cold look and then walked into homeroom and went to my desk. My heart was thumping like a blown tire on the highway. I kept my eyes forward, listened to the announcements, and said nothing to anyone until the bell for class rang. Chastity hurried out ahead of me. She even joined Cathy Starling.

What's with her? I wondered. Suddenly, she was best friends with those girls? Cathy Starling, who compared her to a blimp? I didn't rush to catch up. Chastity never looked back for me, either.

When we sat at our desks in our first class, Chastity leaned over to whisper, "How was your day in the park?"

"It was very nice," I said. "We went to the—"

"I'm glad for you," she said, interrupting, and then turned around to talk to Carol Lee.

It was the same during all of my morning classes. Chastity and the other girls were always whispering behind my back or even directly in front of me, and Chastity did her best to avoid me as much as possible. It caused me to lose my concentration, and Mr. Kendal bawled me out in math class for not hearing his question and not paying attention. By the time I finished my last class of the morning, I felt like bursting into tears. The only thing that buoyed me was knowing that I was going to meet up with Evan. He was waiting at the west entrance. I smiled and hurried to him.

"Let's go outside," he said, opening the door.

I followed him out, and he walked down the path that went around the building. There was a low cement barrier between our school and another building. He sat on it and looked up at me.

"What's wrong?" I asked.

"My mother got a call last night from Carol Lee Benson's mother. They go to a Pilates class together."

"So?"

"Seems somebody told Carol Lee that you have an older sister," he said. "Not an adopted older sister and not a half sister, either."

It was as if I could feel my heart drop into my stomach.

"And it seems she's a prostitute, a famous prostitute."

"She's not famous," I said. It was all I could think to say.

"She has a French name, something about a flower?"

"Fleur du Coeur. Flower of the heart."

"So it's all true? Your sister's a whore?"

"They call it an escort," I said so dryly that it sounded as if I was talking in a tunnel.

"Why didn't you tell me this? Why did you pretend you were an only child? I even asked you what it was like to be an only child. And your father's such a . . . correct, spit-and-polish man. What an act."

"He's not acting. That's how he really is. I didn't lie about him. His father, my grandfather, is a real Army general, and he was brought up—"

"And has a prostitute for a daughter?"

"You don't understand. My sister left our family when she was young. My father threw her out, actually, and . . . I can't even mention her name in front of him now."

"But you know her? You want to be friends with her?"

How easy it would be for me to say no, but I didn't need someone to tell me where lying got you. Evan's face said enough.

"I want to know her, yes. I haven't seen her or spoken to her for nearly ten years, Evan."

"Why would you want to know a prostitute? And why did you lie to me?"

The tears were trapped under my eyelids. I took a deep breath, hoping to suck them back, but they kept coming until they started to flow.

"It wasn't that I was lying to you, exactly. It's the way it is. We don't talk about her, so—"

"But you're trying to get to know her, be with her?"

I took another deep breath. How could I explain this quickly? It took me years to understand what it was I wanted from Roxy, what it was I needed from her.

"She's still my sister" was all I could think of saying.

He got up. "My mother was really hyper about it," he said. "You know, with my father running for Congress and all. I told them I didn't know any of this, but that only made matters worse. I can't bring you to my house now."

"Oh," I said. It was more like a gasp.

"And for the time being, I promised I wouldn't see you. They're terrified that some reporter will find out I'm seeing a girl whose sister is a famous prostitute in New York. That's how politics is now," he added. He looked at my devastated face. "If you had only told me, I might have come up with something."

"But she's not part of our family anymore," I protested.

He shrugged. "She's your sister. She'll always be part of your family," he said. "That's what blood means," he added, and started away.

I watched him go. And then I called after him, even though I knew he was too far away to hear.

"You don't know it, Evan, but you just answered your own question about why I wanted to see and talk to Roxy.

"That's what blood means."

9

Of course, it wasn't hard to figure out where this all came from. When I entered the cafeteria, I saw Chastity immediately turn toward me. There was a look of great satisfaction on her face. She wasn't smiling, exactly, but I could see the pleasure in her eyes. All of the girls at her table stopped talking to look my way. I heard their laughter spreading to nearby tables, rippling through the faces and over the lips of the girls in my class. More students stopped talking to look at me. I could feel the heat come into my face. In fact, the whole cafeteria seemed to go up twenty degrees.

I started toward the lunch line, then stopped and quickly walked out. The way my stomach was churning and churning, I couldn't dare put any food in it. It would just come back up, and the thought of regurgitating in front of my classmates, especially the girls who were already enjoying a good laugh at my expense, was terrifying.

I went directly to the nurse's office and told her I was feeling very nauseated. She had me lie down and took my temperature. I wasn't running a fever, but it wasn't difficult for her to see that I was in no condition to continue with my classes.

"I'll let your mother know," she said.

"I could just walk home, Mrs. Morris," I said, but she wouldn't hear of it.

"There are insurance regulations," she explained. "I can't simply turn you out on the street."

That expression made me wince. Wasn't that what my father had done, turn Roxy out on the street? What were his insurance obligations? Mrs. Morris put a cool cloth on my forehead, and I closed my eyes to wait for Mama. Now I was really feeling terrible. She would surely come in a bit of a panic. I hoped she wouldn't call Papa.

I nearly fell asleep, but when she came into the nurse's office, my eyes popped open as I felt her hand on my forehead.

"I've taken her temperature. She has no fever. If it's a virus, there might not be a fever," Mrs. Morris told her. "How are you now, Emmie?"

"Better," I said. "Just tired."

"I have a taxi outside," Mama said.

"I could walk home, Mama."

"Get your things," she said firmly. There would be no discussion about it.

"Don't worry about your schoolwork. I'll inform your teachers, Emmie," Mrs. Morris told me.

I picked up my books and followed Mama out. She put her hand on my shoulder to stop me as soon as we were alone.

"What is it, Emmie?" she asked. "Why aren't you feeling well?"

I shook my head, but my tears were determined to run freely down my cheeks. She moved me along faster. I didn't look back when I heard the bell to change classes. Moments later, we were in the taxi and on our way home. I curled up against the rear door and closed my eyes. I didn't want to talk.

Mama was too good at reading me, anyway. The moment we entered the house, she stopped and turned to me. "Something happened between you and Evan Styles? Is that it?"

I nodded. There was no point in trying to come up with a false reason.

"What?" she asked.

"He found out about Roxy," I said, and hurried up to my bedroom. When I got there, I threw myself facedown on the bed. I heard her behind me.

"I don't understand, Emmie. Why should that matter to him?"

I turned and looked at her. "I never told him about her."

"Of course not. I understand."

"My best friend apparently told the other girls, and one of the mothers called his mother to tell her. His father is running for Congress, remember? No scandals are permitted, and I'm a potential scandal. I have a sister who is a professional . . . escort."

"Oh," Mama said. She brought her right hand to her face.

The realization that her older daughter was a scandalous person didn't come as any surprise, perhaps, but facing it did. It was the same as saying that the little girl she had conceived was not fit to walk the earth, but it was not only that. Maybe Roxy could contaminate the rest of us, especially me. Whatever faults Mama had found with herself or whatever reasons she had come to blame herself for Roxy's behavior were now compounded by what was happening to me. That was her fault, too, if Roxy was.

"We can't tell your father," she said quickly. "I'm glad I didn't call him when the school called me."

I looked up quickly. "What will I tell him when he sees that Evan isn't calling or coming over anymore?"

"I don't know. We'll think of something, but if he heard this, it would be like tearing off a scab, reopening a wound. *Comprenez?*"

"*Oui,* Mama."

It wasn't difficult to understand.

She walked off, mumbling to herself in French, but I didn't cry. I was tired of crying. My sadness was flushed out by a rush of anger. I wanted to rage against Chastity, call her all sorts of names, ridicule her and insult her until she was drowning in remorse and regret. I thought about all sorts of ways to get revenge. I had once threatened to reveal some of her weird sexual activities and thoughts. It would be easy to turn the tables on her. Those girls who were accepting her now were only doing so because she had some juicy gossip that affected one of the most popular boys in the school. Once they had milked her of all the shocking information, they would turn their backs on her, and she would be even more alone than ever because she wouldn't have me anymore, either.

I slept most of the remaining afternoon, and when I realized that Chastity would be home from school, I called her.

"Why did you do it?" I asked as soon as she said hello.

"Do what?"

"Don't play games with me, Chastity. You told them about Roxy."

"Oh, that. It just slipped out, and once it did, I didn't know what to do," she said, feigning innocence. "Why? Was it a problem? I heard you went home from school sick. What's wrong?"

"You betrayed the wrong person," I said, and hung up.

I went to the bathroom and washed my face with cold water. Mama came to my room just before Papa was to arrive.

"How are you?"

"I'm okay, Mama. Don't worry."

"I don't like telling lies or telling you to lie, but sometimes a little twist of the truth is a nice thing to do, not for yourself but for someone else."

"What lie, Mama?"

"If your father asks about Evan, just tell him he was a little too interested in another girl. Maybe because his father's running for Congress, he's a bit stuck-up right now."

I almost laughed. Mama creating some soap-opera material?

"Okay, Mama. Who knows? Maybe that is exactly what will be happening anyway."

She smiled, gave me a hug and a kiss, and went down to work on dinner. I sat at my computer for a moment. The anger that had been simmering inside me twisted and turned, snaking its way deeper and deeper into my brain. The evil ideas that started to take shape were shocking to me. I never thought I would even consider doing such a thing to someone. But someone like Chastity, who let her jealousy and envy do harm to her closest friend, had to be punished. She had to be made to see that her actions had consequences.

I told myself that Chastity was like a little witch, a Wiccan, and they were always warned that if they did evil to someone, it would come back at them three times.

I turned on my computer. As soon as it was ready, I went into my e-mail. I had the e-mail addresses for most of the girls I spoke with in my class. Which one would be the best for this? I wondered, and then thought the perfect irony would be to choose Carol Lee. After all, it was her mother who had called Evan's.

Hi, Carol Lee, I began. *I have a stunning question for you, a little puzzle for you to solve. Which girl in our class puts lotion on a cucumber and experiments with herself sexually while looking at erotic pictures in her copy of the Kama Sutra? Hint. She likes to eat. There's lots more hints, too. And lots more she does that would make your stomach turn inside out.*

I hesitated, and then I clicked send.

Was it the Roxy in me that had me do it? It wasn't hard to imagine her doing something like this and even more. Whatever, I felt a sense of satisfaction, left the computer on, and went down to help Mama with dinner.

Papa was excited when he came home. He felt as if he had inside information and had told his associates about Evan's father running for Congress. Later in the day, they all heard the official announcement, and everyone wanted to know how he was in on it.

"I told them my daughter was seeing his son socially," he declared with some pride.

We were all at the table. He smiled and then looked from Mama to me. I had my eyes down, and Mama's face was always an open book.

"Something wrong?" he asked.

"Nothing serious," Mama began. "Emmie is a little annoyed with Evan at the moment."

"Oh? What happened?"

"He's full of himself," I said.

"Just a young boy feeling his oats," Mama muttered.

"Oats, huh? Flirting with other girls?"

I didn't say anything. Sometimes it was better to let someone else fill in the blanks using his or her own imagination. That way, it seemed as if you didn't lie so much.

"Well, you don't worry about it," Papa said, patting

my hand. "If he doesn't know how lucky he is to have your attention, then he's not the young man I thought he was. Besides, you're too young to be having love problems."

I nodded. "Yes, Papa. You're right," I said. I gave him the best smile I could muster, and he quickly changed the subject.

As soon as Mama and I finished cleaning up, I went to my room and saw that Carol Lee had bitten on my e-mail. In big block letters, there was a response.

You're kidding. Tell me more about it.

After having dinner, talking with Papa, and listening to him and Mama talk about some of their future plans for all of us, I had lost a good deal of my passion for revenge. Suddenly, it seemed juvenile and quite unimportant. I had started something, however, and I had to do something to end it, at least for now.

It's too disgusting to write about, I told her, and shut off my computer.

Despite what had occurred between us at school, I still clung to the hope that Evan might call. By now, he probably had heard I had left sick, and I thought he would at least care about that and call to see how I was, but the phone never rang.

I tried to put on a pleasant face for Papa in the morning, even though this sense of dread washed over me almost the moment I awoke. School loomed before me like a place of gloom and doom. I was very nervous about how the other students would treat me. Would they all be laughing and hiding their gleeful smiles? Of course, I wondered if Evan would even look in my direction. I didn't care about Chastity. Whatever would happen to her was well deserved.

I walked so slowly to school that I was almost late and had to rush from my locker to homeroom. As soon as I entered, I could see that my e-mail to Carol Lee had already taken effect. Chastity was sulking in her seat and avoided looking in my direction.

I took my seat. When the bell rang, Carol Lee and Cathy Starling were at my side almost before I could rise out of my seat.

"We want you to join us at lunch today," Carol Lee said.

"We've got a lot to tell you," Cathy added as an incentive. "Apparently, you're not the only one she's told these disgusting things."

That surprised me. Was there someone else Chastity had been courting to be her best friend behind my back?

"And you have a lot more to tell us," Carol Lee reminded me.

Their eyes twinkled with glee as they shot off ahead of me. I looked back and saw Chastity walking slowly with her head down.

Patty Marcus nudged me and nodded in Chastity's direction. "They really gave her a hard time this morning. Did you hear?"

"No, I was almost late today. What did they do?"

"Someone put a bag of cucumbers in her locker with a disgusting note," she said, laughing. "Everyone's talking about it now."

At one point during our morning classes, I thought Chastity was on the verge of apologizing to me. I imagined she'd heard the other girls talk about the confab that was going to take place in the cafeteria. I had made up my mind that I wasn't going to add anything to what I had already revealed. I knew I should have felt good about the result I had already gotten, but I didn't. Who really wins when two friends damage each other? It all made me sick, and it was beside the point, anyway.

The point, which no one but me would understand, was that Roxy was still very much in my life, whether she wanted to be or not and whether I wanted her to be or not. And there wasn't very much that either of us could do about it. How I would go about dealing with it was all that mattered now.

The first thing I did when I went to lunch was look to see where Evan was sitting. He was with some of the boys in his class, and they were sitting way off to the right. I stood for a moment to see if he would look my way. He did, but he turned right back to one of his friends as if he had never met me and had no idea who I was. Right now, it seemed our short romance had been nothing more than one of my fantasies.

What did all of those beautiful words he had said really mean? I was a discovery. *Je t'aime. I love you.* Was spending words like spending pennies? How much worse would I feel now if I had gone further with him in his room? How do you know when a relationship is solid and significant? How did Mama and Papa know? Was it something so special that only a very few ever have it? Was this something Roxy had realized? Did she decide to do what she was doing because she knew she would never have a relationship, never fall in love?

How could Evan tell me I was special, enjoy my company, be proud to be seen with me, and want us to be a couple one day and not even give me a second look the day after?

Maybe most important for me was the realization that I didn't see this failure in him. I was naive. Why wasn't there a class in school that would teach us how to recognize sincerity? Wouldn't that be the most important class of all?

I decided not to sit with Carol Lee and the other girls. I sat at another table with girls in the ninth grade, who didn't know much about me or what was happening. They were surprised. I just smiled and started eating. It took Carol Lee a few moments to realize it, but when she did, she came over quickly. I felt her standing there but kept eating.

"What are you doing? I told you to join our table," she said.

I paused and looked past her at her table. The girls there suddenly resembled starving dogs, hungry for my pornographic gossip. I had no doubt that the pack would turn on any one of them if it meant they could enjoy some erotic pleasure. Chastity was just the flavor of the day. Gazing around a little more, I didn't see her. Had she done what I had done and gone to the nurse's office to get herself excused from the rest of the school day? Unlike her, I didn't realize any new pleasure from the thought. I was actually beginning to feel sorry for her, despite what she had done. But I always had felt sorry for her.

"I really don't want to hear any more about her," I said.

"Well, what about what more you promised to tell us? You said it was too disgusting to write about. So?"

"I didn't promise," I said, and continued eating my sandwich.

"You know you're really as sick as she is," she said, her face reddening.

I imagined she had assured them that I had promised to give them some more shocking information. She was like their star reporter.

"I know why you wrote that e-mail," she continued, still practically on top of me. "You wanted to get back at her. You used me. Well, I did it, so now you owe me. I want to hear all about your sister, too, and I mean right now."

She stamped her foot like a little girl throwing a tantrum. The ninth-grade girls at the table all stopped eating. They were mesmerized by the scene being played out before them. Other students at other tables were starting to look in our direction. Suddenly, I saw Chastity way in the rear, sitting with two girls who were about as popular as the measles. She was looking my way, too, probably terrified of what else I was going to reveal.

"Well?"

I folded up the remainder of my sandwich, put it back on the tray, and picked up the tray.

"Good," she said, and turned victoriously toward her table and her friends.

When I rose, however, I turned in the opposite direction and walked toward the refuse slot in the cafeteria wall.

"Where are you going?" Carol Lee shouted after me.

I didn't look back. I deposited my leftovers and my tray and walked out of the cafeteria. There was still a good fifteen minutes to the lunch hour, so I went outside. The day had turned gloomy, overcast. There was that familiar late-fall chill in the air now, the harbinger of winter. I hugged myself and walked slowly around the building.

I hate being here now, I told myself. I was strongly tempted by the urge just to walk away from the building and spend the rest of the day wandering about the city, but if I did that, Papa would definitely be told and what happened would be revealed. Mama would be so disappointed in me. It all made me feel trapped. How could my life be anything but miserable? And whose fault was that?

It's your fault, Roxy, I whispered. *You're like a rock dropped in a pond causing ripples to go out wider and wider. You're like a scream that echoes and echoes.* I hadn't seen her for nearly ten years, but I suddenly hated her anyway. *I don't know why I ever wanted to meet you. Papa was right to throw you out. I wish he had thrown you out before I was born so I wouldn't have any memories of you at all.*

Raging like this, even though it was only in my mind, seemed to bring me relief, but when I saw my reflection in a classroom window, I didn't like what I saw. I saw someone full of venom and fury, someone made so ugly by her sick rage that she was almost unrecognizable. I despised Chastity and loathed the girls in my class. Once so attracted to and enamored of Evan, I was now furious with him. The sight of him, even the mere thought of him, was revolting. I felt as though I would never smile again, but I had no idea how or why that feeling would become even stronger. It was lying out there, waiting for me like some hungry tiger. It had been watching me for a long time, stalking me, anticipating its opportunity.

"Emmie," I heard, and turned around to see Mrs. Morris coming out of the building. Did she think I was sick again? Was she going to call Mama to come get me? Had some of the students told her I hadn't finished my lunch and had practically run out of the cafeteria?

"Yes, Mrs. Morris."

"I want you to come inside, come to my office."

"I'm all right, Mrs. Morris. I just wanted to get some air and—"

"I'm not concerned about your health right now, Emmie. Please do as I ask."

"Why?"

She stood there looking at me. "Dr. Sevenson asked me to find you. Please do as I ask," she said.

I followed her back into the building. She waited at the door and then started down the hallway without saying another word.

"What is this about?"

"Your mother called and asked that you meet me at my office. She's on her way," she told me.

"Why?"

"I think it's better that your mother tell you," she said.

It was as if my body knew the answer before the words entered my ears. I could feel my heart tighten like a hand into a fist and the icy cold rush through my veins. My legs weakened, and my lungs seemed to stop calling for air. Nevertheless, I kept up with Mrs. Morris. When we arrived at her office, she told me to sit on one of the beds and wait, and then, as if I did have a contagious disease, one that frightened even her, she hurried away. I sat there silently, my heart thumping.

I heard the bell ring for the end of lunch hour, and then I heard students hurrying through the hallway, talking loudly, shouting and laughing. The warning bell for the first afternoon class sounded. The hallway grew very quiet, and the second bell rang.

The nurse's office door opened, but it wasn't Mrs. Morris who stepped in first. I recognized the man from the few times I had been at Papa's office. It was Mr. Maffeo, the office manager. Mrs. Morris came in behind him.

"Hi, Emmie," Mr. Maffeo said. "I've come to take you home."

"Home? Why? Where's my mother?"

"She's waiting at home," he said, forcing a smile. "I made the arrangements at the office."

"Why do I have to be driven home?"

"Your mother wanted that," he said.

"Just go with Mr. Maffeo, Emmie," Mrs. Morris said.

I rose slowly. "Something happened to my father?" I asked.

No one spoke.

No one had to speak.

And if they had, I wouldn't have heard, anyway.

There was that much thunder roaring in my ears.

10

"I feel like he really was a soldier," Mama said. She was speaking slowly, with little emotion. "It's as if he was fatally wounded on some battlefield."

"He was a soldier," Mr. Maffeo said. There were more than a half dozen of Papa's coworkers in the house. Someone had made coffee. Others who had been in Papa's division at the firm had brought cakes and cookies and were organizing things in the kitchen. "It's a battle to make a living these days. He was just as much of a hero as any soldier, Vivian, fighting to keep his family safe and comfortable."

Mama nodded, but everything she did was mechanical. She was moving with a robotic demeanor, like someone who had lost all of her senses and her ability to think. I remained stunned and skeptical. This couldn't be true.

Yes, Papa was overweight, and his doctor had been warning him about his cholesterol levels, but he never looked or acted seriously sick. Maybe he walked more slowly, and maybe he slumped over a little more than usual when he wasn't thinking about his posture, but he was still my strong and firm Papa. I kept telling myself that this had to be a mistake. He had just fainted or something, and soon we'd get a call from the hospital telling us that he'd bounced back and he'd be fine.

The phone did ring many times, and almost every time, I looked up, expecting to hear how this was all just some bad confusion, but all of the calls were from friends and more coworkers who had learned what had happened.

"I want you to know that we look after our own," Mr. Maffeo was telling Mama. "We'll be there for you, Vivian. I have my secretary prepared to help on all the arrangements. You just jot down anything you want taken care of, and it will be done, calls made, whatever." In a lower voice, he added, "I know Norton wasn't close to his brother or his brother's children, and we know your brother and two sisters are in France, but believe me, we're your family and always will be."

Mama looked at him with a very strange expression on her face. Was she about to say she had another daughter who lived here? I held my breath.

"Thank you," she replied. "I'll wait to phone my family in Paris."

"If you want us to do it . . ."

"No, no. It's something I must do myself. *Merci,* Nick."

"Absolutely. Just call on us for anything else," he said. He looked at the others and then stood and looked down at me. "You have a great deal on your shoulders now, Emmie. Look after your mother."

Mama reached for my hand and smiled. "We look out for each other," she told him. "Always have and always will."

I started to cry. Until now, I was just as stunned as she was, feeling like the little boy who had his finger in the hole in the dike that in our case held back a flood of sorrow. Thick tears began to zigzag down my cheeks. They burned my face. Mama wiped them off with her handkerchief and then hugged me and rocked me. Everyone stopped talking and looked our way. I was uncomfortable showing my emotions in front of so many people, so I got up and went out to go to my room.

The moment I stepped out, it seemed as if I had gone completely deaf. All of the voices and sounds fell like shattered glass around me, and then it became so still that I could hear myself breathing as I ascended the stairs. I paused for a moment at the top and looked toward Mama and Papa's bedroom. Papa hadn't been sick and home from work very much, but I recalled one time when he had such a bad cold and cough that he couldn't go to the office and couldn't talk much on the phone. Mama didn't want me going into the bedroom. She didn't want me to catch anything, but I did go to the doorway to look in on him. When I did, I saw he was asleep, and I remembered he looked so much smaller to me. She had the cover up to his chin, and there was a humidifier going. It made me smile to think how when Papa was sick, Mama treated him the way she would treat a child, and he put up with it, welcomed it.

"Men really are babies," she had whispered to me. "If they had to go through the pain and discomfort to give birth, there would be no human race."

I had laughed, of course, but I also felt jealous of how Papa would show her his vulnerability and permit her to pet him and fidget around him. He always had to be "the general" as far as I was concerned. Maybe that, too, was a holdover from his time with Roxy. She was so difficult that he was afraid to show the slightest weakness, softness, even for an instant. It occurred to me that she might never have seen him as a human being, someone with real feelings, real pain, and real disappointment. Maybe if she had, she would have behaved better, been more considerate and loving.

But it was too late for any of that now, wasn't it? It was too late for so many things. Too late for Papa to realize that I definitely would never be another Roxy. Too late for Papa to watch me graduate from high school and even college. Too late for Papa to meet the man I would marry and to give me away at my wedding. Too late for Papa to be grandfather to my children. It was too late to tell him one more time that I loved him or hear him say he loved me one more time.

It was too late for everyone in our family. Too late for his brother to mend fences and for his brother's daughters to find out how much of a loving and considerate uncle he could be. Most of all, it was too late for Mama, who had died a little today, too. How lost and alone she already looked. How horrible it would be for her to lie in their bed and listen for Papa's breathing or wait to feel his hand searching for hers under the blanket. Loneliness and loss would take so many forms in our home now, whether it be Papa's empty chair at the dining-room table or the silence in the hallway. No more heavy footsteps coming our way. No more calling out Mama's or my name. Yes, the silences would be most painful of all, the silences and the empty chairs.

What were his last thoughts? Did he realize he was going to die, and did he think, *Oh, no, I have not spoken to Roxy, and I'll never speak to Vivian or Emmie again*? Did he rage against the dying of the light the way Dylan Thomas wrote in his poem? Papa was a soldier, a fighter. He wouldn't simply surrender to death. There was surely a terrible struggle, a battle well fought. His ancestors would greet him with praise.

"You showed him," they would say. "You weakened him good, and like a true Wilcox, you made death pay for his victory. He knew he was in a fight when he chose you."

I smiled thinking about that, and then I went to my window and looked down at the street. Somewhere out there in this great city, Roxy was laughing with someone or having something wonderful to eat, completely unaware of what had happened. Maybe she was wearing that dress Chastity and I saw her try on in the boutique, or maybe she was in a limousine being brought to some man or returning from some man.

Maybe, just maybe, she heard something odd in the air and was confused for a moment.

Was that my name? she would wonder. *Did someone just call to me?*

She might have turned or paused and listened again.

Whomever she was with might ask her what was wrong.

She would shake her head but look a little confused.

"What was it, Roxy?"

"I thought . . ."

"What?"

"I thought I heard my father calling me."

"Your father? What . . ."

"Nothing," she would say, and shake her head. She would go on doing whatever it was she was doing, and she wouldn't think about it again.

Because it was too late.

I sprawled out on my bed and looked up at the ceiling.

The phone was still ringing. I could hear more voices downstairs. I closed my eyes and didn't wake up again until I heard Mama call my name. She had come up to my bedroom and was standing right beside me.

"Your friend is here," she said.

My eyelids fluttered and then opened. I sat up. "What friend?"

Did the terrible news bring Evan back? How could I even care at that moment?

"Chastity," she said. "She wants to come up to see you."

"Oh."

My first reaction was to tell my mother to send her away, but there was a part of me that longed for someone my own age. My father and mother's friends and my father's coworkers seemed to think of me as much younger now. I could hear it in their voices and see it in their eyes. It was as if they thought I didn't understand fully what had happened.

"Okay," I said, and got up to throw some cold water on my face. I stared at myself in the mirror for a moment. Of course, it was my imagination, but I looked as if I had aged years.

"Hi," I heard, and turned to see Chastity standing timidly in my bedroom doorway. Over the past two years, my bedroom and hers were like our private clubhouses. The walls in both rooms were painted with our secrets. There was no formality. Nothing of mine was untouchable, as was nothing of hers. We no longer asked each other permission to do anything in our rooms.

"Hi," I said, and sat at my desk.

She walked in gingerly, looking at me as though she were afraid I might suddenly develop thin cracks in my face and crumble before her eyes.

"I can't believe it," she said.

"I wish we could just do that, refuse to believe it, tell the truth to get out and go find another family, another home."

She nodded. "Once you left, the news spread like some computer virus. Everyone was coming up to me, expecting me to explain it. I told them I was just as surprised. I had never seen your father sick, ever."

"I know."

"Evan wanted me to tell you he was sorry," she said. I looked up quickly. "About your father," she added. "He, too, said he couldn't believe it. He said your father looked like he could stand up to anyone or anything."

I just stared at her.

"I'm sorry I told anyone anything about your sister, sorry it spoiled things for you with Evan."

"It turned out to be a good thing," I said.

Her eyes widened. "What do you mean?"

"It showed me what and who he really was. Most people just use other people to satisfy some need or get something they want. When the person can't do that for them, they move on to someone else. If you had heard him talk when we first met, you would have thought he would sacrifice a kidney for me or something. I'm never going to believe what any man says, even if he writes it in his own blood."

"I bet your sister feels that way now," she said. "There's probably a lot to learn from her."

I looked away. Chastity was still idolizing and fantasizing, I thought. "I don't care about her anymore," I muttered. Then I looked hard at Chastity. "My father suffered inside because of her. I'm sure it hurt his heart."

"Oh, sure, sure. I just meant . . ."

"I don't want to think about her right now."

"Okay. Your mother's not going to tell her?"

"I don't know." I looked at her again. What was

she hoping I would say, "You go find her and tell her"?

"That's up to my mother," I added.

She nodded quickly. "Is there something I can do for you?"

"What can you do?" I asked, a lot more harshly than I had intended. "There's nothing anyone can do for me, Chastity. I've got to help my mother get through this."

"Oh, sure. I'd like to help her, too. Maybe she needs someone to buy things for her or do some errand or . . ."

"You can ask her," I said.

"I will. I promise. Are you going downstairs? There are people there putting out food." It didn't surprise me that eating came to her mind.

"I'm not hungry, and I don't want to see anyone right now."

"You want me to do anything for you at school?"

"No, nothing. I don't want to go back to that school," I told her.

"What? Where would you go?" she asked with surprise.

"Anyplace else."

"But . . . your father wanted you to go there, didn't he?"

I looked away. Suddenly, talking to her was even more painful than talking with the adults downstairs. I stood up. "I'm going down to help my mother," I said.

"Okay. I'll stay with you," she told me, and followed me out and down the stairs.

I didn't know how my mother could continue to do it. She greeted people all day and into the evening. Once in a while, when she turned to me, I could see the exhaustion in her face, but she wouldn't give in to it. I knew that holding herself together like this, keeping herself going, was what she believed my father would want, would respect. This was how a soldier's wife should be at such a time. Apparently, while I was upstairs or while I was distracted, she had excused herself for a phone call in my father's home office. As soon as she had a moment that she could spend alone with me, she told me she had called Uncle Orman.

"What did he say?"

"I thought I was talking to your father's commanding officer," she replied. She didn't sound angry about it. She almost looked amused. "He told me he was about to begin a very important assignment at the Pentagon and couldn't be here for the funeral. He said your father would understand. I left it up to him to inform his children and your aunt Lucy. I'm sure he'll have a military attaché do it. The truth is, you and I were the only family your papa had," she said.

My whole face trembled. She hugged me and kissed my forehead.

"Let's do what we have to do, Emmie. We'll mourn for him afterward and forever."

I took a deep breath and followed her back to the visitors and mourners. Chastity was looking more uncomfortable than ever and told me she should get home. She wanted to tell her parents so they could visit my mother.

"I'll be back every day," she promised. "You can call me whenever you want, no matter what time."

"Okay, Chas," I said. "Thanks."

We hugged.

"Do you know when the funeral will be?" she asked, as if she had just remembered what this was all about.

"What funeral?" I said. "This is just a dream."

She nodded, her eyes flooding with tears, and then she turned and left as quickly as she could. I didn't blame her. When she got outside, she probably felt as if she had come up out of a grave, I thought.

I understood why Mama wanted people to exhaust her. By the time the last mourner had left our home, she was ready to collapse.

"We have a lot to do tomorrow," she told me. "Just try to get some sleep."

I followed her up to the bedrooms. When she paused at mine, I wanted to ask about Roxy. Would she try to reach her to tell her? Did that matter at all to her? Once again, Mama surprised me. She really could read my thoughts.

"We'll think about your sister tomorrow," she said. She kissed me and then went to her bedroom like someone who was stepping out of this world and into another.

I was surprised at how tired I was and grateful that she had been wise enough to exhaust us both. I fell asleep like someone under anesthesia.

She was up ahead of me in the morning and waiting for me in the kitchen. We hugged without speaking. I looked at the breakfast she had prepared and shook my head.

"I know you think you can't eat, Emmie, but you must."

To emphasize, she began to eat herself.

"Your father's company has placed an obituary in the *New York Times*," she told me.

I looked up at her. I felt certain she was telling me this to open the conversation about Roxy. Who else did she care about seeing it?

"You think Roxy will see it or learn about Papa today?"

She glanced at Papa's empty chair as if she thought his spirit was there listening. "Your father and I talked about your sister more and more lately. He was still very angry about her, but he was beginning to soften. I left a message with her service last night," she said.

My heart raced with anticipation. "And?"

"I've heard nothing back. It took a great deal of effort to get your father to find out how to reach Roxy. He gave me the information only two days ago. It was as if he knew what was coming," she said, and took a breath so deep I thought she had reached back into her youth to find the oxygen.

"Why didn't she call you back right away? How could she ignore this?"

"Maybe she didn't get my message yet," Mama said. "Maybe she doesn't care. I did what I thought I should," she added, glancing toward Papa's chair again.

Every time the phone rang after that, I held my

breath, expecting it to be Roxy, but it wasn't. Mama's family in France called as soon as they were up and about. The only one I spoke with was my mother's brother, Alain. I hadn't spent much time with any of her family, and I was very young when I did, but I could recall him the best. He was the nicest and sweetest of them all. Mama had recent pictures of her sisters and brother. They were a good-looking family, but besides being strikingly handsome, Uncle Alain had a softness in his smile that could make anyone he met feel comfortable. As Mama herself said, Uncle Alain had the most positive energy. He was still unmarried, and although Papa had never come out and said it, especially in front of me, he believed Alain was gay. Mama never said anything about that. I knew he was a successful international attorney, but aside from that, I knew little else.

Mama advised all of her French family not to come to the funeral. They were all very busy with their lives and families, and she assured them that she would be fine. She promised that she and I would visit France as soon as we could. When she spoke to them, she spoke only in French. I thought I heard her mention Roxy's name when she spoke with her brother Alain and her sister Manon, but not when she spoke to her younger sister, Chantal.

Papa's company sent a limousine to take us to the funeral parlor and the church to make arrangements. I took it as a compliment that Mama did not try to get me to stay home and avoid all of it. Instead, she made me feel adult and equal. In fact, she gave me the impression that she needed me and leaned on me for support. Because of that, I pushed away any childish thoughts or feelings. It occurred to me that we don't just grow up on some schedule. Events jolt you or drag you into maturity. I was sure that the day Roxy walked out of our home and into the New York streets, she put aside all of her youthful feelings and thoughts and immediately became a young woman. She had no choice. Either she did that, or she would not survive.

Papa hated the idea of an Army career but was the first to admit that it made men of boys and women of girls. "If you have no choice but to grow up, you grow up," he would say.

Nevertheless, I was anxious to get home at the end of the afternoon to see if Roxy had left a message. There were messages, condolences, and offers of assistance from other friends and some cousins on both sides but no message from Roxy. No one at my school had called to leave me a message except for Chastity. She wanted to come over to tell me what everyone was saying at school. Suddenly, all of that meant little or nothing to me. When I didn't call her back, she called again. I was sure she was really more interested in what was happening with Roxy.

I told her not to come over, because both my mother and I were too tired. More visitors came to offer their condolences, however, and some who had been there the day before returned for a little while. People didn't stay as long. Mama wasn't hiding her exhaustion. Enough food had been brought in to feed us for a week. Neither of us ate very much, and it was more difficult to fall asleep this time. I was still hoping to hear from Roxy, even expecting her to show up, but none of the later phone calls were from her or anyone who knew her. When I thought about it, I considered the possibility that she was out of the country or somewhere far away and still hadn't picked up the message or heard the news. I didn't ask Mama about it. I thought it was just adding to her pain to mention Roxy now.

Throughout my father's funeral and the burial at the cemetery, I hoped Roxy would appear. I imagined her stepping up between us and taking Mama's hand and mine, but she never came. I didn't know until the next day that Mama had called her hotel and tried to leave a message containing the details of Papa's services for her that way, too.

"What happened?" I asked her when she told me.

"The receptionist said there was no one by that name living there. She probably has changed her name, or perhaps she has left that place and gone to some other state or even another country. Whatever. I've done all I can about it, Emmie. We have enough to do."

I said nothing. I didn't have the nerve to tell her that Chastity and I had been spying on Roxy and that I knew for certain that she was still living at the Beaux-Arts. I thought that would only make her feel worse.

Mama wanted me to return to school immediately. "The longer you stay out, the harder it will be for you to return," she said.

"I don't want to return ever," I told her. "I hate that school now."

She looked as if she would collapse under the burden of any more trouble and turmoil. I felt terrible complaining.

"Emmie, I don't have the strength to start looking for some other school for you right now. Please," she said.

"I'll finish the year, but I'd like to go to a public school, Mama."

"We'll see," she said.

I told myself I would just grin and bear it, but what I had more trouble accepting was Roxy's complete disinterest in our father's passing and our mother's grief. I was no longer interested in her as much as I was angry at her. I didn't care how she had been treated. She had brought the trouble on herself. She was at least partly, if not mostly, to blame, especially if she could be this heartless now. I was determined not to let her get away with it.

I certainly wasn't going to tell Chastity what I was planning, and I couldn't tell Mama, but that night, I sat at my desk and composed a short letter.

Dear Roxy,

You and I haven't seen or spoken to each other for years. You knew that Papa knew who and what you were now. There's no point in pretending anything. I don't care how angry

you were at him and Mama. Papa died, and
Mama left you a message with your service and
your hotel, and I know you are there. She tried
to reach out to you, thinking you might have
an ounce of decency left. I think it's horrible
that you wouldn't even respond.

    All I can say is that even with your rich
possessions, you're someone I pity.

Your sister,
Emmie

I folded it and put it in an envelope with the charm bracelet she had given me years ago. On the front, I wrote in big block letters: TO ROXY WILCOX.

I told Mama I needed to go for a walk. She nodded and went back to the papers she was studying in Papa's office. Then I left the house and marched with such determination that I didn't see or hear anyone around me until I reached the Beaux-Arts. I stood outside for a moment. Of course, I thought how much Papa would hate me doing this, but it was too important to me. He'd have to understand.

I entered the lobby and immediately stopped. I was sure Roxy was just getting into the elevator. She was with a man, and just before the doors closed, I saw him put his arms around her waist and pull her closer.

The desk clerk looked up. He was a very thin man with large dark eyes and thick dark brown hair. I didn't think he was much more than in his twenties.

"Can I help you?" he asked when I hesitated.

My heart was throbbing so hard I didn't think I could speak, but I stepped forward.

"Yes, you can," I said. I slapped the envelope on the desk. "That woman who just got into that elevator was Roxy Wilcox, right?"

He stared at me for a moment and then leaned forward, his beady eyes looking like two glass ebony marbles. "Who are you? What do you want here?"

"I want you to make sure she gets this, and you don't have to pretend that she isn't here. I know that was Roxy in the elevator just now. I've seen her here before. When you hand it to her, tell her it came from her sister."

He looked at the envelope and then at me. Before he could say a word, I turned and marched out. I can't say I wasn't afraid and trembling.

I made my way home as quickly as I had made my way to the hotel.

There were many ghosts chasing me, Papa's in the lead, all of them bawling me out. Their voices grew louder. I was practically running down the sidewalk, my hands over my ears. I bumped into people, cut between people, even stepped into the street to get past older people who were walking too slowly.

I was sure I looked like someone fleeing, someone too terrified to look back.

11

I said nothing to Mama about it, but for the remainder of the evening and even after I had gone to bed, I listened for either the telephone or the door buzzer. The telephone rang once, but it was Mrs. Maffeo calling to see how we were doing. I heard Mama talking to her. When she came by to say good night, she looked so tired and defeated that I couldn't even think of mentioning Roxy. But thinking about her kept me up most of the night. I tossed and turned, worried that I might have done something that would make things worse somehow. Maybe Roxy's company, or whatever it was called, didn't know who she really was. Maybe someone would be coming around to check up. I knew that would be very disturbing for Mama. Roxy could come here when I was in school, too, and she might be nasty and terrible to Mama.

As much as I hated the very thought of returning to school, I rose as early as I would on any school day when Papa was alive. Despite all that Mama and I had been through during the past days, I still dreamed that I would see Papa sitting in the kitchen, his *Wall Street*

Journal beside his coffee cup. The sight of me dressed and ready that early always had brought a smile to his face. How I longed to see that smile again.

Mama was right behind me. When I saw her, I wished I hadn't risen and dressed before it was necessary. There was no one there to impress. I thought Mama was forcing herself to be energetic just for my benefit.

"I'm all right, Mama. You didn't have to get up this early. You know I can look after myself."

"Of course you can. I've got to see our accountant and our attorney today. I have their first appointment of the day," she explained.

"Why do you have to do everything so quickly? You need to rest, Mama," I said.

"Things have to be done now," she insisted.

I wanted to ask why. Were we in some sort of financial trouble? Surely, with Papa's success and his life insurance, we would be fine. Were there things they had kept hidden from me? Whatever it was, she shouldn't have to bear the brunt of it all alone, I thought, but I could see that continuing the discussion would only tire her out. I ate my breakfast and kissed her before I started out for school. When I hugged her, she seemed to be trembling, but she forced a quick smile and, as usual, told me to be careful. She used Papa's favorite expression: "Stay alert. You're always on guard duty."

"Yes," I said. We smiled at each other even though our hearts were heavy.

Chastity had e-mailed me a list of all the work I

had missed, but I hadn't done a single thing. I had little or no enthusiasm for school and even walked like someone who was walking in her sleep, someone really not sure where she was going. When I saw the school ahead of me, I almost turned away to spend the day wandering the city, maybe hanging out in Central Park. Chances were good that no one at school would call about me, because they all would think I was still in mourning. But Chastity did know I was coming, and if she called to see where I was, Mama would be terribly frightened.

From the moment I arrived, I saw how differently my classmates were looking at me. Some actually seemed terrified to speak to me. It was as if they thought they could say something or do something that would send me into hysterical sobbing for which they would be blamed. They forced smiles, asked how I was, but as quickly as they could, they moved away. Meanwhile, Chastity acted like some sort of bodyguard, answering for me or guiding me along. She was always looking for a way to feel important, and my tragic situation gave her a new opportunity. I couldn't have cared any less about that or anything else involving my classmates.

I didn't see Evan until lunch. The moment he set eyes on me, he broke away from his friends and approached while Chastity was getting our food.

"I was really sorry and shocked to hear about your dad," he began. "Please tell your mother how sorry I am."

"Thank you."

I avoided looking at him, but whether he felt guilty about the way he had treated me or was simply curious, he followed with, "Does your sister know?"

I paused. I had all sorts of angry responses piling up on my tongue, but I shook my head. "It doesn't matter if she does or doesn't, Evan. That won't bring back my father," I said, and joined Chastity at our usual table. He didn't follow.

"What did he want?" Chastity asked.

"Nothing," I said. "I don't want to talk about him or hear about him," I told her so firmly that she quickly nodded. "None of these kids interests me anymore. I don't care what any of them have to say, so don't bring me any gossip."

Because of the look on my face and the tone in my voice, she hardly said a word during the remainder of the lunch hour. I'm sure she thought I was like a tube of nitroglycerin. It would take the slightest nudge to see me explode.

My teachers thought so, too. They were all quite sympathetic and considerate, speaking extra softly. None demanded anything of me. All told me to take my time and come to them if I ever needed some extra help. The truth was, my interest in being a very good student had waned with Papa's passing. I think I achieved my high grades for him as much as for myself. Mama wanted me to do well, too, but I knew she would readily accept Bs, even Cs, now.

Every day that followed seemed as gray and dull as the previous one. They all ran together like one long day, in fact. Once I reached school in the morning, my body tightened. It was as if I had gone into rigor mortis along with Papa. I imagined I looked like someone simply going through the motions. I never raised my hand to answer a question, and none of my teachers called on me. It was as if I was in an invisible cubicle. In fact, it wasn't long before friends who had tried to reconnect began to act as if I weren't there. I suppose I wasn't. I mean, my body was there, but my mind drifted so much and so often that most of the time, I didn't hear them speak. A few times, someone asked me a question and even repeated it, but I didn't respond. They all looked at one another and at Chastity, shrugged, and then went on to something else.

As this continued, I could see their attitude toward me harden further. Whatever pass they had given me because of my father's death gradually disappeared. I was just annoying to them now. It was easier to leave me out of conversations or plans. It reinforced the feeling that I had become invisible. At first, Chastity didn't mind, because she was usually left out of everything anyway, but I soon felt sorrier for her than I did for myself. She was left with only me again, and I wasn't good company. She might as well be alone.

Evan and his friends were another story. I had no idea what sort of things he had told them during the short time we had been seeing each other. I had a dreadful suspicion that he might have exaggerated the way I knew some boys did in order to appear more sophisticated than their friends, bragging about sexual relations or something.

Now that some time had passed since my father's

death, my forbidden sister was fair game again. At least a half dozen of Evan's friends came right out and asked me if Roxy had been invited back into our family. Some of the boys began to make remarks in the hallways.

"Is she working out of your house?"

"What's her number? How much does she cost?"

Dirty notes were left in my desks or slipped into my hall locker. I thought if I ignored it all, it would go away, but it was as if my mere presence in the school was enough to keep it alive forever.

Despite what I had told her, Chastity returned to passing along the gossip she heard. What was too horrible to mention weeks ago in light of what had happened to my family was suddenly headline news again. I didn't have to hear it to know what my fellow students were saying. I could see it in their licentious smiles and the whispering when they looked my way.

Not satisfied with their titillation and sick humor, some of Evan's friends began hitting on me, crudely inviting me to do all sorts of sexual acts. I could sense that this was some sort of new game they had concocted, who could be more disgusting and attract my attention. They might even have taken bets on who would get me to go out with him. Most of the time, I simply ignored them. Some just laughed when I said, "No, thanks," but one boy, Martin Horton, got nasty.

"Who do you think you are?"

"Excuse me?"

"Your sister is a prostitute, and you act like Princess Purity?"

"It's not hard to act that way when someone like you acts like an ass," I said, and walked away to the sound of loud laughter.

How I hate it here now, I thought, and sucked back my tears.

It was doubly difficult because I didn't want to go home looking so down and unhappy every day. Mama was still going through her own depression and sadness. I knew she was anticipating my arrival after school in the hope that I would cheer her up. I had to put on the best act I could and invent good news. What was really upsetting me now was that Roxy had not responded in any way to my letter. Every time I heard the phone ring at home or when anyone came to the front door, I still anticipated her. I always expected that Mama would greet me after school with the news that Roxy had been there, but that never happened.

It got so that even if she was angered by my letter, I'd be happy. Anything was better than nothing, better than treating us as if we didn't exist. Surely, that desk clerk had given it to her. How could she be so cold and unforgiving, especially since she knew I had come to her hotel and could come again?

A few times, I almost came out and told Mama what I had done, but I thought it would upset her even more. After all, she had tried, too. One night, I caught her sitting in her bedroom looking at one of the pictures of Roxy she had hidden from Papa. She was staring so hard at the photo that I expected she would break into sobs, but she just took a deep breath and put the picture back into a drawer.

Chastity tried to get me to talk about Roxy a number of times. She was as subtle about it as she could be, which wasn't very. She would say something like "I wonder if your sister really doesn't know what's happened to your father." Or she would pause when we were walking home and say, "That woman reminds me of your sister."

I never responded, so she didn't continue, but finally, one afternoon when we were studying for a test together at my house, she put down her notebook and glared at me in a way I had never seen her glare.

"What?"

"I know you're going to get angry at me, and I know you might tell me to get out and never speak to me again."

"What is it, Chastity?" I said, putting my notes aside, too. She sat there dumbly. "Just spit it out already."

"I saw your sister two days ago."

"What? Where?"

"Coming out of her hotel and getting into a limousine. She looked very dressed up. I'm only telling you," she continued quickly, "because I thought maybe she really doesn't know about your father. I mean, maybe she doesn't read the newspaper or—"

"You went back there to spy on her?"

"Just for you," she said. "I knew you wouldn't go there, and I thought maybe—"

"Maybe what? What good would that do? You weren't planning on talking to her, were you?"

She didn't respond.

"You were?"

"Just for you, Emmie," she repeated.

I shook my head. "You won't let go of this, will you? You're just as sick as the rest of them."

"No, that's not it. Really. I was thinking about you and your mother and how good it would be if somehow your sister came around and maybe apologized or something. She's got to be sorry your father died, right?"

I looked away.

"I'm just thinking of you," she whined.

Yeah, right, I thought. *You just want something to jazz up your boring life.*

Was there really such a thing as a best friend, or was that just another of life's illusions? I was surely an expert on why best friends could be better than relatives, but the real reason for why best friends did things was often not easy to understand. Maybe we should say "the best possible friend" instead of "best friend."

"I went to my sister's hotel, and I left her a message," I said after a long pause.

"You did? When?"

"About a month ago. I went in just as she was getting into the elevator."

"Did she see you? Speak to you?" she quickly asked.

"No, but I went directly to the desk clerk and told him I had just seen her, so there was no point in his denying her existence."

"Wow."

"So, you see, there is no reason for you to go there anymore, Chastity. In fact, you'd be embarrassing my mother and me if you ever did speak to her, understand? It would be like begging her to give us her time."

"You left her a letter?"

"It was more than a letter. She once gave me a charm bracelet, and I put it in the envelope. I told the desk clerk I was her sister, too. I hoped to stir up some feelings in her."

"And she hasn't responded, called or anything?"

"No. Nothing."

"That's horrible," she said, tucking in her lips and widening her eyes. "I know what you should do now."

"Really, what?"

"You should leave her another message. 'Go to hell.'"

"And what good would that do?"

"Self-satisfaction. You would know that she knew she didn't get away with it."

"Get away with it? I'm not out for revenge. This isn't some sort of childish game. She's my sister, my mother's daughter." I shook my head. "I'm really sorry I ever told you about her."

"That's not fair," Chastity whined. "You should always tell me your secrets. I tell you everything."

I stared at her. At this moment, I felt as if I had left her so far behind on the maturity road that she was less than a dot. Why was I wasting any more time with her?

I looked at the notes for our upcoming test and then flung them across the room.

Chastity jumped in her seat. "Why did you do that?"

"I don't care about this test. Just go home to study yourself. You don't have to fail because of me. Go on!" I shouted at her.

She was too stunned to move.

"Get out!" I screamed, and she rose.

"All right, all right. You are so weird now. I know I should be sympathetic, but I can take just so much, too, you know," she said, tears making her eyes glisten. "I have feelings just like you."

I turned my back on her.

She paused in my bedroom doorway. "You know, everyone asks me why I remain friends with you, Emmie."

"Right," I said. "I know you have a whole lot of them lining up to take my place. Go for it."

She stomped out and down the stairs. I heard her open and close the front door, and then I flopped back on my bed and stared up at the ceiling. Mama was in the doorway. She was in her robe and slippers. Lately, if she didn't have to go out, she wouldn't get dressed all day, and she would do little or nothing with her hair. I was worrying more and more about her, about how pale and frail she was looking.

"What was that all about?" she asked.

"I'm tired of her, Mama. She's such a busybody."

"You just made that discovery?"

I didn't say anything.

She came into my room and sat on my bed. "What is it really, Emmie?"

"I can't stand not having Papa with us," I said.

She sighed. "I know. He was very firm and on the surface seemingly insensitive at times, but you were the apple of his eye, and there was nothing he wouldn't do for you."

"Are we all right financially, Mama?" I asked.

"We're fine," she said, patting my hand.

"Are you all right?" I eyed her carefully.

Her lips quivered, and she nodded quickly, patted my hand again, and rose. "Just a little tired. I'll get to sleep early tonight," she said. She leaned over to kiss me and then walked out.

I could feel the darkness seeping in behind her, following her out of my room. It made my heart skip beats. Here I was feeling sorry for myself when it was Mama who should have all the attention. I was young. I would survive. Roxy survived, didn't she?

Or did she?

Maybe she was more unhappy than it appeared. Maybe that was why she stayed away. Maybe she didn't want us to know how bad things really were for her. Just maybe, she was ashamed of who and what she was, too ashamed to face her mother. Perhaps I had been too quick to condemn her.

Never did I dream that I would be lying in my bed thinking I was too hard on Roxy. Was my desperation for a sister, for more family, so great that I would overlook so much, even the way she had treated my parents? I had tried to forget her. I was still trying to hate her, but for some reason, I just couldn't do it. Somehow, my vague memories of her grew stronger and more vivid. I could see her smile, hear her voice again. It was as if a door had been nudged open in my mind and memories were slipping out.

There was one in particular that I hadn't recalled until now, the memory of Roxy holding my hand as we walked on an avenue. It seemed we were alone, returning from some errand she had completed. Maybe Papa didn't know that Mama had permitted Roxy to take me along. I remembered her being very careful and protective, guiding me along, her grip on my hand so tight that it actually hurt a little. But I didn't complain, because I was so happy to be treated like someone older. Other pedestrians looked at us and smiled. *Look at how responsibly that older sister is behaving.* I felt very proud, too.

The memory brought a smile to my face, but that was followed by a deeper sadness.

It was a precious moment, and it was gone forever.

I turned over and buried my face in my pillow. *I don't want to think about her. I don't want to remember her.*

Papa was right to disown her and forbid my even mentioning her name. How could she leave us like that? How could she be so stubborn and mean?

There was another thought. Was it selfish to think it?

If it was, I couldn't help it. It was the thought that took me to sleep.

How could she leave me?

12

Maybe I was dwelling too much on myself, soaking myself in a gray pool of self-pity. I was walking through the school day with blinders over my eyes, not seeing or caring about anything or anyone else. I sat like a granite statue, barely changing expression, no matter what my teachers said. Finally, after weeks and weeks of this, one of my teachers, Mr. Collins, pulled me aside after class to talk about my work. He was very tall and stout but almost always pleasant with an almost impish smile. I really liked him. Right now, he hovered over me like the shadow of my conscience.

He was the first to do this, but I knew that teachers talked about their students in the faculty lounge, and my other teachers probably would follow his lead shortly. I couldn't say I didn't expect it. This was, after all, a private school, where students had their teachers' full attention. Two of my classes had fewer than fifteen students in them. Mr. Collins, who taught math, had one of those classes.

"I know you and your mother have been through a very difficult time, Emmie," he began, "but I also know how proud your father was about your grades. You and I know you can do much better than you're doing." I looked down as he spoke, and when I didn't respond, he said, "Let's just leave it at that, but you know I'm available anytime to help you. Just ask."

I nodded, but I didn't even say thank you. I was still drowning in self-pity. He had thrown me some rope. All I had to do was take hold, but at the moment, I didn't care. I was still angry about Papa's death, confused about Roxy, and annoyed with my classmates. Doing well at school had lost all attraction for me. It was unfair to treat my teachers with such indifference, I knew, but I seemed incapable of changing. I didn't mind the silence and the self-imposed solitude. For now, staying to myself and pulling my head in like a turtle were more comfortable than anything else. It was truly as though my face had forgotten how to smile. Laughter was a thing of the past, a distant memory. Even when I heard other students joking with one another, I looked at them as if they were Martians.

I did get a similar short lecture from most of my other teachers over the next two days, and finally, Dr. Walter, our school dean and counselor, called Mama and told her to consider sending me to a therapist. At first, all that did was get me angrier. I was angry at myself more than at anyone else for letting this happen and hurting Mama, but for now, it was more convenient to blame the school. Mama, of course, blamed herself.

"I should have been paying more attention to you. Your father was always more involved in your schoolwork than I was," she said after she told me about the call she had received. She had been waiting for me in the kitchen when I returned. This particular day, she had gotten dressed. Lately, she had our food delivered most of the time, and as far as I knew, she rarely left the house. I was sent out to the store whenever something was missing.

"I'm not failing anything, Mama. I don't know why he had to call you and make such a big deal of it."

"It is a big deal, Emmie. You know your father would never have been satisfied with your just passing everything, and you wouldn't have been, either."

She was sipping some tea. Now that she was wearing one of her nicer dresses, I could see how she had become much thinner. She had put on some makeup, but she still looked pale and wan. Her eyes were sleepy all the time, but now they were even duller, her lids quivering to stay open. Everything, even the smallest thing such as lifting a teacup, seemed to require a greater effort.

"I know you are not happy at the school," she continued, "but I thought you would do the good work you always have done until we could find another school for you. You can't go on like this, Emmie. You don't have any friends or talk about anything at school the way you used to. Maybe it's not a bad idea for you to see a therapist."

"I don't need a therapist to tell me what I should be doing in school, Mama. I'm sorry I let it go this far. I'll work harder."

"But you won't be happy, will you?"

"I'll try," I promised.

She nodded softly, but I could see there was something else. I could always tell when Mama had a secret. She had a way of shifting her eyes so that she was looking past me and not at me.

"What is it, Mama? There's something else," I said, thinking that perhaps Roxy had finally contacted her, perhaps had even been there.

"I don't want you getting nervous and all worked up, especially now."

"Why would I?" I leaned forward. My heart, which had been almost hibernating in my chest, came to life and began to thump.

She pressed her lips together and took in a long breath through her nose. "I didn't have a good result on a test."

"What test?"

"I had my annual exam last week."

"I didn't know you were having that done."

"It was scheduled some time ago, and you know how it is with some of these doctors, you don't want to postpone. It would take months to get rescheduled." After another pause, she said, "I didn't want you having something else to worry about," she said.

"What test?"

"The Pap smear. They're doing it over. Lots of times, the first result can be an error."

"What if it's not?"

"We'll deal with it," she said firmly. "Let's not think the worst of everything."

"When do you do the test again?"

"Soon," she said. She smiled. "It's going to be just fine."

"Oh, Mama, with all this on your mind, I'm sorry I gave you something else to worry over. I'll do better in school. I promise."

"Sure you will," she said.

I hugged her. We held each other a little longer than usual, and then she began to prepare our dinner. She tried desperately to get me to think of other things while we ate. She told me about her family in France and how Uncle Alain had called her twice that week already.

"He's always asking after you," she said.

The way she described him and Paris told me how much she longed for family now, longed to go home. Whenever she described a place, she would break into a warm, deep smile, the smile of someone who cherished a memory.

"We should go soon," I said.

"Yes, we will. As soon as . . . as soon as we get a few things straightened out," she said. I knew she was talking mainly about her health but also about me.

I told her to go rest after dinner while I cleaned up. By the time I was finished and looked in on her in the living room, I found she was asleep on the sofa, her right hand on the arm of it the way she had kept it there when Papa was sitting beside her in his chair. Sometimes they had held hands while they watched television. I didn't wake her, although I wanted to. I couldn't stand the look of exhaustion on her face. I needed to see her smile and hear her voice. She had the television on, but the volume was low. I went upstairs to get my homework and then returned and sat in Papa's chair doing it and waiting for her to awaken. When she did, she looked terribly confused.

"Oh, I fell asleep," she said, realizing. "I'm sorry."

"Why should you be sorry? You're tired, so you slept. Good," I told her. "I wanted to finish all this anyway," I added, showing her my books and note-books.

She nodded, holding her smile. Then she remembered something and rose like a woman years older. "I have to do a few things our accountant told me to do. Get some numbers together. Your father did all of this for us, but he made sure to show me how."

"Can I help?"

"No, it's nothing terribly complicated. Just finish your work. I won't be long," she assured me.

I completed my homework and took my books back upstairs. After I dressed for bed, I checked to see if she had come up. She hadn't, so I went down to the office to look in on her. She was asleep in Papa's desk chair, her head in what looked like a very uncomfortable position.

"Mama!" I cried.

She looked as if she had gone beyond sleep, her mouth slightly open. Her eyes fluttered, and she sat up. "Oh." She looked at the papers on the desk. "I finished everything and just . . . I took a pill earlier," she said.

"What kind of pill?"

"A pill the doctor gave me to stay calm. It's nothing,

but it does make me a little drowsy. I'll just go to sleep. Wash that worry off your face," she told me, smiling, and stood up. "Come on. *Allons.* We'll both go to sleep."

I walked alongside her and then behind her as we climbed the stairs. She turned to hug and kiss me good night and went to her bedroom.

What ages someone faster than deep sorrow? When people were together as long as my parents were, what happens to one, happens to the other in subtle ways. It was as though sadness was as contagious as any disease, and death didn't just slip in and out silently. When it touched someone close to you, it left its mark on you, too. A little of the darkness slipped in and settled on your soul, waiting patiently for the rest of it.

I was afraid for Mama, but I channeled my fear into an almost obsessive determination to do well in school during the following days. Suddenly, coming to life again seemed to be the best way to help Mama get healthy and stronger. My hand was up in every class, answering questions almost before my teachers asked them. I aced one quiz after another and put smiles on the faces of my teachers. My new energy and efforts attracted everyone's attention. Some of my classmates began to talk to me again, joining me at lunch or walking with me in the hallways.

Chastity watched timidly from the sidelines, unsure of how I would react to any attempt she made to reconnect with me. I didn't discourage her, but I didn't pursue her, either. Nevertheless, she soon began to attempt some small talk, hesitant to have longer than a ten- or twenty-second conversation because I didn't appear that interested. I just didn't want things to get back to the way they were. I wanted her to understand that I wouldn't tolerate any more talk about Roxy.

One afternoon, I let her walk home with me after school. She parted with "Maybe we can do something together this weekend."

"Maybe," I said, but I didn't pursue it or bring it up again.

Of course, I was eager to get home every day to find out how Mama was and what her doctors were telling her. She told me everything was good. I shouldn't worry. She did seem a little more energetic. She even began talking about our trip to France when my vacation began. Buoyed by this, I even flirted a little with a tenth-grade boy, Richard Erikson. He had dark brown hair, eyelashes that would make any model jealous, and an infectious smile. He wasn't part of Evan's group and was quite shy himself. Right now, that seemed to be the safest type of boy to know. We sat at lunch together a few times. He was a good student and a very good reader, and he seemed to know something about almost any subject I mentioned. But he was far from an egghead or a nerd and very humble about his brilliance.

Chastity was disappointed again when she saw that I was starting another relationship. I knew she was hoping that we'd renew our friendship and be satisfied with just each other. She retreated and worked on a friendship with some other girls in our class who were almost as unpopular as she was. I didn't care at all. I could feel that I had changed in many ways, grown older, yes, but even a little calmer and more self-assured. I was settling into a new groove, finding myself comfortable again in ways I didn't think I would while I remained at that school.

I still looked forward to the end of the day and rushing back to see how Mama was and what she needed. Richard wanted to walk me home, but he was also on the school's basketball team and had to stay after for practice every day. I hung around for a little while occasionally to watch the team practice. He wasn't a starter, but he did get in often and would look toward me to see if I was watching.

And then, one afternoon after I had watched his practice for about fifteen minutes, I left to go home and stopped like someone who had walked into an invisible wall when I turned onto the sidewalk and started to cross the street. She was standing beside the rear door of a sleek black limousine and for a moment looked like a model posing for a photo to advertise the car. Dressed in a green skirt and jacket with her hair pinned up, Roxy beckoned to me.

I hesitated like someone who first wanted to be sure she wasn't dreaming. Papa's angry words returned. He had repeated them more than once, and once not long before he died. "You're never to mention her name in my presence and never to speak to her for the rest of your life. If you do, you're as good as dead to me, too."

Anger, I told myself, causes people to say and do things they wouldn't do if they could think calmly, clearly, and intelligently. I had to believe that. I didn't want to see such venom in my father, no matter what Roxy had done.

I started slowly toward her. When I was nearly there, she opened the limousine door.

"Get in," she said.

I looked into the limousine like someone about to enter enemy territory.

"It's all right," she said when I hesitated. "I won't bite or infect you in any way."

I glanced at her. Seeing her close up now, I realized she had Papa's eyes and that little smile on her lips he formed when he was being playful. But she was also so much like Mama when Mama was her age. Her complexion was as perfect as that of a model who had been airbrushed in a photo. I got in, and she followed.

The driver didn't look back.

"Take us through the park, Jeffery, *s'il vous plaît*," she said. Her use of French raised my eyebrows. She pushed a button, and the window divider between us and the driver went up. The limousine started away.

"You remind me so much of myself at your age," she began. She didn't look at me. She looked out the window. I saw the beautiful, very expensive ring and bracelet on her right hand and wrist. The diamonds and gold glittered. She had matching earrings.

She turned and smiled.

"You walk and hold yourself just like I do. It's the damn rod Papa had installed in us when we were born, that perfect military posture. Ironically, for me it's been an asset. So, what are you, in tenth grade?"

"Yes."

"And I'm sure you're a good student."

"Not lately, although I'm doing better than I was."

She nodded and looked out again as the driver made a turn that would take us to the park.

"How did you find out where I was?"

"Papa found out," I said.

"And he told you?" she asked with surprise.

"Not exactly. I overheard him telling Mama."

"How far from a curse word is my name in your house?"

"It was about the same," I said dryly, and she laughed.

"You're more like me than our father would like," she said.

It had a mixed effect on me. At first, I felt a chill. Papa's fears were true, but then I suddenly thought it wasn't so terrible to have her self-confidence. My mind spun with an avalanche of questions, but I wasn't sure if I should ask any.

"That was clever of you to put the charm bracelet in the envelope. I probably wouldn't be here if you hadn't."

"Why didn't you respond sooner?"

"I'm amazed I've responded now," she muttered. She was quiet. We entered Central Park, and the driver slowed. "I was at the cemetery during the burial," she admitted.

"Where?"

"Way back, too far to be noticed. I even visited his grave."

I was speechless for a moment.

"If he wasn't dead, it probably would have killed him," she added.

"It would have pleased Mama," I said.

"Would it? I doubt she would have shown it. He's gone, but his influence over her is probably as strong as it was."

"That's not true."

"Please. There's so much you don't know. I suppose I shouldn't hold her as responsible as I do. She was a European woman from a family where the women were always subservient to their men, and when you were married to a soldier like your father, you were trained and obedient."

"Papa wasn't a soldier."

"*Excusez-moi?* He didn't enlist or go to officers' school, but he was in the Army from the day he was born. I remember my grandfather. You don't. Emotions like love and compassion are signs of weakness. I never had any doubt that if your father was in his regiment, he wouldn't hesitate to send him to the front lines, and if your father was killed in battle, he'd write a letter to your mother and himself with the same official stamp. That's how your father grew up."

"Why do you keep saying *your* father and *your* mother? They're your parents, too."

She just looked at me and smirked.

"Well, they are!"

"That thought had a quick death the moment I hit the street, M."

M, I thought, and remembered. That was what

she used to call me, not Emmie but just M. A flood of childhood memories started.

She looked away again, and for a while we rode in silence. The limousine emerged from the park. She pressed the intercom button.

"Take us to the address I gave you, Jeffery, *s'il vous plaît.*"

"Very good," Jeffery said.

"How is our mother?"

"She hasn't been well," I said.

"In time, she'll get better. He probably left orders."

"No, I'm worried about her, even though she puts on a good act."

She looked at me and smiled softly. *She is so beautiful,* I thought.

"You sound very mature. I'm not surprised. There wasn't much time for childhood in Papa's house. I have to admit that's a good thing in today's world."

"Are you rich?" I asked, and she laughed.

"Let's just say I'm comfortable."

"I've been to your hotel before. I went there with a school friend to . . ."

"Spy?"

"To see you, learn about you."

"What did you learn?"

"Nothing much, and I felt stupid doing it."

"There's not much for you to learn."

The driver turned down our street. She leaned over to open her purse. I watched her pluck out the charm bracelet.

"You should keep it," she said, handing it back to me.

"Are you going in to see Mama?" I asked when the limousine stopped in front of our house.

"No."

"Why did you come to see me, then?"

"I wanted to see what you were like, how you were doing. I think you'll survive," she said.

"But Mama . . ."

"Mama let me go, M. I can't forgive her for that."

"She loved you, loves you. She takes out your picture often, and she cries," I said.

"He let her keep a picture of me?"

"She kept it secret, but I think he always knew. If he hadn't died, maybe . . ."

"Maybe I'd get an honorable discharge?"

"You went to his grave, you said."

"Not to ask him for his forgiveness but to see if I could forgive him. I couldn't," she said.

The driver came around and opened my door.

"Just soldier on, M, and be the good little girl your father wanted you to be," she said. I looked at the charm bracelet in my hand. "It's better you keep it. It's better I don't have reminders."

"No matter what you do, how far you go, you'll always have reminders," I told her. "It's like trying to get rid of your shadow."

I saw her eyes glisten, her lips quiver, and the muscles in her face tighten. "Yeah, well, I've got an appointment," she said, nodding at the opened door.

I closed my fingers around the charm bracelet and stepped out. The driver closed the door. The windows were tinted, so I couldn't see her anymore, but I had the feeling she was still looking at me. He got in and drove off. I stood there watching until the limousine disappeared around a turn, and then I looked up at our front door.

I put the charm bracelet in my purse.

It's better if I don't ever tell Mama about this, I thought.

It would break her heart.

It had nearly shattered mine.

13

Of course, when I entered the house, I was worried that Mama would take one look at my face and know that I was keeping a big secret from her. I heard someone else's voice coming from the living room. We had company. That was good, I thought. It would be easier to hide what had just happened if Mama was distracted. I hurried in to see who was there. The voice was vaguely familiar.

Mama was sitting on the sofa, leaning against the arm of it as if the person next to her had bad breath. Beside her was my uncle Orman's wife, my aunt Lucy. I hadn't seen her for more than two years and had not seen her very often before that. Uncle Orman was five years older than Papa, and Aunt Lucy was only a year younger than Uncle Orman. She was one of those women who looked put together with superglue. I remembered her with the exact same hairdo, teased and sprayed so not a strand was loose. It looked more like a helmet than a hairdo, which probably pleased Uncle Orman. She was dressed in a gray tweed skirt suit with a white ruffled-collar blouse and wore what looked like shoes made for people with foot problems. They looked like claws. She still wore a little too much lipstick, a little too red for her complexion, and her cheeks were powdered a shade or two away from a clown's. Her strong perfume permeated the room. She was the sort whose aroma remained in an elevator for at least five or six more trips. People who got in after she exited would look at each other and grimace, holding their breath.

"How big she's grown, and how much like you she looks," Aunt Lucy said, as if I were in a fishbowl and couldn't hear her.

"Say hello to Aunt Lucy, honey," Mama said, and sat up straighter.

"Hello, Aunt Lucy."

"I knew Aunt Lucy was going to be close by and asked her to stop in," Mama said.

"Oh?" I wanted to ask why she couldn't have come to Papa's funeral, but I bit my tongue.

I looked from Mama to Aunt Lucy and then back again as I sat across from them. There was something strange about the tone in Mama's voice. She was never good at hiding the truth. I hesitate to say lie because I couldn't imagine her being deceitful, but, like any mother, she would find ways to make unpleasant things sound more pleasant.

"That's nice," I said. "How is everyone in your family, Aunt Lucy?"

"They're all doing well, thank you, Emmie. What a little lady," she said to Mama. Mama smiled and nodded. "They grow up so quickly. Which means we grow old so quickly," Aunt Lucy told me. "So make good use of your time. Orman is always telling me that youth is wasted on the young," she told Mama, who nodded again. It was something Papa would say often, too.

I relaxed. Maybe there was nothing more to this than a nice visit. Ironically, it was a day for family, I thought, having just been with Roxy. Relatives were falling out of the trees.

"So why are you in New York?" I asked. "Seeing a show or . . ."

She looked at Mama for the answer, which started my nerves flickering again.

"Your vacation is coming up at the end of this week," Mama began.

"You want to go to France?" I said quickly. Maybe Aunt Lucy was going with us or something.

"Not yet," Mama said. "Now, I don't want you to get worried or anything, but I have to have a procedure done, and it means I'll be in the hospital a while. I thought I could have it all done during your vacation, and your aunt Lucy is very happy to invite you to her and your uncle's home for that period so you won't have to be alone. I would worry about you if you were left alone, Emmie," Mama added with conviction. She was leaning on me to agree quickly.

I glanced at Aunt Lucy. She had the sort of face Papa would call an interrogator's dream face. Her eyes were like two peepholes through which anyone could see the truth or that she was lying.

"What is this procedure, Mama?" I asked, instead of agreeing to be with Aunt Lucy.

"It's just a hysterectomy," she said.

I looked at Aunt Lucy. She was watching me closely to see how I would react.

"What is that?"

"They remove the uterus. I'm certainly not going to have any more children," Mama said, smiling. "It's a very common procedure."

"Why does the doctor want to do that?"

"Precaution," she said. She hesitated and then added, "I have a small cyst. They're confident that this will prevent any further problems."

"I have two friends who have undergone the same surgery," Aunt Lucy said. "They're both doing fine. One of them has gone back to work. She works for Senator Batch, who's on the Armed Services Committee."

"Why are you waiting until my vacation?" I asked Mama, completely ignoring Aunt Lucy.

"It's only a few more days, Emmie, and it just works out with the surgeon's schedule. If you visit Aunt Lucy during this time—"

"I won't leave you alone," I said firmly. I looked at Aunt Lucy. "Thank you for the invitation, Aunt Lucy, but I'll be fine."

"You're being selfish," Aunt Lucy said sharply. "Your mother won't get well quickly if she is lying there in the hospital worrying about you."

"She won't have to. She knows I'm capable of taking care of myself. I won't leave you, Mama," I said.

She could see the look on my face. I was sure it was Papa's determined look, so she knew it would be useless to argue, at least right now.

She nodded and turned to Aunt Lucy. "We'll discuss it, Lucy. Thank you so much for offering to help and for stopping by," Mama said.

Aunt Lucy bristled. She clearly sensed that she was being dismissed. I was sure Uncle Orman spoke to her that way whenever he wanted to end a conversation or an argument. In fact, she pulled herself up so sharply I thought she might crack her spine. It almost brought a smile to my face.

"Well . . ." she said rising. "You know how to reach me, Vivian. I do have to make some preparations, of course. Orman hates last-minute things, as you know."

Like my father dying, I wanted to say, but swallowed back the words and raised my eyes toward the ceiling.

"I'll be here at the St. Regis tonight," she added. "But I am going to dinner with the wives of some Pentagon officials." She looked at me. "Be a good girl, now, Emmie, and please help your mother get through all this."

"No one has to ask me to do that, Aunt Lucy," I said in the softest, sweetest tone of voice I could manage, but you'd have had to be tone-deaf not to hear my sarcasm, too.

She nodded.

Mama rose to walk her to the door. I waited, my heart still racing.

"I know how you feel, Emmie," Mama began even before she entered the living room, "but she was the closest relative I could think of and the easiest trip for you to manage."

"I don't need to go anywhere, Mama. Really, I'll be fine, and if I'm not here, who will visit you in the hospital?"

"I won't be there that long," she said. "I do have some friends, you know," she added with a smile.

"Not like me," I told her. "I'm not going to leave you. Don't worry about me. All I would do is worry about you and be too far away to see you every day. I don't want to upset you, Mama, but . . ."

"Okay, let's not talk about it now," she said, obviously frustrated. "I just have to check on the chicken breasts I defrosted for us."

I felt terrible being so difficult, but I knew I would feel worse running off to be comfortable and safe with my uncle and aunt who couldn't even be at my father's funeral. I didn't want to continue talking about this, either. I knew that what I would say would only bring Mama more pain. Instead, I went up to my room and, to keep my mind off it all, began to do my homework.

At dinner, I prodded Mama as much as I could about her condition. I easily sensed that she was trying to make it seem less serious than it was, but I didn't pursue it. After I cleaned up and watched some television with her, I retreated to my room.

The day of Papa's death, I was shocked, of course, but I was more frightened than anything. He was truly a rock, our security and protection. Like any young girl, I looked to my father to shield us from danger and to come up with the solution to solve any serious problems. The analogies he used when he spoke about himself weren't so far-fetched. Fathers, he said, were always on the front lines, like guards manning the walls that kept out our demons.

When I lost him that day, one of the first things that came to my mind was how terrified Roxy must have been the day she left our house and stepped into the streets of the city on her own. How naked and vulnerable she must have felt despite what face she had put on. For all practical purposes, as she seemed to insist, Papa had died for her then as much as he had died for me now. He was gone, unreachable, deaf to her cries for help, not that she was used to asking him for it. It simply gave her and all of us a sense of assurance to have such a father. In Papa, there was sanctuary.

Within his embrace, beside him, holding his hand, having his arm around our shoulders shielded us from what Hamlet called the slings and arrows of outrageous fortune. Accidents, evil people, even our own foolishness wouldn't destroy us as long as Papa was there.

Daddies were supposed to be harder, tougher, firmer. They were more capable of facing the gritty and rotten things in our world. Mothers could be strong, of course, and I did know mothers of some of my classmates who made their husbands look like wet noodles, but for the most part, daddies were built physically stronger and could be more intimidating when it came to facing something outright violent.

Now, as I sat there and thought about Mama, I realized selfishly that I could lose all of my protection in this world. I'd be as alone as Roxy, but she seemed to be far better equipped to handle that than I was. I hated being this afraid for myself and not being more afraid for Mama. I felt selfish, guilty, even sinfully so.

Get stronger, Emmie Wilcox, I told myself. *Grow up overnight. Put away childish thoughts. Shove your dolls and teddy bears deeper into the closet. You have to step up and do for your mother what she has done all your life for you.*

I looked at Papa's picture on my dresser. I wasn't telling myself all of these things; he was. If he were there, he would expect me to be more grown-up. I had heard it when he died, and I was hearing him say it again tonight: "If you have no choice but to grow up, you grow up."

No, I wouldn't run off to hide from fear at Uncle Orman and Aunt Lucy's house. I would stay here. I would be alone at night, yes. I would have to take care of myself, yes. I would have to close my eyes and forget that there was no one else in the house, no one to call to if I had a nightmare or if I heard a strange noise, yes. But this was who and what I had to become.

As Papa might say, "Let's get some steel in those veins."

Over the next two days, Mama realized that I wasn't going to give in and go to stay with Aunt Lucy. She accepted it and even complimented me on being strong enough to do it. We didn't talk much more in detail about her condition, but I did my own research in the school library and realized how serious it could be and probably was. I didn't want to show her how worried I was, so I tried to keep as busy as possible, telling her I had big tests to study for, while all the while I sat in my room feeling like someone tottering on a tightrope and on the verge of screaming.

The next day, I made a big decision while I sat half listening to Mrs. Summerton go on and on about our term papers in world history due shortly after our upcoming holiday. When the bell rang at the end of the school day, I practically leaped up from my desk and ran out of the building. I was that determined.

Probably in record time, I shot up the avenue and entered Roxy's hotel. There was a different desk clerk, a much older man with a rust-colored mustache that looked painted above his lip. He obviously trimmed it under a microscope, I thought. He didn't smile. He looked up from what I saw was a racetrack form and tucked in his thin, shrimp-pink lips. Then he sat back, pulling his shoulders so they tightened his jacket.

"And what can I do for you?" he asked.

"I have to speak to Roxy Wilcox."

He pulled his head back and widened his grimace. "Who?"

"Don't tell me she isn't here. I'm her sister, and I have to speak to her now," I said firmly, raising my voice.

"Now, just a minute, young lady . . ."

"I'm not leaving until you tell her I'm here. You can call the police if you want, but I don't think that would please my sister or anyone else connected with this hotel."

"I know all of our guests, and there is no Roxy Wilcox," he said.

"Fleur du Coeur? Is that better?"

"What are you talking about?"

He looked genuinely confused. It occurred to me that the help there might not know all that much about the clients and that the escort service was separate.

"My sister might have a different name here," I said, stepping closer and speaking more softly, reasonably. I then described her. I could see some recognition in his eyes. He might not know everything, but he knew enough, I thought.

"Just a moment," he said, and got up and went into the office behind the desk.

While I was waiting, a tall, thin man with a thick head of light brown hair came in. He was dressed in an expensive-looking dark blue suit and a light blue tie. He smiled at me and went directly to the elevator. Immediately, I wondered if he was going up to see Roxy. If so, this was certainly bad timing.

The desk clerk came out. "Just sit there," he said, nodding at the settee across from the desk.

"Is she coming?"

"Just sit there," he emphasized.

I did what he said. He went back to his racing form, and I kept my eyes on the elevator. It opened, but an elderly lady stepped out, glanced at me, and went outside to a waiting limousine. I looked at the desk clerk, but he was very involved in his racing form now and no longer paid any attention to me. At least another fifteen minutes passed. I almost gave up, but the elevator opened again, and Roxy came out. She had her hair down and was wearing a long raincoat and a pair of sandals. I sensed that she wasn't wearing much underneath the raincoat. The desk clerk looked up at her, but her stern expression chased him back to his racing form. I stood up.

"What are you doing here?" she asked, obviously very annoyed.

"Mama's very sick," I said.

She didn't speak for a moment, but I saw her face soften. "What do you mean, very sick? What's wrong with her?"

"She has a cyst. She's having a hysterectomy done, or at least that is what she's telling me, but I think it might be more serious than she says."

"Are you a doctor already?"

"I know how to read Mama," I said. "She wanted me to go stay with Uncle Orman and Aunt Lucy."

"Orman and Lucy? You might as well be sent to Leavenworth prison." She paused and looked at the desk clerk again. He didn't look our way. "When is all this happening?"

"Monday," I said. "She goes into Sloan-Kettering.

We have a ten-day break at my school beginning this weekend."

"Great. You'll be able to play nurse," she said. "Look, I'm busy right now. I can't stand around and chat. Take care of yourself, and don't go to Uncle Orman's." She turned to go to the elevator.

"Don't you care at all?" I cried.

She pushed the button and looked back at me when the door opened. "Once," she said. "A long time ago."

She got into the elevator and fixed her eyes on me as the doors closed. Her eyes were empty. They were like unlit bulbs. I stood there for a few moments and then looked at the desk clerk. He was staring at me now. I turned and headed out of the hotel, my feet pounding the sidewalk. I was so full of anger and turmoil that I almost went in the wrong direction. A heavyset man bumped into me as if I didn't exist. He nearly spun me around, but he kept walking. I caught my breath, realized where I was going, and crossed the street, walking even faster now.

I shouldn't be so surprised by what had just happened, I thought, or even upset. I didn't really know Roxy or who she had become. It was almost the same as talking to a complete stranger. Love, or the deep feeling we have for each other, is really a very fragile thing. Once it's damaged as much as it was for Roxy, it probably floats down like a leaking balloon and settles under our feet. We step over the memories, even trample them, and go on, hardening ourselves, maybe even hating ourselves for being this way, but it's probably what Roxy had to do to survive. I wanted to hate her, too, but I couldn't. Despite how terrible things were for Mama and me right now, we still had each other, loved each other. What did Roxy have?

A man waiting upstairs, someone paying for her attention and affection?

And when he was gone, what did she have? What were her thoughts just before she fell asleep? What were her prayers? Had she grown so comfortable and indifferent to the darkness and the loneliness that it no longer bothered her or even mattered?

She was traveling alone through her life now, gazing occasionally at those who weren't alone. Maybe she still longed for family, for someone to love and someone to love her, but if she did, she kept it under lock and key, a secret so tightly folded it was as hard as her heart.

I didn't want to waste any more time feeling sorry for her. Yes, I had gone to her in the hope that she would join me, be at my side, worrying and praying for Mama. That she would return to being the sister I once had. That she would embrace both Mama and me. I was doing it for her as much as I was doing it for myself and for Mama.

But she didn't see that, or she didn't want to see that.

When those elevator doors closed between us, it was like closing the lid of a coffin. She wasn't going up; she was going down.

But I wasn't going up, either. I was just hovering like some cloud unsure of which way the wind was to take it, hanging up there alone and afraid, especially of the rumbling on the horizon and the darkness that was seeping over the blue daylight, oozing like oil toward it and threatening to wash it under forever.

14

I didn't sleep much Sunday night. No one from school called me over the weekend. I hadn't told Chastity or Richard about Mama's health problem. Richard had finally overcome his shyness and wanted to do something with me over the weekend, but I made excuses, telling him we had relatives visiting. It wasn't a good time for me to develop a relationship with anyone new, anyway. As nice as he was, I didn't have any warm emotions to spare, and I didn't want to drag him into my difficulties. Chastity had remained aloof, and I continued to avoid her, especially now. Once she got wind of all of this, I was sure she would pounce, hoping that I needed her more than she needed me.

Maybe I did, but I wouldn't admit that to anyone, especially myself. I knew that Aunt Lucy had called one more time to offer her services. Mama mentioned it as casually as she could, hoping that I had somehow changed my mind.

"I'll be fine," I insisted.

I knew she hadn't told any of her family in France about what was happening. All weekend, I toyed with the idea of calling Uncle Alain, but then I thought that if she hadn't done it, she wouldn't want me to do it. Maybe it would alarm people unnecessarily. On Sunday night, she went through some of the details for things she was leaving for me to do around the house and with some of our accounts. None of it was very critical, but I could see that it helped her to think of other things, and she was deliberately looking for activities that would keep me busy, too. Before she went up to bed, she pinned a list of important telephone numbers on the wall in the kitchen.

I was sure neither of us slept much. I played a little game with myself, a game Papa had taught me when I was very young. He told me that it was guaranteed to keep you from being afraid. As soon as something terrible began to come into your mind, you were supposed to count backward from one hundred, and with each number, you were supposed to think of one happy thought, one happy memory, or one thing you loved, such as chocolate marshmallow ice cream. The effort at association eventually exhausted you, and the creeping nightmares ran out of steam. He told me that these were the sort of mental games soldiers freezing on guard duty or captured soldiers might play.

I don't think Papa ever gave up on the idea that there was always some sort of a war going on, whether with real bombs in Bosnia, the Middle East, or Asia or in everyday life. One way or another, we were always in training, always thinking about defenses, and always planting our flags of victory on some hill, whether the hill was real or in our imaginations.

I was sure that Mama would be the first to admit that she was in a battle. As we headed for the hospital that morning, we were like two soldiers in some army. Maybe we were Greeks marching to Philippi, Americans in landing craft approaching Normandy, or Englishmen getting ready to face the Spanish Armada. Later, no one who survived would seem credible claiming that he was not terrified. Honest ones would admit to it but be proud of how well they kept fear chained down. In my mind, fear was like an aggressive dog barking and lunging at us.

Staying with Mama did help her face the day, because she had to keep courageous as much for my benefit as for her own. She didn't utter a single syllable of self-pity. She never shed a tear. She smiled at all those who were there to help her. She treated it all as if she had done it hundreds of times and kept herself looking bright and hopeful. One of the nurses whispered to me not to look so sad and worried. It wasn't good for Mama. I tried hard to be as brave as she was.

"Be your father's daughter," I muttered under my breath.

I kissed her and wished her good luck before they took her to preop, and then I retreated to the waiting area. One of the nurses promised to keep me informed about how things were going. She said they had direct communication with the staff in the operating room. I got myself something to drink and went to sit and distract myself with magazines. Although there was a lot of activity going on around me, including the small children of other patients complaining because they were bored and restless, people gathering to comfort one another, hugging and kissing, and medical personnel going to and fro, I managed to shut it all out by crawling into my own protective shell. I even lost my sense of time. At one point, I closed my eyes and sat back and dozed until I felt the weight of a shadow, someone looking down at me. I opened my eyes.

Roxy stared at me. "What's happening?" she asked.

She was wearing very little makeup and had her hair pinned in the back and flowing just the way I had seen it that day I spied on her with Chastity. Although I would never call anything she wore conservative, she was dressed in a pretty but ordinary light blue jacket and an ankle-length skirt with a dark blue blouse. For a moment, I just stared up at her, digesting that she was actually there.

"Well?" she demanded.

I sat up quickly and looked at my watch. "She went in about two hours ago, I think. I mean, I don't know exactly when they took her into surgery, but . . ."

She blew some air of impatience out through her lips and went to the desk manned by two nurses. I watched her get their attention. After she spoke, one moved quickly to a phone. There was something about the way Roxy carried herself, the air of authority she displayed, and obviously the way she spoke that impressed them. The nurse listened on the phone and then spoke to her. Roxy nodded and started back to me. Maybe it was my imagination, but it seemed to me that even the restless children paused to look at her.

"What exactly did she tell you about her condition, the reason for this surgery today?" she asked, whipping and snapping her consonants and vowels.

"I told you. She said she had a small cyst and had to have a hysterectomy and . . ."

"C'mon," she said, jerking her head toward the hospital entrance. "There's a little coffee shop just down the street. This is going to take some time yet, maybe a lot more time."

"Why do you say that?" I asked.

She glanced at me as if I had asked a stupid question and started out. I leaped up to follow.

"What did those nurses tell you?" I asked, catching up to her at the door.

"You were right to be suspicious. It is more serious than she's told you. She's having a radical hysterectomy, M." She paused. "I know a little too much about it. One of my regulars just happens to be a surgeon, not working here in the city but a surgeon nevertheless."

"What does that mean? What are you saying?"

She kept walking. I was practically jogging to keep up with her.

"What are you saying?"

She paused. "She doesn't simply have a precancerous cyst or something. She has cervical cancer. The operation in a radical hysterectomy is quite a bit more involved. Let's go in here," she said, nodding at a coffee shop. As soon as we entered, she asked me what I wanted.

"Nothing," I said, impatient to hear more.

"I'm having a latte. Nonfat. I'll get you one, too," she said, and ordered at the counter. Then she led me to a table.

"What does this mean?"

"They remove the uterus, the cervix, the top part of the vagina, ovaries, fallopian tubes, lymph nodes, lymph channels, and tissues in the pelvic cavity that surrounds the cervix. That's why I said she'll be in there a while."

"A doctor client told you all this?"

"After I asked him. Someone I knew had contracted cervical cancer, too, and he described what was going to be done. At the time, it was a lot more information than I wanted, but he was not a very emotional man. He treated everything like an operation, and I mean everything," she added, raising her eyebrows in an obvious reference to sex. "Anyway, I was close to this friend, so I wanted to know what to expect."

"How did it all go?"

"She lasted for about six months afterward, but she was a lot younger than your mother."

"She's your mother, too!" I practically screamed.

Roxy barely smirked. She looked away and then turned back, shaking her head. "It wouldn't surprise me to learn that she put off her own health issues to service the general."

"What do you mean?"

"Avoided her annuals, whatever. He always came first," she said as the waitress brought our lattes.

"Can't you stop hating him for a few minutes?"

She smiled and sipped her latte. "Hating him is what kept me going, M. That was his gift to me. You think it's easy to leave someone you don't hate? I kept myself alive thinking I wasn't going to give him the satisfaction of failing or dying. It worked. With a little luck, of course."

"What about Mama?"

"*Je suis ici.* I'm here, *n'est-ce pas? Bien que je préférerais être aileurs.* Even though I'd rather be somewhere else," she translated. I didn't need it, but I didn't say so.

"How did you keep up with French?" I didn't want to tell her about the day Chastity and I had followed her and Chastity had heard her conversing easily in French.

"Someone who helped me a lot after I left home just happened to be French, or should I say ironically was French. She's technically my boss," she added. She continued drinking her latte. I sipped some of mine. "Speaking of French, did she call anyone in France about this?"

"No."

"Just like her not to look to any other family for help," she said. "She's still used to having him around, I suppose."

"She has me," I said, fixing my eyes squarely on hers.

She smiled. "Tough kid, huh?"

"Yes, I am."

She laughed.

"I am!"

"Oh, really? What's the biggest challenge you've had, M? A pimple on your chin, a boy you like ignores you, your boobs aren't big enough?"

"They are, too," I said, and she laughed again.

Then she paused to study me a little. Whatever it was, it brought another smile to her face.

"What?" I asked.

"That expression on your face reminded me of how upset you would get when he came after me. You did all my crying for me back then. Maybe just because of you, he was less severe."

"Yeah, well, you weren't an angel, Roxy. There was a lot going on that I was too young to know about back then."

"He talked about me, did he. Described my sins in detail?"

"Not often." I didn't want to stress how forbidden her name had become. "Almost never. Mama told me the most. Then he found out more about you himself. You had a coworker of his as a . . . what do you call them? Clients?"

"Get to the point."

"One of Papa's coworkers called and got you, didn't he? You picked him up outside the offices, and Daddy saw you in the limousine."

"How can I forget?" She looked away for a moment and shook her head. "The guy was pathetic.

Well, maybe he wasn't as bad as I made him out to be. I couldn't help it. Despite myself, I kept thinking about the way he looked at me."

"Papa?"

"*Oui,*" she said. "I got bawled out for how that one worked out." She finished her latte. "Let's go back. This isn't going to be easy," she warned as she stood. "Especially since it's all coming more or less as a surprise for you."

"I'll be all right," I said.

She smiled softly. "Maybe you will be. You look more like him than I remember."

I followed her out.

We hadn't had any heavy snow yet, even though it was early February, but the air felt like snow, cold and wet. Gray clouds had been shifting about all day, as if they had been playing tag with any piece of blue sky. It was finally completely overcast. I hugged myself. I could have worn something warmer, I thought, but clothing wasn't on my mind that morning.

She looked up. "It's supposed to snow lightly late today. Mostly flurries."

I didn't say anything. The last thing I wanted to talk about was the weather.

"I was planning on getting away for five days. St. Thomas," she continued. "On someone's private jet."

"Planning? What happened?" I asked.

She paused and tightened her lips. "You happened," she said, and walked on. I hurried after her.

We sat and waited for nearly another two hours before one of the nurses walked over to inform us that

Mama's surgeon, Dr. Hoffman, wanted to see us. During the two hours we had spent together, Roxy hadn't talked about herself very much, and I hadn't felt like asking any questions. I was still feeling numb after she had told me what she had learned about Mama.

The nurse explained where we were to go. For the first time, I saw real fear in Roxy's face. Just for a moment, she looked more like a little girl than I did. Then she either felt it or knew I felt it and tightened up again.

"Gird your loins," she muttered.

"What's that mean?"

"Prepare for the worst," she said, and we turned down a hallway to an office. Dr. Hoffman was seated at a desk. He was still in his operating scrubs but bent over his desk writing. Roxy knocked on the opened door, and he looked up. I hadn't met him before. Mama had kept everything quite secret and had never taken me with her to see a doctor of any kind.

Dr. Hoffman was stout, about fifty, with dark brown hair that looked as if it had begun what Papa would call a strategic retreat. I always looked at a stranger's eyes to see if he or she was someone I could like. Dr. Hoffman's hazel eyes were soft and, I thought, full of compassion.

"Which one of you is Emmie?" he asked.

"I am. This is my sister, Roxy," I quickly added.

"Oh. She told me only to expect you."

I could feel Roxy bristle, but why should she be surprised or upset? Mama didn't expect her. Neither had I.

"Please," he added, gesturing at the chairs. We sat. "I don't know how much you two were told."

"Practically nothing," Roxy said. "She told my sister she had a cyst."

He nodded. "Well, we'll wait for pathology, but regardless, she'll have to undergo chemo, I'm afraid. She came through the operation fine."

"Be grateful for the little things," Roxy muttered loudly enough for him to hear.

"Yes." He looked at me. "How old are you?"

"Fifteen."

He smiled. "I have a fourteen-year-old daughter," he said.

I knew he was just trying to make me feel better, feel comfortable, but Roxy would have nothing of it. "With a healthy mother, I imagine," she said.

He looked at her. I could see his whole demeanor change. There was going to be no sugarcoating as long as Roxy was there. He was back to being a scientist.

"I can't give you an exact prognosis yet."

"What stage is she in?" Roxy demanded.

He looked at me again and then back at her. "She's stage four."

"The worst," Roxy muttered. He nodded. "Did she neglect herself, her symptoms?"

"I'm not her primary," Dr. Hoffman said. "You'd have to speak to her gynecologist, but I wouldn't jump to any conclusions. Everyone's different."

"Yes, everyone's different," Roxy said dryly.

"We'll do the best we can. She'll be here a while," he told me. "Right now, she's still in recovery. I'd say give her a few hours before trying to visit. We'll keep her there a few days before moving her."

"How long do you give her?" Roxy asked.

His face hardened. I was sure he didn't like Roxy's tone. The children of most of his patients were nowhere as cold or as tough and surely didn't ask such a question so quickly. For a few fleeting seconds, he was probably wondering about the relationships, but I could see he didn't want to spend any of his time on that. It wasn't the world he worked in. He looked at me again, obviously deciding whether to be evasive. Something told him that Roxy wouldn't let him get away with it.

"Fifteen percent at stage four make it to five years," he replied. "I can't tell you much more than that."

"That's enough. Thank you," Roxy said, rising.

Dr. Hoffman nodded. I looked up at Roxy. I was feeling a bit dizzy. All of these terrible things had been said so quickly. I think she saw it and reached down to take my arm to get me to my feet. None of it felt real to me. It was as if I were in a dream.

"C'mon, M," she said.

I glanced at the doctor. I could see his eyes narrow, his face fill with disapproval.

Roxy didn't speak again until we were almost back to the lobby. "If I didn't push him, he'd have you believing in Santa Claus," she said.

"I don't understand."

She stopped and spun me around. "What don't

you understand, M? Mama might have been sick quite a while. Maybe if she had taken better medical care of herself, it would have made a difference. I don't know, and neither does he. You see how quickly he came to the defense of another doctor. Everyone's different, he said. What a catchall for everything."

"But what was all that about five years?"

She softened. "Where are you going now?"

"Going? I don't know. Where would I go?"

"Right. Where would you go?" she asked herself. She looked at her watch. "I've got to see someone. Go home and take a shower or something. Fix yourself up a little. You look too drab. We'll be back here in two hours and visit her, and then I'll take you to dinner."

"Dinner?"

"We've got to eat, M, and if you go in to visit her looking so overwhelmed and terrified . . ."

"Okay, okay, I get it," I said sharply.

"Maybe you do. Maybe you're smarter than I was at your age." She looked at her watch and said, "I'll meet you in the lobby again in exactly two hours."

"Okay."

She started away. Suddenly, she paused and turned back to me. "I'm sorry," she said. "I've been on my own so long that I forgot what it was like to have someone you cared about and who cared about you. I don't mean to sound so insensitive."

She walked on.

That was the nicest thing she had said to me since we had met again, I thought, and I walked after her, but she was going too fast for me to catch up.

When I stepped out of the hospital, she was getting into a cab.

And the flurries she had predicted had begun.

15

I knew the house would be empty when I returned, but despite the brave face I had put on for both Mama and Roxy, I was simply not prepared for the silence and the shadows. Out of habit, I almost shouted, "Mama, I'm home." For a long moment, I simply stood in the entryway listening. If stillness could be loud, it was deafening there, I thought.

The overcast sky spread thick shadows over the walls and floors. It looked as if a large, solid black cover was being thrown over all of the furniture. It was as if our lives in this home were going to be placed in storage, shut up in vaults that would never be opened. With a vengeance, I began flipping on every possible light and lamp. I would not let the darkness have its way with me. Then I hurried up to my room.

When I looked at myself in the bathroom mirror, I knew Roxy was right. The waiting, the stress of the day, and especially the things Dr. Hoffman had said had drained me of all hope and happiness. I looked like a refugee who had trekked across scene after scene of death and destruction, a young girl without family whom misery had stunned and aged almost overnight.

Show this face to Mama, and you shut down all of her hope, I thought.

I jumped into the shower and then did my hair and put on some makeup. I chose a bright blue dress and some earrings. When I went to put on my watch, I paused and thought of something. I opened my dresser drawer and took out the charm bracelet. It brought a smile to my face. It would surely please Mama to see me wearing it, especially with Roxy right there beside me. I got my nice evening coat from the entryway closet, turned off almost all of the lights, and headed back to the hospital.

I was there before Roxy, but when a good half hour went by, I began to fear that she wouldn't come. I looked up every time someone entered the hospital. When it was more like an hour, I got up and went to the desk to find out where I should go to see Mama. Before I went into the elevator, I paused and watched the entrance. Roxy didn't appear. Angry and disgusted, I started for the ICU. I quickly decided that I could not in any way indicate to Mama that Roxy had been there and then failed to show up to visit her. I thought it was better that she didn't know anything about it.

As it turned out, it almost didn't matter anyway. Mama was under so much pain medication that she barely realized I was there. I held her hand and talked to her anyway. She smiled at me but closed her eyes.

One of the nurses came over to me and told me not to be upset. "She's doing fine and will be better company tomorrow," she said.

I thanked her, but I stayed as long as I could. I was afraid Mama would wake up and not see me or even remember I had been there, even though the nurse assured me that she would tell her. The whole time I was there, I still expected Roxy would show up, but she never appeared. Finally, I kissed Mama and whispered, "I'll be back in the morning, Mama. I love you."

When I returned to the lobby, I saw that the flurries had become a real snowfall. I stood there for a while just looking at it. The flakes were tiny jeweled butterflies surprised by car headlights. They seemed to flee into whatever pockets of darkness they could find, afraid that the light would melt them quicker and their short lives would be that much shorter.

When we are children, everything around us seems alive. We imagine trees and rocks, grass and flowers all have feelings and emotions. Precious possessions certainly do. My charm bracelet looked sad, even a little embarrassed, on my wrist now. I unclipped it quickly and put it in my purse. Whatever feeling my sister had for me when she gave it to me years ago and whatever feelings I had whenever I looked at it afterward were as brittle and dead as an old leaf decomposing between the pages of a book.

Where do memories go when we forget them? I wondered. Do they evaporate and disappear like smoke or crumble into dust and scatter in the wind? Where had Roxy put all her memories? Was she able to crush them or set them on fire with her anger? Was that why she didn't come back? Were her memories resurrected, haunting her and punishing her for forgetting them?

Who was really stronger now, she or I? I recalled how quickly she had left me and hailed a taxicab. Maybe she was the one fleeing; maybe she was the one who wasn't tough enough to face all of this despite the hard persona she had presented to the doctor. If I ever saw her again, I would tell her that, too.

I buttoned up my coat. An elderly man with hair the color of unpolished silverware stepped up beside me and made a clicking sound with his lips. He was about my height and wore a heavy winter jacket.

"We're in for it now," he muttered. "Look at it come down. It's the kind that sticks."

I didn't say anything.

He glanced at me and nodded. "Better button up," he said. He started out, paused, and then walked as quickly as he could, his hands up around his neck as if he didn't want a single flake to touch his skin.

I followed him out.

It was almost impossible to hail a cab in this weather. Every one I saw had passengers in it. There was nothing to do but put my head down and walk. In my eagerness to look nice for Mama, I had put on the wrong shoes for this kind of weather. My feet were freezing by the time I had walked two blocks. I gazed into the windows of restaurants along the way. The people I saw talking and laughing looked completely oblivious to the weather outside. It was as if I were looking through a magic window into a world where there were no sick loved ones, no inclement weather, no fear of what the future might bring, simply no unhappiness.

These people would enjoy one another's company, sit down to a wonderful dinner seasoned with laughter and affection, and afterward, contented and high on their pleasure, step out looking surprised that there was a storm of any sort. It wouldn't matter anyway. Their happiness would keep them warm and safe.

How could I be one of them? Wasn't I supposed to be? Wasn't that what Roxy had said? We would go to dinner, surely at a fancy restaurant? Maybe at that dinner, I would have learned a great deal more about her and about what had happened. Maybe we would have grown closer and been well on our way to being sisters again.

"Maybe, maybe, maybe," I chanted, like someone who had gone mad on the streets of the city. I looked up defiantly into the snow and walked on. I crossed avenues and made turns casually, as if the sun were shining. All of the bad news, the tension, and the disappointment made me giddy. I felt like Gene Kelly in *Singin' in the Rain.* I heard myself laughing and caught the curious, even frightened, looks of some people hurrying by me. By the time I reached our street, my hair was soaked, but I was still oblivious to the cold. When I entered the house, I shook myself off like a dog, threw my wet coat on the floor, and sat right there in the entryway. For a moment, I was dazed, and then I just began to cry. I sobbed hard, so hard that my ribs hurt, until I was exhausted.

I struggled to my feet and made my way up the stairs, using the banister to pull myself along. When I got to my bedroom, I peeled off my clothes, leaving them all in a pile at my feet, and then I went into the shower and ran the water as hot as I could stand. My skin was sunburn red when I stepped out and began to dry myself.

Now truly exhausted, I fell onto my bed and tucked my blanket in around me. In minutes, I was asleep. In a dream, I heard the doorbell ringing and ringing. Finally, I rose and went downstairs. When I opened the door, Papa was standing there.

"What's going on?" he asked. "I leave for a little while, and the place falls apart?"

I quickly embraced him, and he closed the door. I kept my head against his chest and held on to him so tightly that he couldn't move.

"Hey, hey, hey," he said. "It's all right. I'm here. Everything will be all right. The cavalry has arrived."

I laughed and looked up at him. That was just what he would say.

But then he popped like a bubble and was gone.

"Papa!" I screamed. "Papa, where are you?"

I ran through all of the downstairs rooms and then hurried back upstairs. When I looked into his and Mama's bedroom, I saw him lying there just as he was in the funeral parlor. I put my hands on my temples and screamed and screamed until . . . I woke up, gasping.

It was nearly midnight. After a few moments, I was calm again, realizing I had been dreaming. I fell back onto my pillow and looked up at the dark ceiling. I vaguely thought about not having eaten anything, but I really didn't have any appetite. The best thing to do, I told myself, was try to get back to sleep, get up as early as I could, and hurry back to the hospital.

It was something easier thought of than done. Everything came rushing back at me, but I was too tired to cry anymore. Reliving the day finally tired me out again, and I did fall asleep. I woke up with a start, having slept longer than I intended, and then I rushed about, picking up my clothes, dressing, having a glass of juice and a piece of toast with jam because I knew Mama would be upset if I didn't eat anything first. It was probably going to be her first question when she saw me, I thought. I washed and dried my glass and dish, then I started for the front door.

Before I reached it, the buzzer sounded, and I stopped like someone instantly frozen. My dream returned. Was Papa out there? The buzzer went off again and again. With my legs trembling, I stepped forward and opened the door. Roxy was standing there in a jacket and hood. She was in jeans and a pair of nearly knee-high black boots.

"What do you want?" I asked.

"Don't be an ass," she said, stepping in and closing the door behind her. She didn't look at me, however. She stood gazing at the entry and the hallway. "I never even dreamed I would be back in this house."

I folded my arms over my breasts and leaned against the wall.

She glanced at me and lowered her hood. "I came around last night and pressed the buzzer for almost ten minutes."

"I didn't hear it," I said, and thought that probably was responsible for my dream about Papa.

"You have any coffee?"

"I didn't make any, but we have it. Why?"

"I'm knocking on doors in the neighborhood taking a poll. Why do you think?"

She walked to the kitchen.

"She always kept her kitchen immaculate. I was afraid to eat anything, worried I'd drop a crumb or something."

"She's not like that."

"Maybe now," she said.

"Why didn't you meet me yesterday?" I demanded.

She ignored me and looked into the closets. "Amazing," she said. "Everything is exactly where it was when I was here." She turned to me. "I remember every little detail of this place, because the general insisted on everything in his life being organized. Did he bounce quarters off your sheets to see if you made your bed properly?"

"Stop it, and stop calling him the general."

She stared at me a moment and then hooked up the coffeepot and began to prepare the coffee. She spoke as she worked. "Unfortunately, my life isn't all that much freer now. I simply have a different general running things, and just like here, there's little or no room for any opposition or refusals. You get your orders, and you follow them or else."

"What orders? What are you talking about?"

She turned after she had the coffee started. "The people I work for don't want to hear about sick mothers, dead fathers, and destitute sisters."

"I'm not destitute." I sat at the kitchenette.

She took out the coffee cups and saucers and then the milk. "What do you have to eat? Any buns, bagels, muffins?"

"There are muffins in that big bowl," I said, nodding at it.

She took two out and put them on a dish. Then she looked into the refrigerator again. "I should have some juice."

"So have it."

She poured a glass. "Did you have anything?"

"What difference does it make? Stop talking about food. Where were you?"

"I was given an assignment I couldn't refuse. I thought about calling the hospital and leaving a message for you but then thought that might be worse."

"It wouldn't have been."

She smiled. "Did you tell her I came to see how she was?"

"No. I didn't want to tell her anything, since you hadn't showed up and might never," I said. "She didn't need any more unhappiness."

She nodded, then sat and cut a muffin. "What did you do about dinner?"

"Nothing. I wasn't hungry. I probably wouldn't have eaten much even if you had done what you said you were going to do."

"Look, I'm sorry. It couldn't be avoided. I'm here now. We'll have something to eat and go see her. How was she?"

"She wasn't really alert. I don't know if she'll remember that I was there."

"So see? No harm done," she said, and got up to get the coffee.

"No harm done?"

"Don't get dramatic on me," she warned. "You want some coffee? Don't tell me you don't drink it, either. The French love their coffee."

"Okay," I said, relenting.

She poured us both a cup and sat. "What was so important last night?"

"I told you. An assignment."

"Is that really what you call it?"

"Let's not talk about me. You have to go back to school, you know."

"I hate that school. I don't care."

"What would your . . . what would Mama think if you didn't go back?"

I sipped my coffee and nibbled on one of the muffins.

"Well, let's do first things first," she said. "We'll go see her and then talk about the rest later."

"Later? What if you get another emergency assignment?"

She smiled. "I was afraid you and I would be too different even to talk to each other, but I see you have my personality after all."

"Please," I said. "Spare me the compliments, if that was a compliment."

She laughed, then finished her coffee, grabbed another piece of muffin, and got up.

"Let's go."

"First, we'll clean up this mess," I said. I brought the cups and saucers to the sink, turned off the coffee-pot, and began cleaning it.

"Maybe we're not all that alike," she added, and put what was left of the muffins back in the bowl.

When we stepped out, I was surprised to see the limousine waiting.

"You didn't have that last night."

"Reward today for being such a loyal employee last night," she replied. The driver got out to open the door for us.

It wasn't snowing anymore, but there was a good two inches, and the sky was still quite overcast. It was very cold, probably below freezing. I didn't want to say it, but I was happy that Roxy had been rewarded. We got in and were driven to the hospital.

"I hope the sight of me doesn't put her into shock," Roxy said when we got out of the limousine.

For the first time, I wondered how Mama would react to her. Surely, it would be wonderful for her to see her daughter, even like this, but would she smile, or would she burst into tears, and if she did that, would it be very bad for her? Would she look at Roxy and think of all she could have done to keep her home, all she didn't do, and would that make her feel even worse?

When I didn't respond, Roxy paused to look at me. "You're not sure this is a good idea after all. Is that it, M?"

"Of course it's a good idea. You're her daughter. I told you how bad she felt about what happened to you."

"Yeah, you told me," Roxy said, and walked quickly ahead of me. But when we reached the ICU, her step slowed. From the look on her face, I thought she was going to back out for sure.

"She'll be glad to see you," I insisted. "It will be something good after something so horrible."

She turned away.

I put my hands on my hips and raised my voice. "What is it? You were ready to see her yesterday, weren't you?"

"I was going to see her, but I'm not saying I was ready," she replied. She looked at the door. "Don't you think I imagined seeing her again, thought about it, dreamed about it?"

"I don't know. How would I know? You didn't want to before she got sick, and when I came to see you . . ."

"Forget about it," she said. "You wouldn't understand."

She moved quickly to the door, and we entered the ICU. I could see that Mama was raised a little in her bed and sipping something through a straw. When she turned and saw us approaching, she stopped sipping and lowered the plastic cup. Her eyes widened. I moved ahead to kiss her, but she didn't react. She was fixed on Roxy.

"Am I dreaming?" she whispered.

"How are you feeling, Mama?" Roxy asked, as if she had never been gone.

"Roxy," Mama said. "My Roxy."

I looked at Roxy. Her lips trembled, but she sucked in her breath.

Mama reached out for her. Roxy looked at her hand and then took it and embraced her. For a long moment, they held on to each other. I had the feeling that either one would crumble if they let go. Roxy did first, and then Mama released her so she could step back.

"You're very beautiful, Roxy," Mama said. "*Très jolie.*"

"Thank you." She looked at me. "She's not bad, either."

"Both of you . . . together . . . this is my dream," Mama said.

"Yeah, well, you picked a helluva place to have it, Mama," Roxy said.

"Are you all right?"

"Me? I'm terrific."

"I tried to get you to come to your father's funeral," Mama said.

"I was there . . . at the cemetery," Roxy told her.

Mama smiled. "I was hoping . . ."

"Let's not talk about the past now, Mama. Let's talk about your getting up and around again as quickly as you can."

"Yes, yes . . ." Mama smiled, and then her face reflected her discomfort. "I think it's time for one of my pills," she said.

I looked to the nurse, who was watching us. She nodded and started around the counter. We both stepped back as she gave Mama her medicine.

"Has her doctor been here yet?" Roxy asked the nurse.

"Not yet. She's doing fine," she added. She smiled at me and returned to her station.

Roxy tightened the corners of her mouth and glanced at me.

"Are you going to look after her while I'm in here?" Mama asked Roxy.

"Her? You brought her up right. She can look after herself and me," Roxy said.

Mama nodded and smiled and reached for my hand. "You don't have to tell me anything," Mama said to Roxy. "It's just so wonderful to have you here."

"I'm fine, Mama. Just think about yourself for once, will you?"

Mama looked at her and nodded, and then she turned to me. "Have you spoken to Aunt Lucy? Did she call?"

"Oh. I don't know. I didn't check the answering machine, Mama."

"It's all right. We don't know what to tell her yet anyway," Mama said.

I looked at Roxy. Was it possible she knew more?

Mama's medicine began to take effect. I could see

her eyelids weakening. She took a deep breath and lowered herself to the pillow.

"You need to rest a lot right now, Mama," Roxy said. "We'll go get some lunch and return. How's that?"

Mama nodded. She wanted to keep alert, to talk, to enjoy the sight of her two daughters together at last, but her body was shutting down again.

"*Dieu merci, tu as été retourné,*" Mama said, almost in a whisper. I looked at Roxy. She understood, of course. "Thank God, you have come back."

I leaned over to kiss Mama.

Roxy hesitated and then did the same.

We started out together.

"Have I?" she asked herself as we left the ICU.

"Have you what?"

"Come back?"

I didn't know what to say.

I wouldn't for some time yet.

16

Roxy and I returned to the hospital after lunch. Dr. Hoffman had been in to see Mama. One look at her face told us that he had explained everything. She did her best to hide the truth from us, not knowing that Dr. Hoffman had already spoken to us. She told us that he said she would have to stay a while and then come in for some treatments, but everything would be fine. Roxy said nothing to contradict her, and neither did I.

Mama didn't ask Roxy any questions about her life now, and Roxy didn't volunteer any detailed information. She did ask Mama about our French relatives, and Mama went on about them, happy to talk about her family. We stayed until the nurse told us we should let her rest, and Roxy invited me to have dinner with her. She did so in front of Mama so Mama would know we were going to spend time together.

"We'll take you home to change," she said when we left the ICU. "I'll pick you up in two hours."

"Why didn't we tell Mama that we had spoken with her doctor, too?" I asked on the way out of the hospital.

"You have to let her handle this the way she wants to handle it, M," Roxy said. "Otherwise, it will be even worse for her, not that it can get much worse," she added in a softer voice.

We got into the limousine. The driver had been watching for us and had the vehicle right in front of the hospital.

"She looked so small in that bed," I said. "Didn't she?"

"Yes." She looked out the window. "But the last time I really looked at her, before I left home, she looked smaller, more like she was the child and I was the mother. I think what was happening was just too overwhelming for both of us."

I described what Mama had told me about the way she went looking for her, often taking me along with her.

"I wasn't in the city then."

"Where were you?"

"At a house on Long Island."

"Why? I mean, how did you get to be there?"

"It's a long story," she said.

"Didn't you ever think of coming back?"

"Yes, but by then, it was too late."

"Too late? Why?"

"I don't want to talk about all that now, M. It almost seems unfair of me while she's in there so sick. Okay?"

"Okay," I said, seeing how adamant she was.

"We'll have a good dinner," she promised, softening her tone.

When she dropped me off at the house, I hurried in to change. I had so many feelings twisting and turning around inside me. It felt as if I had swallowed a ball of rubber bands. There was the terrible heaviness of Mama's condition driving me to burst out in hysterical sobs, and there was the excitement of being with Roxy and getting to know her again. What she had done, how she had gotten to where she was, all of it was fascinating to me. I was confident that we would draw closer and she would tell me everything, but feeling good about it or what it might mean seemed out of place right now. I felt guilty not thinking only of Mama.

The phone rang while I dressed, but I didn't answer it, nor did I check the answering machine. I didn't want to hear anyone else's voice or speak to anyone. I knew how well dressed and put together Roxy would be when she came to pick me up, and for the time being, at least, concentrating on my own appearance took my mind off everything else. Of course, I was afraid she would cancel on me again, and that was mostly why I wouldn't answer the phone. Finally, just about two hours later, I heard the door buzzer and put on my coat. The driver was there. Roxy was waiting in the limousine.

She did look beautiful. She wore a black coat with a white collar and a black dress beneath. Her hair had been done in an updo so her diamond teardrop earrings were easily seen. I saw she had a diamond bracelet, too.

"Don't you look nice," she said. But then she

added, "I'll have to give you some tips about makeup. I think you can do more flattering things with your hair, too."

"I'm not exactly trying to look beautiful tonight, Roxy," I said, even though I had tried.

"We always try to look beautiful, M. Don't let any woman tell you otherwise."

She took me to one of her favorite small restaurants on the Lower East Side. She explained that it was one of the few places she went to alone. The staff knew her and even knew what wine she liked and where she liked to sit.

"You should return to school tomorrow," she told me after we had ordered.

"It will be a waste of time. I won't be worth anything there," I said.

"You won't be worth anything just sulking in waiting rooms or hovering around her, either. You'll only make her nervous and upset. She has to believe that you can handle this."

"I can," I insisted.

"So prove it to her. Return to school. At least put on a good show. Spend time with your friends again . . ."

"I don't have any friends."

"How can you not have friends?" With a skeptical smile, she asked, "You don't have a boyfriend?"

"Not really. I'm spending some time with someone, but I haven't—"

"Haven't what?" she asked suspiciously.

"Haven't even gone out on a date with him," I said sharply. "I didn't mean anything else."

"So you're a virgin?"

"Yes," I said, maybe sounding a little too defensive. She laughed. "What?"

"I was just thinking of something funny Mrs. Brittany said. 'Are you now or have you ever been a virgin?'"

"Who's Mrs. Brittany?"

She stopped smiling. "Never mind. I thought your generation was even less hung up on all these sexual inhibitions than mine was." She smiled, tilting her head a little as she remembered something. "That was always an interesting contradiction to me with them."

"Who?"

"Papa and Mama. Mama had, what should I say, a more liberal attitude about it all, and Papa . . . well, Papa was Papa, I guess. Wasn't he on your back, checking on everything you did, sniffing around like a bloodhound looking for something not so much sinful as irregular, breaking some code of behavior or something?"

"Yes, thanks to you," I told her.

She wiped away her disdainful smile. "Yeah, I bet. In his mind, I was the poster child for all that was bad. Let's get back to you. She's going to be in the hospital a while, and then she's going to start treatments, and she's going to be in and out often."

"I told you I can take care of myself. I can even pay our bills and balance our checkbook. Mama showed me how to do all that. Besides, the city is full of girls my age running homes, looking after younger brothers and sisters and even parents."

She nodded. "However, there will be a time . . ."

"I don't want to talk about it."

"Suit yourself," she said. "But go back to school. I promise I'll stop in to see her every day."

"What if you get an assignment?"

"Don't be a wise-ass. Here, taste this wine. It's my favorite French white burgundy."

"I know it," I said. "It's Mama's favorite, too."

"Yes," she said, suddenly remembering. "I think that was how I got to know it."

She looked down for a moment like someone who might start to cry. Was I seeing a crack in that armor she had welded around her heart? As if she realized it herself, she looked up quickly and snapped an order at the waitress. Then she looked at me sternly.

"Look, if you go to school tomorrow, I'll pick you up at the end of the day, and we'll visit her together, okay? Will you do it?"

"Yes," I said reluctantly.

"Good. I guess I'll call France," she said.

"You will?"

"Do you want to do it? Maybe it is better that you do it."

"No, it's all right if you do it," I said. "Whom should we call first?"

"The only one I really cared about was Uncle Alain."

"Me, too," I said. "Mama would like it more if you called him," I added.

She thought for a moment and then nodded. "Okay. I can handle it."

They served our food.

"Let's eat," she said. "You need to get a good night's sleep." She looked up with the follow-up question on her lips.

"Stop worrying about it. I'll be fine alone," I said with the same tone she used on me. "I was alone last night, wasn't I?"

She nodded, and we attacked our dinner, stabbing and cutting our food as if it were the enemy. Anyone who didn't know why would think we were starving. We were starving for something, all right, but it wasn't food. We were starving for some hope, some respite from misery and sadness, some detour that would take us off the road of nightmares. I was sure now that Roxy had had her share of them even before all of this sadness about Mama had begun.

Afterward, before she dropped me off, she plucked a light blue card out of her purse and handed it to me. "This is my direct telephone number. It doesn't go through the service or the hotel. Call me if you need anything or if anything . . . just call me," she said, thrusting it at me.

I took it and looked at it. It didn't have her name or anything on it. It was just a number. I nodded and stepped out of the limousine.

"I'll see you at the end of your school day. She'll be happy you went."

"Okay," I said. "I'll call and leave word for her in the morning so she won't worry."

"Very good."

"Tell Uncle Alain love from me."

"I will."

The driver closed the door. I started up the stairs and then paused to watch her limousine quietly move down the street, turn, and disappear. The darkness seemed to see that as an opportunity to close in on me. I hurried into the house and finally checked the answering machine. There were two messages. One was from Aunt Lucy. She sounded very angry and didn't ask for me to call her back; she demanded it. The other message was from Chastity. Someone had found out about Mama, and according to her, the story was bouncing off the walls in the school.

"How is she? I hope she's all right," Chastity continued on the answering machine. "All anyone knows is that she had surgery. What was the surgery? Everyone's worried about you. You know I'm here for you. Call me. I'll come stay with you, if you like. Whatever. Call me."

Reluctantly, I called Aunt Lucy first. She barked a hello and began bawling me out before I could tell her anything. How could I not call her immediately? Didn't I realize she would be waiting by the phone? Didn't I realize she would be worrying about me? My uncle was beside himself with irritation. I recalled that Uncle Orman was never angry. He was always just irritated. I imagined him breaking out in rashes whenever something bothered him.

I let her finish her tirade, and then I began to describe what the doctor had told Roxy and me, but I didn't mention Roxy.

"That man told you all that without an adult present?" she asked.

"I'm an adult, Aunt Lucy. In some parts of the world, I would be married and have my own children by now."

"Don't be facetious. I'll have a word with him tomorrow. I'm coming to New York. You can come home with me."

"I'm going to school tomorrow, Aunt Lucy. I've missed enough work."

"What?" She was speechless a moment. "Oh. Well, I still think . . . that doctor had no right . . ."

"My sister was with me," I decided to reveal.

"Sister? What sister? Roxy was there?"

"She's the only sister I have," I said.

"Well . . . your uncle will want to hear about this. Now she decides to come out of the woodwork? I'm surprised she had the decency to do it. Is she staying with you now?"

"No."

"That's probably good."

"Look, I'm tired, Aunt Lucy. If you're still at the hospital when I go there after school, I'll see you. Roxy will be with me, too."

"She will? I . . . don't think I'll be there that long. I have to get back to prepare for a Pentagon charity ball."

"Have a good trip, coming and going," I said, and hung up.

There was still a good possibility that she could run into Roxy at the hospital. I smiled to myself, imagining the look on her face if she did. It was practically the only amusing thing that I had thought of in days. I debated returning Chastity's call. I even considered her offer to come over to stay with me but decided against it. I didn't have the emotional strength to put up with her right now, I thought, and went up to bed.

Amazingly, I fell asleep quickly, and I almost overslept. When I saw the time, I rushed about to dress and get some breakfast. I called the hospital and was connected with the nurses' station in ICU. The nurse told me that Mama was resting comfortably and promised to give her the message that I was going to school and would see her afterward. I wasn't very eager to go, but Roxy was right. I couldn't just sit around the hospital waiting room all day, and it would upset Mama.

I didn't doubt the truthfulness of what Chastity had told me on the answering machine. Because our private school was so small, serious news about anyone or anyone's family was common knowledge in a matter of hours, a day at most. That was the way it had been when Papa died, so I didn't expect anything less. My teachers were as sympathetic and forgiving as they had been then, and no one was catty or nasty to me. Although he didn't come over to speak to me, I saw a look of compassion on Evan's face. Chastity, as I had expected, pounced. She was all over me the moment I approached my locker.

"How is she? Didn't you get my message?"

"I was home too late to call you," I said, and hung up my coat in the locker.

"So how is she? Is it serious?"

"Any surgery is serious," I said. I started away, but she followed as closely as a conjoined twin.

"But what was it for? There are all sorts of rumors flying about."

"I don't feel like talking about it right now, Chastity. I'd like to keep my mind off it for a while, okay?"

"Okay, sure. I understand. Is anyone staying with you? Because I could really do that," she added quickly.

Fortunately, Richard hurried to my side as soon as he saw me heading for my homeroom.

"Excuse me," I told Chastity, and joined him.

"Are you all right?" he asked. "How is your mother?"

"She's recuperating," I said. "She'll be there a while. Thanks."

"Um, is there anything I can do for you?"

"Yes," I said. "Keep the busybodies off me."

He smiled and was there to escort me whenever he could. He offered to do anything I needed done, but I told him I was fine. He was a sweet and innocent boy who had seemed to fill a gap in my life when I needed it filled, but deep inside, I knew I wouldn't jump into any romance with him, certainly not as quickly and as eagerly as I had with Evan. Why was it that someone as self-centered as Evan was more attractive? Why was evil more interesting than good? Maybe that was because there was more of it inside ourselves than we cared to admit.

The schoolwork did keep me from dwelling on Mama's condition and prognosis. I really didn't want anyone to know how serious the situation was, and by seeming to be interested in my subjects, answering questions, reading my assignments, and spending time with Richard whenever I could, I knew I gave the impression that everything was going to be all right.

Before the school day ended, Chastity tried again to get more involved with me and what was happening. Richard was at basketball practice, so I couldn't use him as a shield. She leaped at the opportunity when I was getting my coat out of my locker.

"I could come over tonight, if you like," she said. "Or we could go to dinner. I'll take you out. My mother suggested it," she added. "We don't want you to be alone, Emmie. Even if it's just for a short time. You'd be there for me, I'm sure. So don't feel like you're putting any burden on me or anything. I want to be your friend. I want . . ."

I thought for a moment before saying it, but I decided that it would provide me with the excuses I would otherwise have to invent.

I took a deep breath. "I'm not alone, Chastity."

"Oh. Who's with you, your aunt from Washington? Relatives from France?"

She followed me to the door. Roxy's limousine was waiting. I didn't have to say any more.

I walked out, and when the driver opened my

door, I slipped in as if I had been riding in a limousine all my life.

Glancing back through the tinted windows, I saw Chastity standing there, gaping after me, looking like a guppy in a fishbowl, its mouth open in anticipation of food particles floating through the water.

17

"How is she?" I asked Roxy quickly.

"Much more alert. She was happy about your going to school. How was it?"

"Tolerable."

"That's the way I always felt about it, tolerable. So," she said as we started away, "guess who I met today."

"Aunt Lucy," I said.

"You knew she would be there?"

"She said she would, but I didn't know when. I told her you and I would be there about now, and she said she would be on the way home by then."

Roxy nodded. "She looked very surprised to see me, so I thought you hadn't told her anything."

"Surprised? Was she nasty to you?"

"Not exactly nasty. Formal. She insisted on calling me Roxanne. She always did, and I would never respond. Naturally, Papa thought I was being disrespectful. Anyway, she pleaded with me to have you go live with them. According to her, they're very concerned about us—about you, I mean. She said if you agreed, they would arrange for Mama to have around-the-clock nursing at home. They would get you enrolled in the school the military's children attend. She told me that if I wanted to do anything for Mama, it would be to persuade you to go."

"Why is this so important to them all of a sudden? Before this, we hardly ever heard from them or saw them. You know they didn't come to Papa's funeral."

She shrugged. "The military takes care of its own. Something like that, I guess. She's simply carrying out orders."

"But Papa wasn't in the military."

"Uncle Orman and our grandfather never accepted that."

"What did you tell her?"

"I told her whether you go or not is up to you, not me."

"Good."

She looked down. I could feel that there was something more.

"What, Roxy?"

"We met with the doctor afterward for a few minutes," she said.

"And?"

"When he first spoke to us, he didn't tell us he had taken a biopsy when they operated. She had another tumor. It's not good news, M."

I digested her words, and then, despite my determination to appear strong, I started to cry. She put her arm around me and held me close.

"Does Mama know?"

"Not yet, but he will tell her," she said.

"So Aunt Lucy heard that, too?"

"Yes. That's why she was so adamant about you not being alone, and she certainly doesn't want you anywhere near me."

"I don't care what she wants. Did you call Uncle Alain?"

"Yes. He was very upset it. Shocked to hear from me but very concerned about you. I called him again before I went to get you at school and told him the additional news. I told him we would call frequently. He sounded as if he was crying. I didn't realize that despite time and distance, he and Mama held on to a relationship that must have been close."

"I know," I said.

"He said he would call his sisters, so you can expect they'll call you, I imagine."

"I barely remember them."

"Look," she said as we continued to the hospital, "maybe you should give some serious consideration to accepting Aunt Lucy and Uncle Orman's invitation."

I started to shake my head.

"I can't be here for you every day, M. In fact, I'm trying to put something off, but it's proving very difficult, if not impossible. I'll probably have to leave tomorrow for five days or so."

"That trip to St. Thomas on a private jet?"

"Yes."

"So go. I can get to the hospital myself," I said sullenly.

"I know you can get to the hospital, and I'm not

apologizing. I have a life I've chosen—or, maybe more accurately, a life that was chosen for me—and I just can't put it on hold like some people can with their lives," she snapped back.

I didn't want to get into all that. Right now, all I could think about was Mama. "Do what you want to do, Roxy," I said. "You always did."

She didn't reply. She turned away and looked out the window. We rode in silence the rest of the way.

"Maybe you should go in to see her by yourself this time," she said when the driver opened the door for me.

"Fine," I said, and got out.

"You haven't spent time alone with her, and you should," she shouted after me.

I didn't look back. I forbade a single tear to leave my eyes and pressed my lips together. I paused when I entered the hospital and worked on getting myself calm. The last thing I wanted to do was show Mama I was upset about anything.

Surprisingly, Mama was in good spirits. Perhaps Dr. Hoffman hadn't yet told her the latest news about her condition. Once she saw that Roxy wasn't with me, she asked me question after question about her, but I didn't have any of the answers she wanted. I didn't know very much more now about the life she had led than I had known before she showed up at the hospital. I did tell Mama how much Roxy regretted what had happened and how much she really loved her. That pleased her. Then she, too, started on Aunt Lucy and Uncle Orman's offer.

"They have no one at their home but themselves. You'll have everything you could want there, Emmie, and you wanted to leave the school."

"Yes, the school, but not you, Mama."

She smiled, but it was the smile of someone who knew that the wish I had was soon going to be impossible. Maybe the doctor had been there after all. Mama was too good at hiding things.

"At least think about it, *ma chère*. Will you?"

"Okay, Mama, I'll think about it."

"Good, good. Now, tell me about school, about the house, any calls, bills, and what you're planning to have for dinner," she recited, and closed her eyes to listen. I stayed until the nurse pointed out that Mama was fast asleep.

I went home to make myself some dinner. Finding things to do was the best way to keep myself from thinking. I was grateful for all of the homework I had to catch up on and the new assignments, too. Every once in a while, I would pause and listen to the stillness in our house, still not accepting that everything had changed and would change even more. I had to go down to the living room and sit reading the way I would when Papa was alive. He would be settled in his chair, and I would be right across from him on the sofa with my legs pulled up and folded under me. He called me a contortionist.

I smiled, remembering. The chair was creased and worn where Papa's large body had fit comfortably. I ran the palm of my hand over the arm of it as if I were stroking his arm. One time, he had fallen asleep in it.

When I got up to go to my room, I paused and kissed him on the cheek. His eyes opened. He realized what I had done, and he smiled and said, "Trying to turn a frog into a prince?"

"You're no frog, Papa," I had whispered. I whispered it again as if he were there and it was all happening.

I still could hear his laugh as I ascended the stairs and then heard him telling Mama why he was laughing. It was as if their contentment and happiness could carry me up like some magic carpet and gently put me to sleep, wrapping the sense of security around me like an invisible blanket. Would I ever sleep like that again?

Roxy called me just before I went to bed to tell me that she was indeed leaving. She would try to call from St. Thomas. She asked how Mama was, whether I could tell if the doctor had spoken to her yet. I told her I wasn't sure.

"She asked a lot of questions about you," I said. "Questions I couldn't answer."

"You don't want the answers, and neither does she," she told me. "Take care," she added, and hung up.

The five days she was away seemed more like weeks, because every day was long to me. I woke up much earlier and, dreading going to bed, stayed up much later. Ironically, I did some of my best schoolwork and was ahead of everyone in all of my classes. I didn't tell Richard any more about Mama. In fact, I was so into my work and shutting everyone else out that he began to drift away. Whatever spark of interest he once had in me was snuffed out. I couldn't blame him. As mean as it might sound, the truth was, I didn't care.

That was especially true about Chastity. Despite her persistence, I said little to her. My indifference dropped the final curtain on our rocky friendship. We would look through each other in hallways and class-rooms. It became that way with more and more of the friends I once had. Although I was there, doing my work, going through the motions, I began to feel as if I was really disappearing, slowly, perhaps, but fading away like some very, very old photograph in a carton in some basement. I moved in my own silent capsule, shut off from almost everything and everyone. The phone rarely rang, and when it did, it was usually one of Mama's friends or one of the wives from Papa's firm who were still vaguely interested in us. I promised to pass on their best wishes and told them little or nothing about Mama's condition. I couldn't find the words for that, and they seemed to understand. They were what I called "get guilt off my back" calls. But I couldn't blame them.

Roxy did call me from St. Thomas on the second night. I told her I had called Uncle Alain and that he had told me he was working on coming to America soon. None of my French aunts had called yet.

"They're getting everything from Alain, I'm sure."

"Aunt Lucy called, too."

"Oh? How did you handle her? They won't give up on you, you know. It's a matter of military pride or something."

"I told her I would think it over. That shut her up for a while."

Roxy laughed. I was going to ask her if she was having a good time, but I didn't want to know. She told me when she thought she would come around again, and we ended the conversation with her saying, "You're stronger than I was at your age."

How could I be? I wondered. She was just a little older than me when she had stepped out alone in the world, when she had the courage to take so many risks. Did her anger alone give her the power to do that? How did she survive? It seemed so long ago when Chastity and I were so fascinated with Roxy and wanted to know everything about her. That interest had waned for me, but it was returning, maybe because of Mama's questions. Perhaps I would start asking more personal questions, I thought.

Two days later, I was surprised when I arrived at the hospital and Mama said she would be coming home the next day. She had been walking a little and was sitting up. I saw she had done her hair and put on some of the makeup she had asked me to bring.

"But don't you have to stay to have some treatments?" I asked her.

"No, no," she said. "I've got to build myself up now. That's all. Don't worry. You go to school. Everything has been arranged."

"Of course I won't go to school. I'll have to help you settle in, Mama."

"No, I'll have a nurse with me until you come home. She's going to pick me up here. A limousine will take me home. I told you, it's all taken care of. You'd just be sitting around most of the morning, waiting. It's a waste of time. Go to school."

"Aunt Lucy arranged it?" I asked. That was probably her way of inserting herself and pressuring me, I thought.

"Aunt Lucy? No. Your sister made all the arrangements," she revealed.

"My sister? Roxy? When?"

"Yesterday." She smiled. "She's called me every day this week."

"She has? She never said . . . well, I haven't heard from her for a few days."

That meant that Mama had told Roxy what was happening before she had told me. Suddenly, a surge of pure green envy flowed into my veins. Why would Mama confide in Roxy more than she would confide in me? Roxy was the one who broke her and Papa's hearts, not me. Roxy was the one who had run off and not shown her face again until I forced her to.

And this wasn't the biblical prodigal child's return. Roxy had not found herself. She hadn't changed one iota. She was still Fleur du Coeur, wasn't she? She was still what Papa had shouted that day, a high-priced prostitute.

"What is it, Emmie?" Mama asked. It didn't surprise me that, as sick as she was, she could still see into my heart and mind.

"Nothing," I said. I tried to smile. "I'm just worried, that's all, and want to be there to help you."

"You will be. I'm not having a nurse around the

clock, no matter what anyone says. Most of the time, it will just be the two of us. Like always," she added.

I couldn't stop the tears now, but I didn't make a sound. I was like one of those dolls that can cry. Mama reached for me, and we hugged. I held her as tightly and as long as I could before I left. I was really feeling depressed now and thought the long walk, even in the cold weather, would do me good. It was dark by the time I arrived at the house.

For a while, I just sat in the living room, sulking. Then I opened my purse and plucked out Roxy's blue card. I hoped I would be interrupting her and made the call. After four rings, I was about to hang up when I finally heard her say, "Roxy."

"It's me."

"Oh. Anything wrong?"

"Why didn't you tell me you had made arrangements for Mama to come home?"

"She wanted to tell you all about it herself. Why, what did she say?"

"She said you had called her every day."

"Right." I heard some music start somewhere behind her. "I'll see you tomorrow," she added, hoping to hang up.

"No."

"No?"

"Why is she coming home without any treatments? She said all she has to do is get stronger."

The music got louder. "Shit," I heard her say. "Wait a minute." I could hear her close a door. "Why don't you wait until I get home tomorrow," she said, "and we can spend more time together? It's really a bad moment for me. I have to go down to the patio and . . ."

"Oh, so sorry to have interrupted your work."

She was silent. I thought she was going to hang up on me. I knew that what she said next was coming from her anger. "You're the whiz kid, M, the A-plus student. Why can't you figure it out?"

"Figure what out?"

"Why she's coming home so fast. She doesn't want any treatments. She heard it all from her doctor."

"What do you mean?" I said, my voice cracking. I knew what she meant. I was just hoping that by driving her to say it, she wouldn't, and somehow it wouldn't be true.

"She weighed the options and decided she would rather have some quality time at home."

I didn't respond.

"Damn it, M, she's coming home to die," she said. "I gotta go. I'll see you as soon as I can tomorrow."

Then she hung up.

I didn't. I stood there holding the phone. The child in me wanted to pretend that I hadn't called Roxy and didn't have this conversation. I wanted to imagine that none of this was happening. It was all a bad dream. All I had to do was put the receiver back on the cradle, and everything would be back to the way it was. Papa would be alive and waiting for me downstairs. Mama would be finishing her dinner preparations. They were going to open a new bottle of red wine that Uncle Alain had sent from France. There was music, Mama's favorite, Edith Piaf. We'd speak in French to add to it all. It would be one of those rare nights when neither of them would think about Roxy or any unhappiness.

I would feel as if I were along with them when Papa was courting Mama. Before my soul was plucked out of that cloud of souls to enter the body that would form in Mama, I was given a preview. These two lovers would become my parents, and I would inherit their histories. I'd favor Mama's, because Papa's wasn't as charming and romantic, but his influence would be there. As they talked and laughed, toasted old friends and old memories, I would sit silently, smiling and thinking how lucky I was to have them and how much I loved them.

Why couldn't I just walk downstairs to that? Why did I have to walk down to the silence and the shadows? *I won't walk down,* I thought defiantly. *I won't give in to reality.* Curling up in bed, I hugged myself and shut my eyes as tightly as I could. I held my breath as long as I could, and then I screamed a long and piercing "NOOOOOO!" My throat hurt when I stopped, but I wouldn't open my eyes, and I wouldn't go downstairs.

Darkness crawled up to me, however. It slipped past any light, slid along the walls and over the floors, oozed into my bedroom, and then fell over me, shutting out the last glimmer of hope.

Mercifully, sleep also invaded, and I didn't wake up until the first light of morning sent shadows retreating to wherever they go to wait for their time to return. I decided that I would not go off to school as if it were just another day. Instead, I worked on the house, vacuuming, polishing furniture, washing windows, and making sure Mama's bedroom was prepared. I put on fresh linens and went down the street to buy some fresh flowers. I defrosted a roast and began to prepare it, following her recipe. She had warned me that it would take most of the morning before she would be released. Hospital paperwork, waiting for the doctor, whatever would click off the hours. I nibbled on a little lunch and hovered by the front window, waiting for the sight of the limousine.

A little before one o'clock, it pulled up to the curb in front of our town house. The driver got out and opened the door for a tall, light-brown-haired woman who looked manly from the back because of her wide shoulders and thick upper arms. She came around to help Mama out. The driver got the bags. Mama looked up at the house. She looked much smaller and thinner to me.

I rushed to the front door and opened it as they started up the stairs. They both paused, surprised. The nurse had large, spoon-shaped dark eyes and a U-shaped face because of her plump cheeks. The driver was just about to step ahead of them. He had the door keys in his hand. He stopped, too.

Mama shook her head. "I should have known," she said. "This is my daughter Emmie, Mrs. Ascott. She was supposed to be at school," she added, feigning a little anger.

"I'm way ahead of everyone in my classes, Mama. Besides, welcome home," I said.

She smiled. As I took her other arm to help her in, she whispered in French, "*Je suis content que tu sois ici.* I'm glad you're here."

"I took some French classes," Mrs. Ascott said. I didn't know if she said it to mean that she was proud of it or that we shouldn't try to say anything behind her back.

"*Très bon,* Madame Ascott. You're sure to learn a lot more here."

Mama laughed. She could give me no better gift than the sound of her laughter.

Maybe, if we ignored everything and everyone else, we could have a miracle, I thought.

Hope still had a place at our table.

18

The weeks that passed were filled with days like slow-dripping icicles. Did an hour suddenly become more than sixty minutes, a day more than twenty-four hours, and a week more than seven days? I think this feeling came from the way Mama wound down, with even the smallest of her gestures seemingly in slow motion. She looked like one of those elderly Chinese ladies doing tai chi in Central Park. I helped her with her needs as much as I could. Mrs. Ascott was there while I was at school and some days stayed until after dinner, but I got the impression early on that she was there mainly to dispense painkillers.

Roxy visited a few times during the first two weeks. Sometimes she came when Mama was asleep and didn't stay long. Her first visit was the longest and the best, because Mama revealed that she had kept more of Roxy's things than either Papa or I knew. She directed me to a carton in the small storage attic. I brought it down, and the three of us went through the pictures, some of Roxy's little drawings when she was four and five, and some birthday cards she had bought for Mama and that Mama had bought for her. There were some memories they could laugh about and some stories about me when I was little that we could all laugh about, but after it was over, the three of us grew quiet. No one wanted to say anything that would resurrect the bad times and the complete break that Roxy had made with her family.

"How did you get along?" Mama finally did ask. "Where did you go?"

"I'll tell you sometime," Roxy said, smiling. "You're tired now, Mama. You get some rest. I'll return as soon as I am able."

Mama simply nodded. She knew that Roxy probably would not talk about those days, not now, maybe not ever, at least with her. On the way out, Roxy gave me the first real sisterly hug since she had come to the hospital.

"Why is it," she asked me, "that it's the hardships and sadness that do the most to make us grow up?"

"I don't know, Roxy."

"No, no one does. Try not to be too bitter," she added as she started out. She turned on the steps to look back at me. "In the end, the only one who suffers because of that is you. That's something I learned the hard way."

I watched her leave and closed the door. It was the same door either Papa had closed on her or she had closed behind her on him. The effect was the same. She was gone, and whether he wanted to admit it or not back then, so was a part of himself. And for that

matter, so was a part of Mama. Perhaps Roxy was trying to give that back to her before it was too late.

Or perhaps she was trying to get Mama back for
herself.

Over the next month, Mama and I had many good
days like that first one with Roxy. I shopped for food
and prepared dinners following her recipes. She ate
less and less after a while and ate mostly to please me,
but at least we were able to enjoy some quality time
together. Roxy was able to come to dinner only once,
but she said I was already an impressive cook. She revealed that she never cooked anything. She either ate
out or had food delivered, often even her breakfast. I
thought she would start talking more about her life,
but she seemed to realize that she was revealing too
much and stopped talking about herself, almost in
midsentence.

I wasn't sure how much anyone outside our family
knew about Mama's illness. From time to time during
those first few weeks, Chastity and some of the other
girls asked me how she was. I always said, "Fine," and
left it at that. The way they suddenly stopped asking,
however, suggested that the gossip mill had ground
out the truth, maybe with some added embellish-
ments. Bad news always had a way of rising to the
surface. The worse the news, the faster it would pop
up. I sensed it in the way Chastity and the girls looked
at me and whispered. Evan couldn't even look at me.
Ironically, it was Richard, the shy boy, who eventually came right out one day in the hallway to ask me if
there was anything he could do for me.

"Why do you ask?"

"I heard about your mother, how sick she really is. I just thought you might need something."

Need something? I thought. *Where do I begin?*

"Thanks, Richard. I'm fine," I told him. He nodded, and I kept walking a little faster to get away from him.

A part of me wanted to stay to talk to him, to revive the potential romance, to have friends again, and to participate in school activities the way a girl my age should. Instead, I felt I was living in a strange state of mind, half awake, half dazed. Too often now, I would drift away in the middle of my classes or even when I was walking in the hallways. Everything I did became more robotic. It was truly as if I was losing all feeling, my emotions drying up like flowers pressed between the pages of a book. Touch them too hard, and they would crumble to dust and be gone.

Maybe I was disappearing with Mama. Watching her now, I felt I was seeing someone in a boat pulling away from shore. I had dreams in which Roxy and I were waving good-bye to her and watching her grow smaller and smaller as she headed toward the horizon. Did my fellow students see me the same way? Was I shrinking and shrinking until I would be out of their sight? It was surely uncomfortable for them to see me and uncomfortable for them to talk to me. How many young people my age did they know who had lost both parents? I didn't blame them for wanting me to disappear. I didn't blame anyone for anything anymore. There seemed no point to it.

Eventually, Mama became so weak that she couldn't get out of bed. Finally, one day, Mrs. Ascott recommended that she be returned to the hospital, especially since I was the only one there after she left each day. I didn't want that. I wanted to forget about school and just be with her, but Mama wouldn't hear of it. She agreed with Mrs. Ascott, and arrangements were made for her return.

"Just for a while," Mama said, but I knew she wouldn't be coming back, and she knew I knew. For now, it was easier for both of us to pretend.

I called Roxy to tell her.

"Have you spoken with Uncle Alain recently?" she asked.

"Two days ago. He said he was about to make reservations for next week."

"Might be better if he came this week," she said.

I couldn't speak for a moment. My throat tightened so firmly that I could feel the blood rush to my face. "I don't want her to go to the hospital. I can take care of her here," I finally said.

"Let her go, M."

She said it without a hint of any emotion. Was that because she was older and more independent, or was it because she didn't love Mama as much as I did? It made me angry but also strangely jealous. How lucky she was if it was true that she wouldn't cry ever over anyone. I once read a poem that said, "You can't love anyone without pain, the pain of jealousy and the pain of loss. It will always be under your skin and in your heart waiting to pounce."

"You mean let her go like you did?" I said sharply.

"Hating me won't help," she replied. "I'll be there tomorrow."

"She'll be in the hospital tomorrow."

"That's what I meant," Roxy said. "We'd better start thinking about you. You should call Aunt Lucy."

"I'll never go to live with Aunt Lucy and Uncle Orman. You went out in the street. I will, too," I said, and hung up on her.

After I gathered my thoughts, I called Uncle Alain. It was late in France, but I thought I should call him anyway. He was silent for a moment after I described Mama and what the nurse wanted us to do now, and then he said he would be here the day after tomorrow and would keep his return ticket open.

I couldn't help myself. I finally began to cry, and cry hard. I felt terrible that I was doing it on the phone with someone who was too far away to reach out and embrace me. He tried with his words. He spoke softly, lovingly, in French and then in English. I listened, choked back my tears, and thanked him. Afterward, I went to tell Mama that he was coming. She surprised me by saying she wished he wouldn't.

"I wish he would remember me only as I was," she said. She wanted to say more, but her pain medicine kicked in, and she fell asleep.

I sat up most of the night, in the living room looking at albums. I saw the blank places from which Papa in his rage years ago had ripped out pictures of Roxy. Some of those pictures Mama had rescued, but there were many I imagined he had torn up or burned. For Mama's sake, I went into the carton of pictures and things she had shown us and began putting some back in the albums. I would bring the albums to the hospital, I thought. It would give us both something to do. I was sure she would want to see them again.

Mrs. Ascott was at the house earlier the next day. The ambulance was not far behind. I felt helpless watching her get Mama ready. Every time Mama saw me watching, she smiled.

"You should just go to school, Emmie," she said.

"No. I'm going with you."

"Your mother's right. They won't take you, too, in the ambulance," Mrs. Ascott told me.

It put me in a rage, and I stormed out and marched up the street, walking with my arms folded, my head down. It didn't take me much longer than it took the ambulance to get to the hospital. They hadn't even placed Mama in a room yet when I arrived, but they wouldn't let me see her until they had. Finally, I went up. She was already hooked up to an IV bag and in and out of consciousness. I sat watching her, the rage I had felt earlier still thumping at my heart.

"How dare you die on me?" I whispered. "Papa is gone; you can't go, too. How dare you leave me?"

I sat sulking like a little girl and didn't even realize that Roxy was in the doorway.

"You should have gone to school," she said.

I turned away from her, and she entered. "Is that what you would have done?"

"This could go on for a while, M. You can't sit here day and night."

"Don't tell me what I can and can't do," I said. I glared at her.

She sighed and looked at Mama. She was wearing a new winter coat now. It was red with a white fur collar. She had a white fur hat with splashes of red in it to match her coat, and she had another pair of knee-high polished leather boots. She wore dark blue slacks and a blue sweater beneath the coat. She took off her designer sunglasses and pressed her thumb and forefinger into her temples. All I could think of was that she didn't look anything at all like a daughter grieving over her mother's terminal illness.

"How many different outfits do you have?" I demanded.

She looked at me and laughed.

"What? Why are you laughing at me? My question is silly? You wear something expensive and new every day."

"One of my clients is high up at one of the more exclusive department stores," she said. "I get gifts in addition to spending my money on clothes. I like clothes. I'm not apologizing for—"

"For anything, I know. Why are you here, Roxy? Why did you come back now?"

"What do you mean? You came to me, didn't you? You sent me letters and that charm bracelet."

"Yes, I did," I said. I looked at Mama. "I thought it would help her."

"Maybe it has. I told you not to become bitter, M. It won't change anything."

"This isn't right," I said. Tears burned under my eyelids.

She nodded and looked at Mama again. "Maybe she can't live without him. I've been told we're all living with one terrible disease or another dormant inside us, just waiting for our immune systems to weaken. Grief does that, grief and great loss."

"Then you'll live forever," I said.

She looked at me, shook her head, and walked out.

I didn't speak to her again until Uncle Alain arrived and insisted on seeing her. He was taller than Mama, very slim, with hair a shade darker and eyes that seemed to go from blue to green depending on his moods. Green was for the more serious ones. Mama and he shared some of the same facial features, their noses, high cheekbones, and perfect lips. I remembered that Uncle Alain was always dapper, elegant, and fastidious about his appearance. Everything always matched perfectly, with clear, correct creases in his pants and no wrinkles in his shirts. He loved shoes, especially soft Italian leather, and always wore a subtle cologne, not too sweet but always interesting, like the discovery of a new flower.

He called me when he landed. I waited for him at the house, but I didn't call Roxy.

"How grown up you are," was his first comment when I opened the door. "Petite Emmie." He hugged me and kissed me on both cheeks. Then he looked past me. "Roxy isn't here?"

"No, she doesn't live here, Uncle Alain."

He nodded and closed the door. I took him to our guest bedroom.

"Are you tired?" I asked.

"No. I had a good flight. I'll shower and dress, and we'll go over to the hospital. Then I was hoping I could take you both to dinner."

"Both?"

"You and Roxy," he said.

"Oh. I'll see if she's available," I said, trying to disguise my bitterness.

I left him to get himself ready and called Roxy. She answered on the second ring.

"What?" she asked in a clipped voice. I knew what she was expecting.

"Uncle Alain is here. We're going to the hospital soon, and he was hoping that afterward he could take you and me to dinner. Are you free for dinner tonight, or do you have a client?"

"I'll be at the hospital, M. And yes, I'm free," she said.

She hung up to show me she wasn't going to tolerate any more negativity from me. I was out of my class when it came to competing with her, anyway, I thought. She was the expert. Anger and hate were infrequent companions of mine. The battles they brought along with them were battles I was not used to waging. She was a veteran of those wars.

I made some coffee for Uncle Alain and some toast with cheese so he could have something before we left.

"You've been here by yourself whenever your mother is in the hospital?" he asked.

"Yes. It's no problem, Uncle Alain."

"Tell me about Roxy. When did she come back? Where is she living? What is she doing?"

Roxy would always be more interesting than I was, I thought. Why should it come as any surprise? I was still more interested in Evan than I would ever be in Richard. I had wondered if that meant evil was always a strong part of us and if life was a constant battle to keep it subdued. I was wondering about it even more now. Who wasn't more excited about breaking rules in school, disobeying their parents, and experiencing the most forbidden things?

"She came back because I sent a letter to her about Papa's death. I thought that might bring her around to see Mama, but for a long time, she didn't respond. She was as angry at Mama as she was at Papa, because Mama didn't stop him from throwing her out."

"I know. Your mama has always regretted that."

"Finally, Roxy broke down and came to the hospital when Mama was in surgery."

He sipped his coffee and nodded. "She has your father's headstrong ways. Your mother always thought that was why they didn't get along. They were too alike. So where is she living?"

I described the hotel. He knew she had the name Fleur du Coeur.

"This is what she still does?"

"*Oui.* She makes a lot of money, has beautiful

clothes and expensive jewelry. She gets taken in private jets to warm places."

"You sound jealous. I'm sure you have a boy-friend, no?" he asked, smiling.

"No. I did for ten minutes," I said, and he laughed. We both looked at the clock. "Should we go?"

"Yes."

I put everything away.

He looked about the house and told me I was doing a good job of keeping it nice. "My sister must be pleased with such a mature, responsible young lady for a daughter."

I pressed my lips together and nodded. *Can't cry now*, I thought. I wanted Uncle Alain to concentrate on Mama and give her all of his affection and atten-tion, not me, and certainly not Roxy.

We left, and when we arrived at the hospital, Roxy was waiting for us. I looked at Uncle Alain when he saw her, and I was immediately jealous of his reaction. I was sure that Roxy looked more beautiful than ever to him. They hugged and kissed, and he told her how pretty she was.

"But you always were," he added.

"You look very well, Uncle Alain. Still living in the Saint-Germain area of Paris?"

"Where else?"

"And Maurice? Where is he working now?"

"He's at Pierre Gauguin, a very upscale restau-rant."

"Still throwing chopping blocks at the sushi chefs?"

Uncle Alain laughed. "You know how he thinks

of his kitchen. It's a work of art, and he will not tolerate mistakes. He's no different at home, although he doesn't throw anything at me."

I looked at Roxy. How did she know so much about Uncle Alain and his partner? Had they kept in touch secretly all these years?

"He would have come along with me, but he's under some pressure. New owners."

"Too bad. We would have gotten a good meal."

Uncle Alain laughed again. "That you would," he said.

"Mama is upstairs," I muttered, as if I had to remind them why we were there. They both glanced at me.

"Oui. Allons," Uncle Alain said, and we headed for the elevators.

Before we entered Mama's room, Uncle Alain took both our hands. He lowered his head, perhaps in prayer, and we walked in. I could see in his face that he wasn't prepared for what he was seeing, even though he was well aware of Mama's condition. I had been living with it for a while, so her gradual loss of weight and her gaunt look were surely much more of a shock for him. It occurred to me that the last time he had seen her, she was vibrant and alive.

She was awake and smiled at him. He didn't speak. He took her hand and kissed it and then sat beside her and spoke in French. Both Roxy and I stood back and watched until he turned to us, telling her still in French that she had two very beautiful daughters. We drew closer, but we didn't interrupt his telling her all about their family in France. The nurse appeared to check her IV bag. She had the look of someone just going through the motions. Uncle Alain asked her about Mama's doctor, and she told him he was on the floor.

Soon afterward, Mama fell asleep, and we left.

"That's her doctor," Roxy said, nodding at Dr. Hoffman, who stood by the nurses' station.

Uncle Alain approached him, and they talked. Roxy and I stayed back. Neither of us wanted to hear what the doctor had to say.

When Uncle Alain returned to us, he looked pale, but he forced a smile.

"Take me to an expensive restaurant," he told Roxy. I was sure she knew the best.

I didn't think I would have any appetite, but Uncle Alain was an amazing shot in the arm for both of us. He was funny and interesting. Like an expert pilot, he navigated through the minefields that would bring on any sorrow or displeasure. He didn't ask Roxy any questions that would make her defensive, and he didn't dwell on Mama's condition. For a moment or two, I wondered if the doctor had given him some reason to be hopeful, but he laid that idea to rest when we all left the restaurant and Roxy hailed a taxi for herself.

"This won't go on much longer," he told her. She nodded. I could see the way they were looking at each other and then at me.

"One of us has to call Aunt Lucy and Uncle Orman," she said.

"You do it," I told her. Aunt Lucy had given her their telephone number.

Roxy nodded and left. We hailed our own cab and headed home. I could see that Uncle Alain was pretty exhausted, both physically and emotionally, so I told him just to go to sleep and not worry about keeping me company. I said I had homework to do.

"That's good," he said. *"Bon nuit, ma chère."*

"Bon nuit."

As I watched him walk off, his shoulders slumped, his head down, I remarked to myself how effective grief was when it came to making you look older. Maybe that was because minutes and hours, days and weeks, suddenly became so important that you wished they would last forever. He was up ahead of me the following morning. He said it was the jet lag, but he had a nice breakfast prepared for both of us.

"You might as well go to school today," he said. "I'm here now, so I'll be at the hospital waiting for you when you are done."

"Is Roxy meeting you there?"

"I'll call her."

"Don't be surprised if she's busy. She's very popular doing what she does," I said.

He heard the disapproval and anger in my voice but held his soft smile. "It's never good or right to judge each other, but especially not now," he told me.

Maybe he was right, but it felt like a reprimand. He should at least have pretended to agree with me. I didn't care how nice Roxy was being to Mama now and how beautiful, elegant, and refined she was.

She had broken Mama's heart for years. Uncle Alain should at least acknowledge that, at least to me, I thought, and I left for school carrying rage along with my books. For now, it was comforting to be angry.

It kept me from being sad and feeling sorry for myself. I supposed I was being more like Papa. I needed him, needed his firmness, his unemotional military demeanor, and his intolerance of anyone or anything that would break ranks.

I pitied anyone who crossed my path that day, and entered the school as if I were stepping onto a field of battle.

I would take no prisoners.

19

No one, including my teachers, dared to ask anything that might upset me. They even avoided asking me questions about the subject or homework. I supposed that was because of the look on my face, but I became paranoid about it, and when I looked around, I began to wonder if everyone knew even more about my mother than I did. Maybe because of my desperate need to cling to some hope, I was blind to the inevitable. I wouldn't listen, and I wouldn't see what others could. I would never accept it.

When I walked toward a group of my classmates, they parted like the Red Sea to let me pass, no one speaking. Of course, I had my gaze on the floor and didn't pause. Perhaps I was imagining everything, but when I grazed against people or bumped into them, they jumped back as if I had touched them with a Taser. Finally, Chastity came to speak to me at lunch. I was just sitting, staring at nothing and barely eating. I didn't even realize she was standing there.

"Emmie," she said.

I blinked and looked at her. She was holding her books against her breasts tightly, like someone anticipating an earthquake or something. I never noticed until that moment that she had cut her hair. I don't know how many times I had warned her not to, not with a face as round and plump as hers. It made her look even fatter.

"Mistake," I said.

"What?"

"Your hair."

"Oh. My mother thought I would look better."

"Did she?" I looked away, leaving my words out there, drifting, looking for receptive ears.

"Are you all right?" she asked timidly.

I looked at her again for so long that anyone would think I didn't recognize her and was trying to figure out who she was. I saw that it unnerved her. She looked back at the girls she was hanging with these days, grimaced, and then turned back to me.

"Huh?"

"Huh what?"

"How are you?"

"Why do you ask?" I said. I wasn't in the mood to make anything easier for her or anyone else.

"I just thought . . . you're sitting here alone and . . ."

I looked around the cafeteria. "I'm hardly alone."

"You know what I mean. Look," she said when I continued just to stare at her, "I know you're going through a very bad time. I've tried to help you, offered to be with you. I don't know what I've done to make you so angry at me. Maybe I don't say the right things all the time, but I'm not trying to be mean to you or anything, and if you would . . ."

I was so unaware of my own reaction that I didn't know for a moment why she had stopped talking. Now she was the one who was just staring. When the tears began to drop off my cheeks and chin, I finally realized that I was crying. As if I instinctively knew its significance, I glanced at the clock on the cafeteria wall. I would always remember this moment, exactly what time it had been. I stood up, scooped up my books, and walked out of the cafeteria.

Chastity didn't call after me or follow. I had no idea where I was going, but when I made the turn and headed toward the main entrance of the school, I saw Roxy walking toward Dr. Sevenson's office. She stopped when she saw me.

"M?"

She couldn't believe I was there, either.

"Did Uncle Alain call the school or something?"

I didn't say anything. I didn't move.

"Because we decided I would come here for you."

I shook my head and backed away. "Go away," I said.

"Don't be difficult, M, not now."

I kept shaking my head. I saw how much I was frightening her. She looked helpless.

"You need to come with me. Uncle Alain wants you to be with him. Mama was amazing. She had all her arrangements done behind our backs, all the phone numbers, all the people to contact. He's at the house calling his sisters and—"

"I want to see Mama," I said. "She wants me to visit her today, but I'm not waiting for the end of the school day. I hate the school day."

"What? Aren't you listening to me? Okay, okay," she followed before I could speak. "Just come with me. Wait here a moment. I'll tell them," she said, and went into the office.

I was at the door when she came out, and without speaking, we headed for the front of the school, where she had a taxi waiting. The driver looked at me quickly and started away as soon as we had closed our doors. I saw the route we were taking. It was the way home.

"I want to go to the hospital," I said.

"There's no reason to go there now, M. She's no longer in her room. You'll see her afterward," she said softly.

"But she has to be in her room. We were talking to her last night."

"If you want to call it that," Roxy said. "You certainly didn't want her to be like she was much longer. It was horrible for her. It certainly wasn't living."

I was going to start shouting at her again. How dare she say such a terrible thing? Who did she think she was? Of course Mama was still in her room. She was waiting for me to visit after school. She wouldn't die before I came to see her, would she? *Stop saying that!*

All of this came to mind, but I stopped myself before I voiced any of it. These were the thoughts of the young girl in me who wanted to scream at her, the young girl who had died with Mama, the one who believed in a world in which anything broken could be repaired, anything lost could be found, and anything wonderful could happen. Things that frightened her or made her unhappy could be driven away with a mother's kiss or soft, soothing words. That young girl would not believe or accept such sadness and disappointment.

Instead, I continued to say nothing. We rode in silence, and when I got home, Uncle Alain greeted me with a tight, long hug. I held on to him as if I might sink through the floor if I didn't. Finally, he kissed my cheek, and I released my hold on him.

"I spoke with your aunt Lucy and uncle Orman," he said. "They'll be here for the funeral. They want to take you back with them immediately afterward, Emmie. It makes the most sense." He glanced at Roxy, who I was sure was nodding in agreement. "At least, until you're old enough to be on your own. I owe it to your mother to make sure you're taken care of."

"It doesn't look like I have much choice," I said. "Whatever."

He described the arrangements Mama had made for her own passing. I listened, but I didn't really hear anything. I was suddenly very tired and felt as if everything inside me had collapsed or stopped working. Even my heart was on pause, my blood frozen in place. I said nothing about it, just that I was going up to my room to lie down. Roxy was leaving, and Uncle Alain returned to the phone to speak to our French relatives. I went up to my room and, no longer strong enough to cry, just fell asleep hugging myself.

Aunt Lucy arrived first. She and Uncle Orman were going to stay at the Plaza. He was coming the night before the funeral. She made a point of saying that it was all the time he could spare. Friends were calling all the next day. I spoke with Mama's sisters in France, but they were not coming. Because of their own problems, it was just too difficult. I heard their excuses, their words of sympathy and sorrow, and thanked them.

From the moment she arrived, Aunt Lucy took over the wake arrangements at our house. I didn't really care about any of that, and Uncle Alain looked relieved that he wouldn't have to do anything. Other people volunteered to help, but he turned them over to Aunt Lucy.

Chastity visited by herself. She was crying, and I realized that she really did like my mother very much. Mama had always treated her well, and she had always felt comfortable at our house. I broke the news about my leaving. I told her I would be moving and attending a different school, which was in Washington, D.C. Despite how little we had been seeing each other, she looked devastated. We talked about her coming to visit. I told her that would be nice even though nothing in my future seemed important at this point.

Roxy called Uncle Alain, but she didn't come by, and neither of us saw her until the day of Mama's funeral. Aunt Lucy and Uncle Orman were at our house in the morning. He kissed me on the cheek, but his lips made the sound of a snapped rubber band.

"You've got to hold yourself together," he advised—or ordered, I should say. "It's what your parents expect of you," he added, as if they would be standing right beside me.

Neither he nor Aunt Lucy spoke much about Roxy. Aunt Lucy wasn't happy about what I had decided to wear, but I didn't change. It was a dress Mama and I had bought together, so it had special meaning for me.

As the morning wore on, I saw how Papa was so different from Uncle Orman, despite them sharing the same military-style upbringing. There didn't seem to be any softness under the layers of authority in Uncle Orman. He was a slightly taller man, with a firmer build and sharper, more sculptured features. He carried himself like a man who had been at many funerals. Dignity and poise were far more important than any show of emotion. When it came to dealing with other people, Papa was softer, friendlier. Uncle Orman spent most of his time talking with Uncle Alain, but Uncle Alain didn't look very happy about it. I overheard some of their conversation. It was more as if Uncle Orman was interrogating him.

I wanted to shout, "Don't ask, don't tell!" but just walked away from them after Uncle Alain and I shared a knowing look.

Finally, Roxy appeared, and for a moment, when my uncle and aunt looked at her, I thought there would be some nasty words exchanged. Roxy was wearing black, but she looked as if she was going to an elegant event, with her cape, jewelry, and matching black fur hat. Her face was as made-up as ever. I was sure Uncle Orman was expecting to see a young woman who had abused herself and been abused, looking mousy and frightened, certainly not someone who could be on the cover of *Vogue*. He seemed to bristle and harden like a threatened alley cat at the sight of her.

Aunt Lucy did not hide her displeasure. "Well, I would think we would all practice some restraint when it came to our cosmetics on a day like today," she said.

"And so you have, Aunt Lucy," Roxy said. "I'm proud of you."

I thought Aunt Lucy would explode. Her whole face seemed to fill and balloon, and her shoulders rose as if some very strong man had put his hands under her arms and was lifting her off the ground.

"Let's get a move on," Uncle Orman commanded.

Our stretch limousine was parked and waiting outside to take us to the church. No one said another word until we arrived and took our places. Aunt Lucy made a thing of where each of us should sit. I thought she was putting on a good show for the mourners, proving that she was not only a concerned relative but also quite capable of taking control to make it all run well.

There weren't as many people at Mama's funeral. Many of Papa's colleagues and their wives and husbands had already forgotten about us, and I imagined few wanted to be there. It was too much too soon. I didn't blame them. I didn't want to be there, either. The service went very smoothly. Mama was buried beside Papa, and when it was all over, we returned home, where Aunt Lucy and Uncle Orman took it on themselves to greet people and accept condolences. With him in his uniform, I was sure people thought they were at some official event.

Chastity and her parents were at the funeral. None of my other classmates attended. Chastity was obviously fascinated mostly by Roxy and introduced herself as my best friend. Roxy glanced at me and saw my small smirk.

"Your sister is even more beautiful close up," Chastity whispered. I didn't respond.

When people began to leave, Aunt Lucy came over to tell me when we would be leaving.

"Your uncle would like us to go early in the morning tomorrow. We'd like you to pack just two suitcases for now. Fold everything properly. Make sure you have enough underthings, and if you're near a monthly you-know-what, pack what's appropriate. Don't bother bringing any makeup. There's no makeup at all permitted in the school you'll be attending, and your uncle detests young girls wearing a lot of makeup. Would you like me to help you choose what to bring?"

"No," I said quickly—too quickly to please her, of course.

"Yes. Well, there'll be plenty of time to return to get other things, proper things. You'll be wearing a uniform at school now anyway, and I don't expect you'll be going to anything social for some time. We do have strict house rules when it comes to looking after your own things and putting things back where they belong."

"Did you say school uniform?"

"School uniform," she said, nodding. "Exactly. You will find many differences between the school you are now attending and where you will attend, differences for the better. Now, anticipating all of this, we've had your room prepared."

"What do you mean, prepared?"

"Repainted. Carpeted. I thought a nice color like coffee would work. Your uncle agreed. I'll warn you now, there's no television in your room, and we will not be providing a separate phone, either. Your uncle doesn't believe in that. We never did that for our children," she added, and looked at Roxy. I hadn't realized that she had stepped up beside me to hear Aunt Lucy's short speech.

"Where are your children?" I asked.

"What?"

"Didn't they hear about my mother?"

"Of course they heard, but they have full, busy lives. Now, you'll need a physical before you can attend the school. We've arranged that for you, too. He's actually a military doctor. Your appointment is the day after tomorrow. There's no time to waste. You'll have a lot to catch up on, I'm sure."

She threw a cool smile at Roxy and returned to stand beside Uncle Orman.

I looked at Roxy. She was glaring at them both

with lasers for eyes. "Forget about them," she suddenly said.

"What?"

"You heard me. You can tell her later that you won't be going to live with them after all."

"I won't?"

"No. You'll be living with me," she added, and went to speak with Uncle Alain.

I stood there stunned for a moment, and then, for the first time in days, I felt my face break into a smile.

When Aunt Lucy and Uncle Orman heard that I'd be living with Roxy, they were even more stunned than I had been. Roxy came up beside me when she saw that I was giving them the news.

"She's old enough to be my legal guardian," I added.

"Roxy? Someone's guardian? Ridiculous," Aunt Lucy said, looking at her. "She's not capable of that, and besides, no court would permit it. Why, she could turn you into someone just like her, and then—"

"Let it be," Uncle Orman suddenly said sharply. I had been anticipating his threats and anger.

"What?" Aunt Lucy asked him.

"You heard me. If this is what the girl wants, fine. Only know this," he continued, giving me his officer's firm glare. "You don't come back to us if you discover you've made a mistake. We're no second choice. Is that understood?"

"I can't come back to you if I've never been with you in the first place, Uncle Orman."

He said nothing for a moment and then came the

closest to a smile. His lips merely creased, and his eyes widened slightly. "You're just like your father, pigheaded," he said.

"Thank you, Uncle Orman. That's about the nicest compliment you, especially you, could give me."

Roxy laughed.

Uncle Orman turned away. Aunt Lucy continued to stare, astounded, and then he called to her and told her to prepare to leave. She went directly to Uncle Alain with her complaints. When he heard what was happening, he looked at us with a slight smile, but he pretended to listen sympathetically to Aunt Lucy. He said nothing, and she turned away from him in a huff.

Finally, they were gone. We realized that everyone else was, too. The silence took all three of us by surprise, and for a few moments, no one spoke.

"Are you both sure about this?" Uncle Alain asked us.

"I am," Roxy said, and she turned to me. "If she listens and obeys the rules."

"What rules?"

"There'll be rules," she said. "Don't think there won't."

"If you can live by them, I can."

"They're not rules for me. They're rules for you."

"What about this house? Are you going to live here?" Uncle Alain said.

"No, that won't be possible," Roxy said. "We'll put it up for sale. The funds could provide her with college expenses. I have someone who can help us with everything, an attorney," she added. "You don't have to worry about any of that, Uncle Alain."

"*Très bon*," he said. "I'll plan on returning to France soon, then."

"You can go tomorrow, if you like," Roxy said. "We're not chasing you away, but we'll be fine."

"I think you just might be," he said, smiling. She had said it with such firmness that I thought we would be, too. "I'll expect you both to come to Paris soon."

"First chance we get," Roxy promised. "Well, I've got some preparations to make. I'm going to have to live with a teenager."

Uncle Alain laughed.

"You all right?" she asked me.

"Yes," I said.

"You can bring more than two suitcases and whatever pathetic makeup you have," she said.

We watched her leave, and then he and I both felt we needed to hug. Everything was happening so quickly now that I felt as if I had been shoved out of the space station and was floating helplessly. Soon he would be gone, too, and I'd have no one but Roxy to go to for advice.

And then there was the realization that I would be leaving my house. Even when I had been contemplating going to live with Uncle Orman and Aunt Lucy, I had not really understood that I would be walking out our front door forever and leaving behind all of the memories a warm, loving home could provide. For a moment, I stood in the living room, turning very slowly to absorb every little thing, from the figurines Mama had collected to every piece of furniture, every crease in every chair, especially Papa's, and every picture on every wall.

Maybe Roxy would want some of this, I thought, but probably not. It wouldn't fit into her world, and she wouldn't be as fond of the memories. No, this eventually was going to be a permanent good-bye.

Mama had once told me of a similar experience when she had left her family home in France. She was excited about marrying Papa and coming to America, of course, but "it was as if another umbilical cord was being cut," she told me. "A home is truly a lifeline, a place where you feel safe and secure, a place to run to when you've been hurt or frightened by something or someone. Everything in it is part of your family and so part of you. The aromas of the food my mother prepared. The smell of my father's pipe tobacco, my sisters' perfumes, my brother's cologne, and the fresh scent in washed linens and towels. All of it lives inside you. It was a lot to leave behind," she said, her voice drifting into almost a whisper. I could easily imagine the expression on her face when she had turned to look back, and I could feel her sadness.

Now I was feeling the same sadness.

Surely, despite Papa's self-confidence and abilities, she was also a little afraid when she left France to live in America. She would have to learn new customs, more English, and new rules that governed everyday life. It took almost as much courage as love.

For me, the prospect of going to live with Roxy was probably not so far from the prospect of going to live in another country. I was excited and intrigued, but I would be lying if I didn't admit to being afraid. Would Uncle Orman and Aunt Lucy be right? Would I find myself in an even more terrible situation? Where would I go then?

Once I was terrified of merely talking to Roxy because of what Papa would think and how betrayed he would feel.

If a corpse could really turn over in its grave, Papa might do just that the next time I went to visit. He would show me his back.

Or would he?

Maybe, just maybe, this was a way to bring Roxy home and not vice versa.

Maybe all that was Papa in me would be welcomed and loved again.

Maybe we would be sisters in every sense of the word.

I hoped so. Then Mama's and his passing would have some meaning for both of us.

I would soon know.

20

Even with Roxy's limousine driver helping me carry out my suitcases and bringing them into the hotel, I felt like a trespasser. I could see the curiosity and what I thought was disapproval in the eyes of the desk clerk and the bellman. Roxy didn't even look their way. I told myself I had to learn how to ignore people the way she did.

When the elevator doors opened, I saw that there were only three apartments on her floor. Hers was to the right. It had a short marble entry with a small but expensive-looking teardrop chandelier. There was a coat closet on the immediate right and a work of art on the opposite wall. It was a picture of a flower cut out of black velvet with pink cloth petals. There were artificial flowers everywhere.

Fleur du Coeur, I thought. The room was designed to fit her image.

The entryway opened to a surprisingly large living room with elegant leather and wood furniture. The centerpiece was a softly curved, L-shaped sectional that consisted of a sofa, a corner back, and a loveseat.

Directly across from it was a swivel accent chair with a round bottom frame. Accent pillows were on everything. A matching coffee table and end table filled out the center of the room. To the right was a large panel window that looked east, and down from it was another, smaller window. A set of four different versions of what looked like the same flower were hung high on the far wall. The walls were painted white with swirls of soft red and pink. The wooden floor was covered with a very large area rug that matched the furniture.

My eyes took in everything quickly. I saw the sculptures, the lamps, and the bouquets of artificial flowers, but there was a fresh real plant at the center of the coffee table. The flowers on it looked heart-shaped.

"What are those?" I asked. "They look like hearts."

Roxy laughed. "They are. They're called dicentra or bleeding heart. I have a client who has them shipped in from Japan. He's actually very sweet. Okay, let's get you settled in," she said, and nodded at the small hallway down to the right. Her driver was already heading there. The floors were marble everywhere but in the living room, and the walls were painted with the same white with pink swirls. I followed him into a large bedroom. There was a king-size four-poster bed with oversized pillows and a comforter, plus a nightstand, dresser, and mirror. Everything had a cherry veneer. There was an en suite bathroom with a small vanity table and an oval mirror in a cherry frame.

"Just leave the suitcases, Mark. We'll take care of it from here."

The driver nodded and headed out without saying a word.

Roxy opened the sliding closet doors. "As you can see, you'll have plenty of space here," she said.

"It's a beautiful place, Roxy."

"Actually, it's the biggest apartment in the hotel. Mrs. Brittany saw to that."

"You mentioned her before. Who is she?"

She thought a moment and nodded to herself. "I should deal with all that first. Mrs. Brittany is the head of the company I work for. She wasn't happy about your coming here to live with me. I had to make a number of promises to her about you and how you would behave here. You can't violate any of these rules I'm setting down."

She walked to the window and opened the drapes. My windows looked out on the avenue, but the panes were thick and almost soundproof.

"She will probably stop by soon to see you and how I'm managing this," she continued, and turned back to me. "First, whenever I have a client visiting, you can't leave this room. I'll tell you way in advance so you will have time to get anything you want and bring it in here. You'll keep the door closed and not come out until I let you know you can. Is that clear?"

"Yes," I said. "How often do you have clients?"

"I'd rather you didn't ask me any questions about any of this, M. When I think it's necessary for you to know something, I'll tell you, okay?"

I shrugged. Was she embarrassed, ashamed, or just secretive? "Okay."

"There's a restaurant on this block that sends up dinners. I'll show you their menu, and you can order anything you want. We'll do our own breakfasts when we're here for breakfast. Should I have a client staying overnight, I'll have you put up in a room on another floor. You'll know in advance so you'll have time to get your things together. You have a television in here and a phone, but be sure not to use the television when I have a client. It's important."

"Why?"

"Let's just say some of these clients want to be very discreet and would rather very few, if any, know they've come here. It would especially spook them to know there was someone else in the apartment."

"Are they famous people? Would I recognize them? Is that why?"

"What did I just say about questioning me, M?"

"I'm just curious."

"Yeah, well, contain your curiosity under lock and key for a while, will you? Now," she continued, walking toward the door, "I really don't anticipate Aunt Lucy making a thing of this, but you never know what someone as self-important as that will do. So you have to do well in school and stay out of trouble. I know you've been doing well, but what I mean is, you can't suddenly change for the worse because you're with me. Understand?"

"Yes."

"I've made an appointment for us with this attorney,

Steve Whitman. He handles estates and all that and will process Mama's will. He's also connected with some real estate people, so he'll get the town house on the market very quickly for us—for you, I should say. How do you get to school every day?"

"I walk."

"You have to walk farther now," she said.

"I know how much farther this is, Roxy. I've been here before, remember?"

"Right," she said. "Good."

I wanted to tell her about Chastity and me spying on her, but I didn't think it was a good time to do that.

"Well, do you want help unpacking?"

"No. Can I see your bedroom?"

She smiled. "Okay, but no jokes," she said. Now I really was curious.

We went through the hallway to the living room. She showed me the dining room and the kitchen, and then we went down another short marble hallway to a double-door bedroom. It was about one and a half times larger than mine, but the centerpiece was her blazing red bed shaped like a heart. The walls were papered with depictions of beautiful gardens. There was a mirror on the ceiling above the bed. The area rug was a tight-threaded crimson. The wood in her dresser, vanity table, and nightstands was rich cherry. Her en suite bathroom was twice the size of mine, with a Jacuzzi, a large shower, and a second bathtub.

"Flowers and hearts," I said. "Fleur du Coeur."

"Mrs. Brittany takes her themes very seriously. Okay, go unpack, M. I'm expecting Mrs. Brittany in a few hours, and I'd like everything settled. I'm sending out for some lunch. What would you like?"

"Just a salad with some chicken, maybe."

"Okay. Let me know if you need anything else. Oh," she said as I started out of her bedroom, "there's a maid here every day, of course. She'll make your bed and change the linens, the towels. We send everything out to be washed, dry-cleaned, whatever. There's a hamper in your bathroom. The maid will see to what has to be washed."

"I'll get so spoiled," I said.

"So what? Don't you think Aunt Lucy is spoiled? There are plenty of women like her."

"I don't ever want to be like her."

She smiled.

"I doubt that you'll ever be. Get going."

I returned to my room and began hanging up my clothes and putting things in the dresser drawers. I had my favorite teddy bear, the one Papa had given me when I was only five. I wondered if Roxy would remember it. As I did in my room at home, I placed it between the pillows on the bed. Just having it with me brought me some comfort. I heard the buzzer ring. A delivery boy had brought up our lunch. I didn't step out until he was gone.

"You don't have to hide from everyone, M. It would be silly to try, anyway. I'm only concerned about my clients," Roxy told me.

I joined her in the dining room. She had set the table.

"Don't think because I did this much that I'm any

sort of homemaker," she said. "I don't wash dishes, polish furniture, anything."

"Can I ask how long you've been here?"

"Some other time," she said. "I don't feel like talking about myself right now. I suppose I'll have to go to your school and register as your guardian or something."

I shrugged. "I guess."

"Well, don't expect me to step into this big-sister role easily. I've been on my own too long."

"What about friends?"

"What about them?"

"Don't you have any close friends?"

I didn't want to mention the young woman I saw her with that day when Chastity and I followed her.

"Close acquaintances," she replied.

"What about when you were in school, living at home?"

"You don't think I kept in touch with anyone I knew back then, do you?"

"No, I guess not." I paused. "You sound as if you've been very lonely, Roxy."

"I survived," she replied, but I saw I had drawn a little emotional blood. She looked away. "I was too friendly with someone once, someone else who worked for Mrs. Brittany. Things didn't work out for her."

"What happened?" I asked.

"Let's just say she took one of her clients too seriously and leave it at that."

"You don't see her anymore?"

"She died," Roxy said, and slammed her fork down

on the plate. "I asked you not to ask questions, M, and the first thing you have me doing is talking about things I don't want to talk about."

"I'm sorry."

"Just do your own thing, and don't interfere with me," she said sharply.

"All right. Maybe this was a mistake," I said, looking at my salad.

She was silent, and then she reached for my hand. "I'm sorry. It's not a mistake. You'll be all right. You'll finish school, go to college, and marry a millionaire."

"Yeah, right," I said. "I don't want to marry a millionaire. I want to marry someone I love, just like Mama did."

"Okay. Here's to that," she said, raising her glass of white wine. "We all need some fantasy, I guess."

I looked at her, still feeling fury inside me. Maybe I would soon get to understand exactly how she had gotten so under Papa's skin that he could throw her out.

"And what's your fantasy, Roxy?"

She thought a moment and shook her head. "I've run out of them," she said. Then she surprised me with a smile. "Maybe you'll bring some back."

I wasn't particularly in the mood for fantasies, either. Reality was a bully. It shoved and pushed its way into your mind, driving rainbow dreams down or out. Dared I think of what my future would be now? Did ambition matter? When would I think about romance again? Roxy had this lovemaking hideaway, the most beautiful dresses, the most expensive perfumes, probably the best hairstylists in the city, but it all seemed more like ways to trap and entice and had nothing to do with love and romance. Did I dare ask her if she had someone special, ever dreamed of someone special or wanted someone special? What did she see as her future? How long could this go on?

I returned to my room to finish up organizing my things. Soon after, I heard the door buzzer again and listened at the door. It was a woman. She had an English accent. A moment later, I heard footsteps coming my way and stepped back from the door. Roxy opened it, and she and a woman who looked about fifty but was probably older stepped in. She was a few inches taller than Roxy and had her light blond hair parted in the middle and curled at her neck. The most striking feature of her face was her crystal-blue eyes. There probably wasn't a more perfect nose on any woman in the city. I thought her lips were recently injected with Botox. Actually, she looked like someone who had a plastic surgeon on call. If she looked in the mirror and saw something she didn't like, she picked up the phone and left the house immediately.

"This is M," Roxy said. "M, this is Mrs. Brittany."

I said hello, but she didn't reply. Instead, she walked in farther and looked me over the way I imagined Southern slave owners at a slave auction looked over new Africans brought into the country.

"With a little work, she could be prettier than you," Mrs. Brittany said.

I glanced at Roxy and thought I saw fear ripple through her face.

"She's only fifteen," Roxy said.

"You weren't much older," Mrs. Brittany replied quickly. Roxy forced a smile.

"I was much, much different," she said.

"Maybe. In my experience, we never know what lies under a young girl's skin. Are you sexually active?" she asked me.

"What? No."

She looked surprised and smiled skeptically. Then she grew serious again. "Sorry about your mother. I understand you have horrible relatives."

"Let's just say it wouldn't have been difficult to leave them on the *Titanic*," I replied, and she laughed.

Her laugh was deep, more like a rumbling in her chest. Now that she was closer to me, I saw the small birthmark on the bottom left of her chin and the strands of hair with gray roots beginning to expose themselves. Her face was tight, plastic-surgery tight, so that her smile seemed more like a folding than a relaxed movement in her cheeks and lips. How old was she? I wondered.

"Okay. We don't want to send you back on the *Titanic*. You can stay here with Roxy, but you will have to obey the rules your sister and I have set down."

"I know. I'm not going to cause any trouble. I know how to keep to myself," I said.

She tilted her head, gave me an appreciative smile, and looked at Roxy. "I'm surprised you didn't talk more about her."

I looked at Roxy, too, to see what her answer would be.

"You knew my memories of my family were painful, Mrs. Brittany. If anyone knew, you did. I wasn't about to talk about anyone."

"Yes. Well, let's see how it goes." She stared at me again and then smiled. "If she stays looking this young, she could be our Lolita. I get a lot of calls for a Lolita these days, you know. The older men get, the more they look to youth. There's nothing a man fears more than losing his erection, and most of these men have wives who could discourage the most psychotic rapist. Youth is a valuable commodity. It always has been and always will be."

"She's going to college, Mrs. Brittany. She's got a good inheritance coming. She's far from the state I was in at her age."

"Um," she said, still considering me. "We have college girls, too, you know." She turned to Roxy. "Clair de Lune has a BA from Columbia. Anyway," she continued, starting to look bored, "I don't want to see or hear about any problems, Roxy."

"You won't."

She looked at me again. "You mean to stand there and tell me you're a virgin, then?"

"Yes," I said. "I haven't met the right young man for that."

"The right young man? I thought you kids today weren't as discriminating and treated sex as just another recreation."

"I don't," I said firmly.

She shook her head. "It's amazing how two girls from the same home can be so different," she said, and laughed. I saw how uncomfortable Roxy was becoming.

"I'm sure there was no one in your family exactly like you, Mrs. Brittany," I told her, and she lost her smile for a moment. The silence that fell was heavy. It felt as if all of the oxygen had left the room.

Then she relaxed. "I see in you one quality you share with your sister, being headstrong, fearless. That could be good, or . . ." She turned to leave, then turned back at the door. "It could be disastrous. The trick is knowing when to watch your mouth." She smiled. "Maybe that's something you'll learn while you're here, and it won't be a total waste." She looked at Roxy. "Let's talk," she snapped, and walked out.

Roxy glanced at me, nodded, and followed her.

I let out my breath.

From a distance, Mrs. Brittany looked like an attractive, elegant woman, but up close, her true nature showed itself. She wasn't just tough; she was street tough, with those rough edges of someone who had clawed and scratched her way out of the gutter. Maybe she had learned how to appear dignified, aristocratic, and cultured, but as Mama might say, scratch her skin, and you'll find an alley cat lurking.

If the devil came as a woman, it would be someone like her, I thought. Roxy wasn't sensitive to it or perhaps was deliberately blind because of her situation, but I sensed a cruel coldness under her suave, sophisticated appearance. Despite my bravado, she chilled my blood and made my heart thump when she scrutinized me the way she must have scrutinized Roxy.

I hoped I wouldn't see much of her.

Roxy returned nearly a half hour later. "We're all right for now," she said. "She was impressed with you, but she's very careful about everything. This is a very big enterprise involving very important people, M. I'm just telling you all this so you won't feel bad about the way she spoke to you."

"I didn't feel bad about the way she spoke to me, Roxy. I don't know her, and she doesn't know me. I felt bad about the way she spoke to you."

"Forget it," she snapped. "I can handle her. Don't make trouble."

I looked away.

"One thing I didn't bring you here to do, M, is judge me, understand? Go on about your own life, and don't try to interfere with mine."

"Okay, okay," I said.

She stood there staring at me.

"I'll do what you say," I promised, and she relaxed.

"We're going out to dinner tonight. There's a little Italian restaurant I frequent uptown. I like it because the food's good and it's out of the way. You'll have a good time, but I think we should go to your school tomorrow and get you started again. You can't mope around here all day. Okay? Okay," she repeated harshly when I didn't respond.

"Yes."

"Good. Take a bubble bath or something, and . . ." She paused. "Stop acting like Papa. Get off your high horse," she told me, and left.

There I was, immersed in luxury and comfort, but

it didn't bring me happiness and security. The reality seemed clear to me despite the act Roxy performed. She had tried to make it all seem like nothing, but I knew in my heart that I had entered her world, and there were dangers there that I probably had never imagined.

21

"You'll like these people, and the food is great," Roxy told me when we got into the taxi to go to the Italian restaurant. "I've been going there for a few years. In case any questions come up, you should know that I told them my family was in Los Angeles," she added. "It was just easier."

I didn't say anything, but I realized that Roxy had to invent a lot of things to get along with people she met, not that her so-called clients were really interested in her, I imagined. She had already clearly implied that it was a no-no to talk about herself and tell anyone what was true. Mrs. Brittany surely insisted that her girls remained mysterious. I understood that was the combination that made them so desirable: beauty and mystery.

The restaurant was cozy. It felt more like eating at someone's home because of the soft-cushioned chairs, the personal pictures, and the family artifacts. The couple who ran it, Ed and Mary Diana, were both in their mid-sixties and obviously very fond of Roxy. From their conversation, I gathered that they hadn't the faintest idea of what Roxy did or how she lived. Between the lines, I picked up that they assumed that she was involved with clothing since she always wore such beautiful and expensive-looking clothes. I realized that she let them believe that she was a buyer for a department store. However, I thought I saw some awareness in Mr. Diana when Roxy introduced him to me. Roxy was careful about what she told them about me, never really saying that I had moved in with her.

I imagined that inventing so much about herself when she spoke to people other than her clients and Mrs. Brittany made it difficult for Roxy ever to grow close with anyone. That was why she had no real friends and, as long as she was doing what she was doing, never would have any. I had to be careful about these thoughts and conclusions. Roxy was as proud and as defiant as ever. She wouldn't tolerate anyone feeling sorry for her, especially me. She had made that clear today.

The following morning, she took me to school so she could meet Dr. Sevenson and establish herself as my guardian. She had the limousine available to her. When we arrived, we turned a lot of heads and, as Mama would say, set tongues clapping. Roxy tried to look like someone's guardian, I know, but despite our age difference, she still looked as if she could be the one registering to attend high school. She was in her black fur-lined coat and hat, with her hair in an updo, and very tight slacks with thick high-heeled black shoes. She did restrain herself when it came to her makeup, but Roxy didn't really need much makeup, anyway. Heads continued to turn our way when we entered the building and started for the principal's office.

Our principal, Dr. Sevenson, always struck me as being quite aloof. Everything that had to be done on a day-to-day basis seemed to be delegated to someone else, such as Dr. Walter, Mrs. Morris, or one of the teachers. Most of Dr. Sevenson's time was spent in public relations, getting funding and new students for the school. She was a stout woman, with teased dark brown hair that looked as if it had been styled and sprayed twenty years ago. The joke was that there were bedbugs living in it. She had a clipped way of speaking, especially if she was speaking to someone from whom she didn't expect much in the way of funding or anything else. I don't think I had spoken a half-dozen words to her or she to me since I had begun attending the school.

Her secretary opened the door of her office for us and stepped away, smiling as if she had accomplished some great feat. Roxy barely glanced at her.

Dr. Sevenson looked up from her papers and sat back. "Please," she said, nodding at the chairs in front of her desk.

We sat.

"I was sorry to hear about your mother," she told me.

"Thank you," I said.

"It takes great strength to continue doing what would certainly have made your parents proud, but I'm sure you will continue to do so. At least, I hope so."

"Me, too," I said.

"What can I do for you?" she asked Roxy.

"I'm Roxanne Wilcox. I will be Emmie's guardian. I was told I had to inform the school of our situation and leave contact information. I was also told that we had to see you personally, so I made this appointment."

"Right. Well, that is the protocol. Where are you and Emmie residing?"

"We're at the Hotel Beaux-Arts."

"Hotel?"

"I have an apartment there."

"I see."

From the way she was scrutinizing Roxy, I wondered if she had picked up on the student gossip and knew exactly who and what Roxy was.

"There is no other relative to take on this responsibility?" she asked. "One with a real home, perhaps?"

Roxy bristled. "Why would we even think of another relative? I'm her sister, and I'm well over eighteen. We do have a real home. I said I had an apartment, not a hotel room in some fleabag joint, either."

"That's good," Dr. Sevenson said, not even blinking at Roxy's indignation. "We usually don't have very much to do with social services, the child-protection agencies, and the like. Our students come from well-to-do families, but when something like this occurs, there could be a lot more scrutiny. I do appreciate the recent family tragedies Emmie has experienced, but—"

"We both experienced," Roxy interrupted.

"Yes, well, as I was saying, I appreciate the pain and suffering, but we do hope your sister's admirable behavior and good schoolwork will not change dramatically for the worse. That could lead to more scrutiny and, as I said, not simply by me or the guidance counselor."

"Are you threatening us? She's paid up here for the remainder of the year, isn't she?" Roxy asked sharply.

"Yes, she's fine, and I'm not threatening you. I'm just doing my job and informing you that we have high expectations for our students, both in their academic behavior and in their social behavior. I would tell this to any new parents or guardians when they brought in their child for enrollment."

"I doubt you would say it the same way," Roxy pursued.

"I'm sorry if I've offended you, but that is just the way it is."

She turned to me.

"Please come see me if you have any difficulties, Emmie, any at all," she added, looking pointedly at Roxy. "I don't have the forms for you to fill out here."

She pressed her intercom to tell her secretary to provide them for Roxy.

"Well," Roxy said, rising, "since everything we need to do is out there, we won't waste any more of your time or mine and keep Emmie out of her classes. Thank you."

I stood up, too. It was clear to me that no one could intimidate my sister. She seemed to know instinctively how to speak and deal with people, no matter who or how high up they were. Where did she get her poise and self-confidence after becoming a street kid? How did she develop into this beautiful and accomplished young woman? Did I want to be more or less like her? When would she tell me more about herself, especially the journey she took to arrive at this place in her life?

Roxy and I paused at the counter, and Dr. Sevenson's secretary handed Roxy the forms to fill out.

"You can go to class," Roxy told me. As I turned, she added, "And watch your ass. You can see how everyone else will be," she added loudly enough for even Dr. Sevenson to hear behind her closed door. I smiled at her and left.

When I entered my class, Chastity's eyes nearly exploded, as did those of some of my other classmates. I took my usual seat and opened my notebook, pretending that nothing at all was different. I could feel the curiosity practically boiling over and out of the minds of those around me. When the bell rang to end the class, Chastity nearly leaped over desks to get to me.

"You're here!" she cried. Some of the others gathered around us.

"Yes, it does seem like I'm here," I said, and started out.

"But . . . I thought you were going to live with your aunt and uncle in Washington, D.C."

"That didn't work out," I tossed back. "They don't have MTV."

"What?"

I laughed to myself, wondering how long I could keep her dangling. She hurried to walk beside me.

"But where are you living? I mean, who are you living with?"

"Whom," I said. "You're never going to improve your grades in English."

"I don't care about my grades in English," she whined. "Where are you living? Are you at home? Who's with you?"

I paused. The other girls were still hovering around us.

"If Dr. Sevenson hears that sort of disrespect for our English class, you'll be dangling on your participles," I said, and kept walking.

I saw Richard ahead of me with two of his friends and quickly caught up. He was excited to see me but didn't ask many questions. I used him to waste as much time between classes as I could and entered the next class just as the bell rang. I glanced at Chastity. She looked as if she might explode with frustration. The moment she had an opportunity to whisper, she leaned over. "You're living with your sister, aren't you?" she asked. It sounded more like an accusation.

I didn't reply. I pretended not to hear her because I was too involved in my work, but her question hung in the air until the bell rang again.

"Well?" she asked immediately.

"Yes," I said.

"In the hotel?"

"That's correct," I muttered, and kept walking.

"But how can you . . . I mean . . . with what goes on and everything?"

"Where there's a will, there's a way," I said, and went on to my next class.

For a while, I actually enjoyed the curiosity and excitement swirling around me. It was mostly stirred up by Chastity in the beginning but soon developed until I was the topic of conversation everywhere. I knew that once Chastity told others where I was living and with whom, the news would fly through the school. Everyone was after me to sit at her table in the cafeteria at lunchtime. Suddenly, I was fascinating to those girls who were previously intimidated by my grief and my family tragedy and wanted to do everything to avoid me.

Handfuls of questions were thrown in my direction. "You're living in a hotel? What's it like? Are you really on your own? What kind of people are you meeting there? Do you have anything to do with your sister's work? Are you going to meet rich and famous people?"

I was deliberately vague with my answers, making all that they thought was exotic and exciting seem very matter-of-fact, if not outright boring.

"I have to walk farther to school and back," I told them, as if that summarized it all.

Frustrated and annoyed, they stopped asking questions and peeled away like beggars who realized that the one they were following would give them nothing. Naturally, Chastity expected that I had reserved the truth only for her ears. She smiled and was at my side as soon as she could be.

"Can I visit you at the hotel?" she asked. "I could come today."

"No, I can't have any visitors," I said.

"Really? What, is it dangerous there?"

"No, of course not."

"Does the school know where you're living?"

"Yes. My sister brought me today, and we met with Dr. Sevenson."

"Your sister came here with you?"

"I'm surprised no one told you. We attracted enough attention."

"She met with Dr. Sevenson?" she asked, her face soaked in incredulity.

"She's my legal guardian now, Chastity. What did you expect?" I left her with her mouth frozen in the shape of an O.

Although I teased and frustrated my classmates when they asked me questions during the next weeks, their curiosity about Roxy and me didn't wane. The more I evaded their questions, the more they came to their own nasty conclusions. I should have anticipated it, but I was really feeling aloof, finding myself floating above them. I did my schoolwork as diligently as ever, but I avoided social contact almost as much as I had when Mama was suffering and my thoughts were always with her. Maybe I helped to bring about the things that began to happen. Maybe they were inevitable.

Roxy's decision to "improve" my wardrobe certainly didn't help defuse the situation. Now that spring was almost here, she decided to update my fashion and brought me to her boutiques, where I was fitted for a blue T-back drop-sleeve dress and a red double-bikini-string halter dress. She also bought me sexy heels and boots. Of course, when it was finally warm enough to wear my new outfits, other girls were fascinated with my new clothes and wanted to know where they could get them, too.

That was all short-lived, however, because Dr. Sevenson called me into her office to tell me that what I was wearing to school was inappropriate.

"We do have a dress code," she said. "I've left a message for your sister. I mean to enforce our standards here," she added firmly.

"There's nothing wrong with my clothing," I insisted.

"Maybe out there, but there is something wrong with it in here. If you wear anything like this again, I will be forced to send you home. That's all." She dismissed me with a flick of her wrist.

Roxy was upset about it, but she didn't put up any argument. I was more unhappy now than ever and wanted to leave the school, but Roxy was taking her "motherly" role very seriously these days, checking on my homework and my grades, making sure that I came back to the hotel when school was over for the day, and demanding to know where I planned to go on weekends and whom I was with. I wasn't doing much at all, but she was still hovering over me.

"I don't have a social life at this school and never will," I told her.

"Just finish up there, M, and we'll get you into another school. Mama and Papa paid for it. You told me yourself that it was important to Papa."

Reluctantly, I returned to wearing what I always wore, but the damage had been done. Although Evan was the only boy I had gone out with from the school, his earlier stories about me now were more believable. I had been guilty simply by being related to Roxy. Now I was condemned forever because of where I lived and whom I lived with. I could see it in the lustful looks boys gave me at school and hear it in the remarks they mumbled when they were near me.

How could I live in a hotel with a sister who was a professional escort?

The truth was that in the beginning, life at the hotel wasn't unpleasant or uncomfortable at all. Twice a week, Roxy had a guest—or a client, as she called him—and I stayed in my room and read or did my homework, just as I was instructed to do. There were three occasions when I had to leave and stay in one of the other hotel rooms. They were nowhere as comfortable as mine, but I did what I was told. So far, after a few months of this life, I had not yet seen or spoken again with Mrs. Brittany, and I wasn't sorry about it.

Roxy was successfully keeping me sheltered from the life she was leading and the things she was doing. I obeyed her wishes and asked no questions. I wouldn't say I wasn't curious and tempted to sneak a peek or listen to what her clients were saying, but I was too frightened of being discovered and bringing some terrible problems to both of us. I was terrified that it would lead to my being sent to live with Aunt Lucy and Uncle Orman after all.

Then, finally, the situation simmering at school for me boiled over in ways I couldn't anticipate.

And Roxy was not happy about it.

22

It was Mrs. Brittany who came personally with the complaint. Roxy and I were having the dinner we had ordered from the restaurant on the avenue. I had set the table, and we had just sat and begun. Almost the way Papa would do it, Roxy would cross-examine me about my day at school at dinner every night. In fact, her questions were so similar that I almost broke out into laughter at times. She also wanted to see my tests and comments made on my homework.

"Why are you so worried about my grades, Roxy? You weren't any sort of student."

"What I did and what I do is not your concern," she said. "You're not me. You have other opportunities out there."

I shrugged. "I don't know what I want to do."

"You will. What about your social life? You haven't been invited to any parties, asked out on any dates?"

I looked away. She had been tiptoeing around this ever since my return to school. My answers were always vague, with a show of indifference.

"What's going on?" she asked. "None of that is important to you?"

"It's important."

"So?"

"The sort of invitations I've been getting are not what either of us would appreciate."

"What do you mean? I'd like some answers, M," she insisted when I didn't respond.

"What do I mean?" I sat back. "Okay, here's what I mean." I rose, went into my bedroom, and returned with an envelope that I tossed onto the table.

She looked at me curiously, picked it up, and looked inside. Slowly, she took out the two ten-dollar bills and the note. She looked at me again. I sat back with my arms folded under my breasts and waited for her to read the note.

"What is this, a joke?"

"Yes, it's a joke, or maybe it isn't. Maybe that idiot thought I would respond."

She read the note again and then read it aloud. " 'This is for the first ten minutes. There's more if I can last longer'?"

I nodded.

"I don't get it."

It suddenly occurred to me that Roxy never knew what Chastity had done and what I had done with Chastity. I had backed myself into a corner and finally had to confess.

"It's not your fault. It's mine," I said.

"Explain," she demanded, and sat back with her arms folded, too.

I shook my head and leaned forward. "After Papa had seen you in the limousine waiting for one of his coworkers, I would hear them talk about you often. That was how I learned that you lived in this hotel and what you were doing."

"So?"

"So I was curious about you, Roxy. I used to think I might walk into you on a New York street. I know Mama hoped for that."

She relaxed, looking less angry. "If I wanted to get in touch with you and them, I would have."

"I'm sure you wanted to," I said.

She looked at me sharply. "Oh, you are, are you?"

"Yes, now that I've gotten to know you more, I'm sure. But you didn't because you were . . ."

"What? Don't tell me I was embarrassed and ashamed of myself."

"No, I think you were just afraid."

"Afraid? Of what?"

"Of how much you would realize you needed them, maybe not me as much but definitely them."

For a moment, she just stared at me. "So what are you going to be, a psychiatrist?" she asked belligerently.

"Maybe. I have a good background for it now," I fired back.

She continued to glare at me, and then she smiled. "Okay, but that still doesn't explain this," she said, holding up the envelope with the money and the note.

"I said I was interested in you. Neither Mama nor

Papa talked about you with any of their friends, of course."

"Of course."

"And those who did know about you didn't mention you in their presence. Papa wouldn't have stood for it."

Her eyes got smaller. "And?"

"And I didn't talk about you in school, either, except with the girl who was my best friend at the time."

"That fat girl at the funeral?"

"Yes, Chastity Morgan. I was always planning with her to see if we could see you. I told her where you were and what you were doing."

"What did Papa say about your doing that sort of research?"

"He didn't know about it. Neither did Mama. Finally, one day, we came up here after school and stood across from the hotel, waiting to catch a glimpse of you. I was afraid to ask for you, of course."

"Of course. Papa would have disowned you, too, if he had found out."

"We were about to give up when we saw you come out and followed you to a boutique. We watched you try on a dress, that black one you wore two nights ago, and then we followed you to where you met a woman for coffee. An older man joined you. I stayed far enough away, but Chastity overheard you speaking in French."

"Mr. Bob," she said, nodding.

"Who is he?"

"The man who saved my life, I suppose. He brought me to Mrs. Brittany. I still don't get this," she said, holding up the envelope.

"I got involved with someone at the school, Evan Styles."

"Martin Styles's son?"

"Yes. You keep up with politics?"

"I know who he is. So?"

"Chastity became annoyed because I was ignoring her and wouldn't go back to spying on you. One day, she told someone about you at school, and it spread very quickly. Evan's father was running for Congress, and when his parents found out, he broke up with me, not that we had gone together very long, but it wasn't pleasant. More stories were spread, nasty things said, and stuff like that."

"I see. And now it's worse because they know you're living here with me?"

"Yes."

She looked at the envelope. "So that's the joke? They think you're—"

We heard the front door open and close. I knew there was only one other person with the key. We both froze in anticipation until Mrs. Brittany sauntered into the kitchen. She was wearing a dark brown pantsuit with a frilly collared blouse. Her hair was shaped and styled, and she looked made-up to attend an important event.

"Sisters having a bit of dinner?" she asked, disarmingly pleasant.

Roxy recognized something frightening in her voice and demeanor, however. "I had nothing on for tonight, Mrs. Brittany."

"Oh, I know, although if we followed up on the requests for you, you'd have something every night."

"What do you mean?" Roxy asked.

Mrs. Brittany looked at me, and her face hardened, her eyes turning to ice cubes, her lips tightening. "We've been inundated today with requests for Fleur du Coeur."

"What? What do you mean? Who's calling?"

"Obvious nuisance calls. Ridiculous and at times filthy statements. I had someone put a trace on them for us, someone with authority," she added. She turned to me. "Do you know who Evan Styles is?"

I felt the air rush out of my chest and the rock tumble into my stomach.

Roxy turned to me. "You told them my telephone signature name, too?"

"I didn't. Chastity did," I moaned.

"What is this, Roxy?" Mrs. Brittany asked. "What is she talking about?"

"Sometime before my sister came here, she and her girlfriend spied on me. They found out I was known as Fleur du Coeur, and the girlfriend told her friends. She was just revealing that to me when you came, Mrs. Brittany."

"I've taken action to put a stop to it. I think Martin Styles will see that it's done," she added, "but this is not very good for us, Roxy."

"I know. I'm sorry. We'll deal with it."

"I don't like my business threatened," Mrs. Brittany said, mostly for my benefit.

"I'm sorry," I said.

"If you were so intrigued with what your sister does, perhaps you should think about it for yourself," Mrs. Brittany told me.

"No," Roxy said, a little more sharply than she had intended, I'm sure. Mrs. Brittany turned to her angrily. "I mean, she has other opportunities. Please, Mrs. Brittany, let me handle things."

"This is already more of a problem than I had expected," she said. "I wouldn't want to see anything else, any more surprises. Who knows what else she has done? Maybe sweet sisters bunking together isn't as innocuous as we hoped."

"It will be. I'll handle it. I promise," Roxy repeated, sounding more like someone pleading.

"I have an important charity event at the mayor's mansion," she said. "We'll talk about this later."

She turned and started out. Roxy looked at me and then leaped up to follow her and speak to her again at the door. I put my elbows on the table and lowered my head to my hands. I should have told her everything much sooner, I thought. It takes so long for two people to build real trust between them, even two sisters. Maybe it's even harder for two sisters.

Roxy returned, looking quite subdued.

"I'm sorry," I said.

"Stop saying that. After a while, it has no meaning. I learned that from Papa a long time ago." She sat.

"What's going to happen?"

"Nothing. Yet. But you had better be extra careful about what you say and to whom you say it, especially in school," she warned.

"I hate being there."

She thought a moment. "Maybe it would be easier if you started in a new school. Let me look into it. In the meantime, you have a spring vacation coming up soon, don't you?"

"Two weeks."

"Maybe we'll go to France," she said.

"Really? I'd like that."

She nodded, and we returned to our dinner.

I knew my life at school wasn't going to get any better, especially now that Evan had gotten into trouble. The looks of lust and the dirty humor directed my way turned into angry and hateful glances when he had told his friends. Exaggerated stories circulated about me. Every morning, I felt as if I was entering a nest of vipers, the girls in my class hissing at me, the boys smirking, and even my teachers looking at me suspiciously. By now, they all knew I was living with Roxy, and I was sure they knew who Roxy was and what she did.

It got so I felt self-conscious when I put on makeup. I eventually stopped wearing even lipstick, and I would spend far too much time agonizing over what blouse or skirt to put on. While other girls were actively trying to be prettier and sexier, I was trying to look more like a girl from some extremist group who thought sex was the path to fatal sin. I was hoping that the plainer I looked, the less attractive I made myself, and the more uninteresting I became, the closer I would be to invisible. Not only would they not see me, but they would stop talking about me. I felt so shut up inside myself, so tightly wrapped, that when the school day ended and I stepped out of the building, I was like a prisoner who had been released from solitary confinement. The moment I was back on the street, I let my hair down, unbuttoned the top buttons of my blouse, and felt my whole body defrost.

As soon as I arrived at the apartment, I practically ripped off the clothes I had come to despise. It felt so liberating to be naked. When I looked at myself, at how my figure had developed, I grew even angrier. Once I had wondered if I would ever be pretty, attractive, and exciting to boys. Now I knew that I was head and shoulders above most of the girls in my class, and yet I had to hide it. Even Richard, the shyest, sweetest boy I knew at school, avoided me. How ironic all this was.

I lived with my sister, who had to be beautiful and sexy, who had to be someone men were proud to have beside them, men who wore her like some expensive piece of jewelry, the trophy girl who made them the target of other men's envy. And then there was me.

I had to be the exact opposite, hidden in my room, gagged and tied and shut behind doors. I couldn't have sexual feelings, fantasize about any boy, or dream about a wonderful love affair. I couldn't look at any boy with interest or smile or flirt. Alarms would sound. Fingers would begin pointing. What everyone expected would occur. I would show that I was the sister of Fleur du Coeur, a budding second flower drawing the innocent to peer between her blossoms and then, like a Venus flytrap, close around them and steal away their reputations, corrupting them forever.

When Roxy first said I would live with her, I had felt a surge of excitement come into my body. I was going to be permitted to enter her exotic and glamorous world. I was going to learn about real life and be freer than ever, living in an expensive hotel, going to the finest restaurants, wearing the most exciting clothes. Merely walking with her on the street would make me feel special.

But instead, I had put myself in a different kind of prison. I was more restricted than I had been under Papa's stern supervision. I had to laugh to myself thinking about his reaction now. He forbade my knowing Roxy. He was always afraid that I would turn out to be too much like her, but here I was, because of her, being almost the exact opposite. I'd probably have more of a normal teenage girl's life if I had gone to live with Uncle Orman and Aunt Lucy.

I couldn't help being bitter about it. What would I become? Where would I eventually go? What kind of romantic life would I ever experience? Would transferring to a new school, even a public school, really make a difference? What would happen if someone there also discovered whom I was living with? How fast would the stories spread? How quickly would boys, maybe one I fancied, start to look at me as no one to have a relationship with but only someone with whom to have a one-night stand?

Once Roxy was my forbidden sister.

Now I was the forbidden girl.

One night a few weeks later, I put on my robe and sat on my bed feeling sorry for myself, mumbling like some bag lady on the street. It was a school night. I had plenty of homework to keep me busy and help me avoid thinking about all of this, but I was in a foul mood. Defiance washed over me. I rose and went out to Roxy's bar and poured myself half a glass of straight vodka. It was the one hard liquor I had drunk and, in smaller amounts, enjoyed, especially with some fruit juice. Tonight I wanted the buzz faster and longer. I sat at the bar and sipped it, and then I put on some music.

I hadn't spoken to Roxy since the night before. She had overslept, and I had left for school without seeing her in the morning. She hadn't left me any notes when I came home, telling me about where she was or what she was doing. Usually, she was very concerned that I knew her schedule well in advance, especially if it would involve me sleeping in the hotel room instead of in the apartment. I thought she had a lot on her mind since the confrontation with Mrs. Brittany, however. She seemed more distracted with her own thoughts, even a little more secretive at times.

I was half through with my drink when I heard our door buzzer. It was too early for any dinner delivery, I thought. Perhaps something had been sent to the hotel for Roxy or me, maybe something from Uncle Alain in France. I tightened my robe and went to the door.

A man only an inch or so taller than me, dressed

in what, thanks to Roxy's tutoring, I knew to be a Giorgio Armani two-button gray pinstripe suit, stood there with an ever-widening smile, showing small teeth and large nostrils. He had dark brown hair and one of those perfect tanning-salon complexions. On his left pinkie finger, he wore what I thought was an overly big diamond ring. He also had a jeweled Rolex.

Roxy taught me always to look at a man's shoes closely. If they were polished and/or Italian leather, you knew that he was closer to the real thing, the real thing meaning wealthy.

"Those who fake it most often overlook their shoes," she said.

Walking with her, watching people moving on the sidewalk in front of a café window, or scrutinizing men and women when they came into restaurants was how she taught me about clothes and people.

"When you've lived the way I have, you have to rely on good instincts, but you need to read people faster and more accurately. Often, there's no time for corrections."

"Corrections?" I asked.

"Defensive moves," she added. She didn't go into what they might be or why they would be necessary.

"Yes?" I asked the man at the door.

"Yes? I'd say yes," he replied. He looked at his watch. "I don't think I'm too early."

"Oh."

My mind reeled with the possibilities. Did Roxy

mess up an appointment? Had she forgotten? Was it this man's fault? Did he make a mistake?

"Oh? Don't panic. I can come in and wait," he said.

"No. I mean, you're here to see Fleur du Coeur?"

"That's the plan," he replied, still holding on to that wide smile. It looked as if he had a walnut in each cheek.

I considered what to do. I couldn't just turn him away. I had to call Roxy on her cell phone to tell her he was there and see where she was and what was happening.

"Yes, come in," I said, stepping back.

"Nice place," he commented immediately. He looked at me as I closed the door. "So what's the story? You need help getting dressed? That part of the night's activities?"

"No, no," I said, pinching the sides of my robe closer. "I'm not Fleur du Coeur. I'm . . . someone else."

"What do you mean?" He looked into the apartment. "There's someone prettier than you here?"

"Yes, but . . . she's late. I'll call her. Why don't you fix yourself a drink?" I added, nodding at the bar. "Everything's there."

"Late? How late?"

"I'll call her right now," I said, hurrying into the kitchen.

Roxy answered on the first ring. "What's up?"

"There's a man here to see you."

"A man? What man?"

"A client, Roxy."

"I have no appointment tonight," she said. "Where is he?"

"I had to let him in. I told him to make a drink for himself while I called you."

"What's his name?"

"I didn't ask."

"It's a mistake," she said, but she didn't sound confident of that.

"Where are you?"

"I'm only ten or so minutes away."

"What should I tell him?"

"Tell him . . . I'm on my way," she said. "M."

"What?"

"Don't tell him anything about us. I mean, don't tell him anything true."

"I understand."

"It's important," she said.

"Okay."

She hung up. I stood there for a while. My heart was thumping. I had no idea what I would say or do if he asked any questions. He was sitting at the bar and turned quickly when I entered the living room.

"What's going on?"

"She's on her way," I said.

"Yeah, well, I don't understand why she wasn't here waiting. Time's money," he added. He downed what looked like a glass of straight whiskey. Then he looked at me. "So who are you? How do you fit into this? You another flower girl or something? I didn't know about you. I like younger women, especially pretty younger women."

"No, I'm just a . . . roommate."

"Just a roommate? I don't know how you could be just a roommate," he said. "You got a date tonight?"

"No, I don't . . . I'm not . . . I'm just a roommate," I said. "You want another drink or maybe some cheese and crackers?"

"No, I don't want cheese and crackers, and I'm not here to get bombed, Miss . . . say, what's your name?"

"My name's not important," I said.

"Oh, more mystery, huh? I like that." He gave me that wide smile again.

"I have to get dressed," I said, and started away, but he reached out and seized my wrist.

"Naw, you don't have to get dressed yet. You just told me you're not going on a date. You can keep me company."

"Well, it's not a date, but I'm meeting someone."

"That's not a date? More mystery?" he said, and pulled me a little closer. "You smell fresh. Just take a shower or something?"

"Please. You're hurting my wrist," I said. He was holding me very tightly, his grip burning my skin.

"Oh, sorry," he said, releasing his grip on my wrist, but then he seized the belt on my robe. "What are you really, the warm-up girl? Like an act before the main act or something? Because I don't mind."

I shook my head.

"You invited me in for a drink. Is this some role-playing game, part of the service? Because if it is, I like it."

"No."

I backed away, but he held on to my robe's belt.

"Please, let me go," I said.

"I like that. Pleading. Sexy," he said, getting off the stool. He tugged my belt and then reached for me, taking hold of the collar of the robe. "How about we get it on first, then?" he said. "Pass the time?"

When he brought his lips toward me, I pushed on his forehead, and then I spun, slipping out of the robe and running naked to my bedroom. I heard his laughter as I locked the door behind me. Shivering with fear, I hurried to put on a blouse and a pair of jeans. He came to the door and tried the knob.

"Hey!" he yelled. "What is this?"

"Please. Go away," I said, crying now. He rattled the knob. I thought he might break the lock, but suddenly, he stopped. I held my breath, and then I heard Roxy's voice and him walking away from my door.

23

I didn't leave my room. Still trembling, I returned to my bed and sat waiting to see what was going to happen. I heard the music get turned off, but I didn't hear any voices. The silence made me even more nervous. What was going on out there? Did Roxy realize she had forgotten a date? Was there a real mix-up, and was she explaining it to him? Would it matter to him?

I began to worry about Roxy. Although the man wore expensive clothes and jewelry, there was something very common and streetlike about him. My mind spun with images from mobster movies. I paced in my room, stopping when I thought I heard someone shouting. It grew quiet, and then it sounded as if something hit the building. I held my breath and listened. This time, I heard footsteps, and then I clearly heard the door slam. Was it the front door or the door to Roxy's bedroom?

I went to mine and pressed my ear against it, listening. It was very silent again, ominously silent this time. If the man had left, why didn't Roxy come to see me? Terrified but seeing nothing else I could do, I unlocked the door and opened it slightly. Still, I heard nothing.

My first thought was to close it again and wait for Roxy. Of course, she could have left with the man, but if she had, she surely would have come by to tell me she was going, wouldn't she? There was no point in her pretending there was no one but her there now. I waited and listened, and then I began to move slowly toward the living room. I kept as quiet as I could. There was no one there—no one at the bar and no one in the kitchen or the dining room. The apartment was still dead quiet. Nothing looked moved or touched. His whiskey glass was still on the bar.

I paused and listened for voices again but heard none. *Dare I do it?* What else could I do? I had to find out what was happening. I practically tiptoed to Roxy's bedroom. The door was closed. My heart was racing so hard and fast I thought I might faint in the hallway. After every few steps, I paused to listen. It was too silent. Roxy must have left with him, I concluded, and went to her door. I stood there for a moment, and then I pressed my ear against it to listen for voices, sounds, anything. I thought I heard a sob.

I certainly didn't want to confront that man again, but I had to do it. I had to take a chance.

"Roxy?" I called. "Are you there?"

It grew silent again.

"Roxy?"

"Go back to your room, M. I'll talk to you later."

"Are you all right?"

"Go back to your room," she ordered.

I started away but then stopped and brought my ear to the door again. I didn't hear the man's voice. I thought I heard the water running in her bathroom sink. Very gingerly, I turned the doorknob and opened the door a little more than an inch. Through the crack, I could see into her bathroom. The door was open, and she was bent over her sink. I heard her gag and spit, and then, when she raised herself, I could see her in the mirror. She had what looked like a black-and-blue mark on the left corner of her mouth, and her lip looked swollen. I pushed the door open. There was no one else in the room.

"Roxy!" I called.

She spun around. "Get out!" she screamed, and slammed the bathroom door closed.

I stood there, even more terrified than before. "What happened? What did he do to you? Who was he?" I asked.

She didn't reply, but I didn't move. Finally, she opened the door and looked out at me.

"This is the first time this has happened to me," she said. "There was a real screw-up. I had no appointment tonight and certainly wouldn't have had one with someone like him if I knew anything about him." She pressed a cold washcloth against her mouth.

"He hit you? Why did he hit you?"

"I wouldn't do what he wanted."

"What did he want?"

"Forget about it, M. It's over."

"No. Tell me," I said.

She sat on her bed. I went over and sat beside her. She kept her gaze on the floor.

I put my hand on her shoulder. "Should you go to see a doctor?"

"No, of course not." She took a deep breath.

"Did he hit you anywhere else?"

"No. This was enough to satisfy him," she told me.

"What did he want, Roxy?"

She studied me a moment and shook her head. "He wanted me to bring you into the room."

"What?"

"You know, a *ménage à trois*. Satisfied?"

"I thought you said the men, the clients you have, are all well screened, that this sort of thing can't happen."

"I told you. This was the first time." She thought a moment and then said, "Maybe it wasn't such a screw-up." She rose and went to her window to look down at the street.

"What do you mean, maybe it wasn't?"

"Mrs. Brittany has funny ways of making a point. She's been on me about this sister-act idea of hers ever since she came here to bawl me out. She's always reminding me about how much she has done for me, pressuring me. I owe her. I can't say no."

She turned to me.

"So you see, Papa was right to tell you to stay away from me," she added.

"No, he wasn't right," I said, shaking my head. "You only tried to help me."

"Right. I'm a big help. You should have gone off with Uncle Orman and Aunt Lucy. None of this would have happened. We both would have gone our own ways and not hurt each other. I only made trouble for myself."

I felt the tears building around my eyes. "That's not so, Roxy. I wanted to be with you. I needed you."

She looked up sharply. "No one needs me, except Mrs. Brittany."

"You're wrong."

"Yeah, well, it wouldn't be the first time I was wrong. Just go about your schoolwork, M. Dinner should be up soon. Eat it yourself. I'm not very hungry, and it probably will hurt to chew anything for a while."

"What about the man?"

"What about him?"

"Are you just going to forget about this?"

"I'm not about to call the police or anything, if that's what you mean. He's gone. I'll deal with it in my own way."

She returned to her bathroom and closed her door. I heard her running a bath. I left, and on the way back to my room, I heard the buzzer. I was afraid the man had returned, but when I looked through the keyhole, I saw that it was the delivery boy from the restaurant. I opened the door and took the food, but I had lost my appetite, too. I tried to eat a little, taking my time and hoping that Roxy would come out for something, but she didn't. I was certainly not in the mood to do any homework.

Later, I heard her come out, but before I could say anything, she told me she was leaving. I imagined that she was off to see Mrs. Brittany. I didn't know who else she would go to for anything. I watched the clock, tried to work, but couldn't concentrate on anything. It was nearly eleven by the time she returned. As soon as I heard her come in, I charged out of my room.

"What happened? Where were you?"

She took off her jacket and flopped onto the sofa.

"I was right. She sent this goon up. I think she really believed that I would involve you if I was faced with it and knew it would please her."

"What did you tell her? What did she do when she saw your face?"

"She was sorry about that, but she said I'd live. Mrs. Brittany is not big on sympathy, especially if she thinks you are partly to blame. She reminds me a lot of Papa."

"But what did you tell her about her idea? I mean, involving me in . . . ?"

"I told her I would work on the idea."

"You did?"

"Sure. I can stall her and get her off our backs for a while. Maybe after time passes, she'll forget about it."

I didn't believe it for a moment. One thing Papa had taught me was never to fool yourself. *"Burying your head in the sand, even for a short time, is self-defeating. Prepare yourself, and train for trouble. Face your problems and challenges head-on and defeat them,"* he often preached, as if I really was in his army. I was sure it was advice his own father had given him.

But I saw that Roxy wanted me to believe that she had things under control, so I kept quiet.

"I told Mrs. Brittany you had a holiday coming up and I would use the time to work on it. I told her we were going to France. That was part of what I was doing today. I made our ticket arrangements. You're out on Friday, and we're off on Saturday. I've called Uncle Alain. He's very excited about it."

"Me, too," I said.

"Good. Just put this out of your mind. It won't happen again. I promise," she said.

"Okay. I left food in the fridge for you," I told her.

"Yeah, maybe I'll nibble on something. Thanks." She rose and then paused just before going into the kitchen. She kept her head down. "I'm sorry I said what I said before in my bedroom. I'm glad you're here."

Before I could respond, she went into the kitchen. I returned to my room, finally believing that I would be able to get to sleep.

In the morning, I brought her a cup of coffee before I left for school. The trauma on her face looked worse, but her lip wasn't as bad.

"Don't worry about this," she said, seeing how I stared at her. "Makeup does wonders."

"Is it really the first time something like this has happened to you, Roxy?"

"Some men are a little rougher than others, but no one has deliberately hurt me before this."

"How can you . . . I mean . . . how do you . . . ?"

"Go out with so many different men?"

"Yes."

"After a while, they all look the same to me. I don't have sex with all of them, M, if that's what you're wondering about. Some really are just looking for an escort, someone to make them look better at an event. It's an ego thing."

She paused and looked away and then turned back to me.

"I shouldn't say they all look the same. I've been with some very nice men, elegant men, men who treat lovemaking like a symphony. At least, that was the way Mrs. Brittany put it when I began. They're gentle, loving, and tender and then, like in some musical piece, bring it to a crescendo. You know, like in the movies when they show fireworks going off when people make love."

She paused again.

"You have a look on your face that reminds me so much of Papa."

"I'm sorry. I . . ."

"It's all right. I know who and what I am. See, this is why I didn't want to talk about myself right now, M. You understand?"

"Yes."

"It won't be the same for you. I mean, sex and love. It will be different, better."

"Can't it ever be for you?"

"I don't know." She smiled. "He'd have to be one helluva liberal-minded guy." She sat up. "I could get used to having my coffee brought to me every morning."

"I would do it."

"I know. Look, we're going to change things for you, M. We'll get you into a new school. You'll meet a new crowd of friends, everything. I'll get you out of Snob Central, and you'll be able to wear the clothes I bought you, too."

"I can't wait. You going to be all right today? Because I can stay home. It's no big deal."

"To do what? Take care of me? Believe me, I went through worse in the early days before I hooked up with Mrs. Brittany."

"You ever going to tell me about all that?"

"Someday, when you're desperate for nightmares," she replied, and I laughed.

"I'll see you later."

"We're going out tonight. A new place," she called after me.

"Great," I shouted back, and left the apartment.

We were having a beautiful spring morning in New York. The air was fresh and the breeze gentle, bringing hints of the warmer weather to come. I felt like smiling at people on the street and enjoying my walk.

How strange, I thought. I felt buoyed up because of our heartfelt and candid conversation that morning. I was full of new hope for Roxy and myself, even though we had both had a very bad experience, and in my mind, neither of us was well out of the difficulties that Mrs. Brittany could create. Last night was only the beginning of what could happen.

I smiled, thinking of how Chastity Morgan would react if I ever told her about it. The danger, of course, would be that she would spread the story so fast that it would reach Dr. Sevenson's ears. I had no doubt that she would put the child-protection service on us and get me away from Roxy. Maybe Aunt Lucy or Uncle Orman had left her their phone numbers just in case anything untoward occurred. She could call them, and despite Uncle Orman's threat, he would have me brought to them and locked up in their world. No, I had to be very careful about what I said to Chastity or anyone else.

That didn't bother me right now. I felt above it all. The prospect of leaving for a new school soon and our vacation trip to Paris to see Uncle Alain put even more bounce in my steps. My whole demeanor changed when I entered the school building that morning. I said hello to classmates who thought looking at me would turn them into pillars of salt, raised my hand frequently in my classes to answer questions, and even though no one invited me, sat with other girls in the cafeteria.

Chastity couldn't help herself. The dramatic change in my behavior stirred her curiosity. She had to approach me to ask how everything was. I should have snubbed her. Look at the trouble she had caused by telling Evan and the others about Roxy. But I didn't want to give her the satisfaction of knowing it.

This time, instead of replying with a grunt or a monosyllabic "Fine" or "Good," I went into a vivid and enthusiastic description of the services at the hotel that were at my beck and call, the wonderful meals we had brought up for our dinners, including those delicious pastries she loved, and the luxury of Roxy's apartment. I explained all I was learning about fashion, the boutiques we explored, and the clothes Roxy had bought me, clothes I certainly couldn't wear there. Then I went into reviews of some of the restaurants Roxy had taken me to for dinners and lunches. Finally, I told her we were going to Paris for our vacation.

"We're going to stay with my uncle Alain and see old relatives but then go to shows and dinners and do some of the fun tourist things. We're going to be like real sisters traveling together, and since we both can speak and understand French, we should have a great time, don't you think? Money is certainly not a problem."

I saw how I had overwhelmed her. She was practically speechless, chanting, "Wow, that's great," after almost everything I said. Then I told her that when I returned from Paris, I might be able to invite her up to the apartment.

"Really?"

"Yes, but only you. Unless, of course, your parents wouldn't want you to have anything to do with me now."

"Oh, no. They've never said that. Besides, why do they have to know anything?"

I laughed to myself. Chastity was as easy to look through as an open window.

"We'll see," I said, but it was enough to get her very excited.

I shouldn't be toying with her like this, I thought. The Emmie Wilcox who was best friends with her not that long ago wouldn't be so cruel and conniving, but I couldn't help myself. She and the others had been so quick to condemn me, so eager to prove that they were better.

When I turned her loose on the other girls, she was eager to describe how exciting and wonderful things had become for me. The words exploded from her lips like tiny firecrackers, and her hands went everywhere with dramatic flair. I was sure she embellished everything to make it sound as if I had finally confided in her and told her the most secret and forbidden things.

They all looked my way. The depressed, forlorn, and pitiful Emmie Wilcox they had grown used to seeing, the girl they had beaten down with their remarks and disapproving looks, was suddenly more cheerful and happier than they were. I could see the confusion on their faces and almost hear the debate going on in their soft ice-cream brains. Should they become friends with me again? Was it worth the risk? Could they still be contaminated? Suddenly, they looked willing to risk it in order to hear about this illicit and dangerous world.

Sorry. It's too late for you all, I thought. *I'll be leaving this school and probably not setting eyes on any of you again.* But I wasn't leaving with a tail of shame between my legs. I was leaving even more confident and stronger. After what I had been through, no challenges or obstacles lying in my path would frighten me.

At least, that was what I hoped.

24

I was both excited and sad when Roxy and I were driven to the airport to fly to Paris. It had been so long since I had gone to France, and I had been so young, that my memories were vague. It was exciting because everything would be like new, seen for the first time. Also, I was looking forward to spending quality sister time with Roxy. Even though I had been sharing her apartment with her, we saw little of each other from day to day because she was out and often busy at night. Until now, there was a thick veil of secrecy hanging between us. After the candid talk we had the morning after she was beaten, I felt there was a rip in the veil. What she did, whom she saw, all of it, had been on a need-to-know basis. I had to be careful about what I said and what I asked. Maybe that was about to change.

Despite the act I had put on for Chastity and the others to make my life seem glamorous and fun, living in a hotel, even in an apartment in that hotel, still felt strange and uncomfortable to me. I had trouble calling it home, even in my own thoughts. I would think, *It's time to get back to the hotel* or *I'd better get back to the hotel,* never *I'd better get back home.*

The desk clerks and bellboys all had gotten used to seeing me, but I never failed to detect some lustful thought hiding behind their nods and smiles. I imagined they believed that either I, too, was in Mrs. Brittany's employ or I was being trained by her, soon to be one of her own. No matter when I entered the lobby, I felt I was running the gauntlet of lewd stares and comments. They undressed me in their minds and groped me in their dreams. Maybe that was why the first thing I usually did when I returned from school was to take a shower. By the time I had reached the elevators, I imagined their saliva and their eye prints stuck on my skin.

This trip that Roxy and I were taking was the first time in a very long time that I had left the city. I loved New York, just as Papa and Mama had, but escaping from the sad memories and getting away from the school and the hotel were like opening the windows in a house after a fresh rain. Maybe it was because of my French heritage, but I thought of France as home, too. I had family there. I knew the language and the customs almost as well as I knew my American customs and language. I was confident that none of it would feel strange or terribly different for me.

But I was also melancholy and wistful. This had been a trip that Mama and I were going to take. We had talked about it often. I knew she had been looking forward so much to seeing her family again. Now that I was older and could appreciate everything more, she had been eager to show me places and things she loved. She often said seeing something again through the eyes of your daughter was like seeing it anew. She had wanted to share in my wonder, my pleasure and excitement.

To ease the sadness and the pain, I told myself that I was taking her with me. She was inside me and always would be. Maybe when loved ones died, they didn't go off to another world but instead slipped inside you and curled up, waiting to be remembered or to do just what Mama wanted to do, live life through your eyes.

I was eager to know if Roxy had any of these thoughts and feelings. When I spoke about some of it on the plane, she became a little melancholy herself and revealed that she had been to Paris a few times but always on a trip with a client and therefore unable to make contact with any of our family. She said especially bothered her that she couldn't call or see Uncle Alain, but it was just not possible.

I wanted to ask why it wasn't possible, but I knew. It was because she didn't want him to know how she had gotten there, whom she was with, and what she was doing. She hated saying it, probably even thinking it, but despite the face she put on, she was ashamed. Right now, I could see that remembering that made her sad.

However, she also remembered places and things Mama had loved. She admitted going to the Left Bank on one of her trips to search for a particular café Mama had described to her when she was just a few years younger than I was and still living with our parents.

"I found it, and I was able to spend an hour there, sipping coffee and watching people and thinking of Mama sitting there just as I was. We'll go there," she promised.

Perhaps it was wishful thinking or just my over-working imagination, but as we traveled farther and farther from America, from New York in particular, I thought I felt a change in Roxy, a softening. She looked more like someone who was escaping than I did. I could see it in her smile and hear it in her voice when she spoke to flight attendants and to me.

Was it possible? Could we erase all of the ugly and nasty things that had happened to us simply by taking this trip together? Was it our own private pilgrimage, our religious journey, that would cleanse us and renew us? Were we like visitors to Lourdes or some similar holy place looking for miracles? Perhaps it was wrong to put too much weight and pressure on a two-week vacation, but I could at least tell myself that it was a transition to something better.

We had already decided before we left that even though I had only two and a half months remaining in the school year, I would transfer to a public school when we returned. She promised me that I wouldn't even have to go back to my old school for one day. She would take care of it all.

"I'll deal with your Dr. Sevenson," she said, obvi-ously eager to confront her.

She told me that she had someone working on the

arrangements and paperwork for us while we were away.

Roxy always seemed to have someone in some high place doing things for her. The lawyer she had hired to handle Mama's estate and the sale of the town house was very efficient. The town house had been sold two weeks before our trip, and the proceeds were placed along with my other inheritance in funds and accounts that would earn interest and provide for all of my needs and my college education. Roxy was determined that I go further in education than she had and have a profession.

"You need to be able to support yourself. It's only when you are dependent on others that you are forced to make compromises you later regret," she said in a very pensive moment. "That was one of Papa's lessons that I refused to learn, and I suffered for it. Make something of yourself, and whatever you do, don't put all your hopes on a man."

"You sound as if you hate men," I told her. I thought that was ironic for someone who was so involved with so many men.

She laughed. "I'm a fisherman who hates fish," she replied, but then she became very quiet. I saw that she didn't want to talk anymore, so I didn't push her, even though my mind was under an avalanche of new questions.

Was there someone during the earlier years, someone she thought might rescue her, love her? Did Mrs. Brittany somehow prevent it in order to keep her working for her, perhaps telling her that she owed her, just as she had recently done? Or did this man simply learn too much about her and flee?

Without any formal education, how had she learned so much about people, places? How did she know how to hold a conversation with these obvious financial princes, captains of industries, wealthy entrepreneurs, and highly educated men? Was it all just sex?

She had told me it wasn't just sex, that sometimes she was really just an escort. Well, how did she know how to compose herself and be part of a conversation with people who were so successful? What did they think of her? Did she meet any really interesting men, men with whom she could at least dream of having a long relationship even if that was not possible? What were her fantasies now, her goals and hopes?

How often did she come back to her apartment and just cry? How often did she cry about losing her parents and me? Did she ever consider coming back to us? What stopped her? Was it just her pride, her stubborn pride, or did she think it was too late?

All the time I had been with her, I had lived with these questions buzzing around in my head like bees in a garden. Sometimes they were so close to the tip of my tongue that I actually uttered the first word and then choked back the rest. When I was younger and she was gone and I would think about her out there in the city, I felt sorry for her. Actually, when I learned that she was living in an expensive boutique hotel, buying expensive clothes, looking so beautiful and accomplished, I became angry. After all, she had defied Papa and hurt Mama when she had run off.

I had wanted her to be a ragtag young woman pan-handling in the parks or at the bus and train stations. I envisioned her sleeping under bridges, living in some hobo village, scratching and clawing her way into some safe place but always sleeping with one eye open, anticipating a drug addict or drunk taking whatever she had managed to scrounge together and maybe attacking her sexually. She wouldn't have beautiful hair and a beautiful complexion. She would suffer from some disease, always look in desperate need of a bath, and have bleeding feet because of shoes that didn't fit.

In short, she would be what Papa expected her to be, too, a victim of her own foolish and disruptive ways. Maybe that was why he was even more upset when he saw her that day in the limousine, flush and beautiful, healthy and enticing. She defied him and was not suffering. On the contrary, she was flourishing.

These thoughts zigzagged through my mind as we flew to Paris. Except for the times we ate together, Roxy and I rarely spent so long with each other with no one else competing for her attention as we did on the flight. She fell asleep, but I couldn't. When she was asleep and she didn't know I was studying her, I thought she looked even more vulnerable than I was. There was still something young and sensitive in her face. Asleep, without her guard up, she resembled me more. I saw movement under her closed eyelids and could only imagine what sort of nightmares she might have.

It was then that I realized why Roxy wanted to do what she did or how she could work for someone like Mrs. Brittany. She might never admit it to me or anyone else, but she was desperate for Papa. She threw herself at other men, luxuriated in their arms and under their kisses with her eyes closed, imagining that Papa had embraced her again. He was back. He would protect her.

These thoughts brought tears to my eyes. Without her realizing it, I laid my head softly against her shoulder and closed my eyes. I, too, fell asleep, and I was sure that if she woke up before me, she wouldn't move. My eyes did snap open when the lights came on and the flight attendants began making preparations for our landing in Paris.

"You okay?" Roxy asked.

"Yes, fine."

"*Oui, bien,*" she said, reminding me that we should rely on our French.

As soon as we retrieved our luggage and headed out, we saw Uncle Alain waving among other friends and relatives of other passengers.

"That's Maurice," she said, referring to the curly-light-brown-haired man beside him. He was a little taller than Uncle Alain and stouter. He had soft, almost rust-colored eyes and a smile that involved every part of his jolly round face. He looked like someone happily surprised at the sight of his own rarely seen relatives. In fact, he was waving at us as enthusiastically as Uncle Alain.

"*Bienvenue,*" they both shouted. Uncle Alain held out his arms, and Roxy looked to me to go to him first. Maurice kissed Roxy on both sides of her face and then embraced me and did the same while Uncle Alain kissed Roxy and took her bags. Maurice took mine.

"How was your trip?"

"*Très bien,*" I said.

"Oh, no," Maurice said. "If they speak only French, how will I improve my English?"

All four of us laughed.

"Maurice has made a spectacular dinner for you tonight," Uncle Alain said. "It is his day off today, but he's like . . . what do you say, a busman?"

"Yes," Roxy said. "It's called a busman's holiday when you do on your vacation or your day off exactly what you do when you work."

"Making dinner for two beautiful women is not work for me," Maurice said in perfect English. I complimented him on it, and he embraced me tighter and kissed me on my cheek. "I like her."

"You like anyone who gives you compliments," Uncle Alain told him, and, turning to us, he added, "He's always looking for praise."

"So? This is not French?" Maurice asked, and we laughed again.

How quickly I felt at home with them, and from the look on Roxy's face, she had, too.

We all got into Uncle Alain's Peugeot sedan and started for the Saint-Germain area of Paris, where they had their apartment. It was located on the famous Left Bank, known for its bohemian lifestyle. Their apartment was off the Boulevard Saint-Germain, a beautiful wide street that stretched for nearly two miles. There were cafés on the boulevard and near it. As we rode, Uncle Alain felt obligated to point out sights such as Saint-Germain-des-Prés, the oldest church in Paris.

"It was first built in 542 to house holy relics," Uncle Alain told us. "And then it was rebuilt in the eleventh century, the nineteenth, and again in the 1990s."

"Your uncle should be a tour guide, no?"

"He is just very proud of where he lives," I said, and Maurice turned around to look at me.

"*Voilà!* She is truly a special *jeune femme, n'est-ce pas?*"

"*Oui, mais oui. Elle est ma nièce?*" Uncle Alain said.

"Such an ego. Giving you credit for being special just because he's your uncle," Maurice said in English, and we were all laughing again.

They had what I understood was a very large apartment for Paris. It was on the top floor of a five-floor building that had been constructed before the United States was in existence. Of course, it had been refurbished many times. Their apartment had three bedrooms, a good-size living room, a dining room, and a very updated kitchen, which Uncle Alain called Maurice's studio.

"After all, a chef like Maurice is a true artist. You two rest up. Then we'll have cocktails and hors d'oeuvres and one of Maurice's signature meals. He's made the dessert, too."

Maurice stood next to him, looking very proud. We knew he had done much of the planning. The apartment was filled with delicious aromas. Roxy and I looked at each other gleefully and then went to our bedrooms. Just before she got to hers, she turned to Uncle Alain, who escorted us, and thanked him for what he was doing.

"What am I doing? Only what an uncle should do, *n'est-ce pas?*"

She leaned into him and in hardly more than a whisper said, *"Aucun d'autre ferait ce que vous faites."*

She hugged him and went into her room. He glanced at me.

Why was she so emphatic about it? I wondered. She told him that few uncles would do what he was doing. Doing what? Letting us be his guest for our vacation? I wasn't making little of it, but she made it sound life-saving. Then again, I thought, maybe in a way it was. Things weren't going so smoothly between Roxy and Mrs. Brittany now. Who knew what awaited her on our return? I put the thought aside and went to rest, shower, and dress for Maurice's dinner.

They had wonderful wine, and Maurice had made duck *à l'orange*. It was something Mama made on special occasions, but I had to admit, hers didn't taste as good as Maurice's.

"You're going to make his head explode with these compliments," Uncle Alain said, but when Maurice brought out his soufflés, it was impossible not to rave.

"Are we going to eat like this every night?" I asked.

I never drank as much wine as I did that night, and after our day of travel and all of the excitement, the bed looked like a cloud. I drifted into one of the most pleasant sleeps I had enjoyed since Mama passed away.

Uncle Alain was up early to go to his office. During breakfast, he told me about some of the work he was doing with international law, mainly involving businesses. From time to time, it took him traveling to China, South America, and other European countries. He had even done work in Russia. I told him how exciting it all sounded to me.

"Travel is wonderful. It fills your life, Emmie. It's important to be open to other cultures, other ways of thinking. I'm sure you'll find your way."

Maurice left shortly after he did. Preparation was critical for his cooking, and we could already see how much of a perfectionist he was. We were invited to his restaurant that evening. He warned us not to eat very much for lunch.

"You'll be given the chef's menu," he said.

"What does that mean?" I asked Roxy.

"You sample everything he's made for the evening, and with each serving, you get a different wine."

"How do you know these things, Roxy?"

She laughed. "I was trained like a seal. I've had the chef's menu in some of the finest New York restaurants, but I'm sure this will be extra special for us. Let's get going," she told me, and we were off for our touring.

I was jealous of how well Roxy knew her way around Paris. We took the Métro to the Arc de Triomphe and walked the Champs-Élysées, where Roxy splurged on some new French dresses for both of us. Neither of us used any English the entire time, and then she took me to have lunch at a restaurant not far from the Eiffel Tower. We decided we couldn't go up the tower right then because the lines were so long.

"Maybe before we leave, we'll have dinner at the Jules Verne," she said. "That's the restaurant on the Eiffel Tower."

"You've been there?"

She laughed. "Once or twice."

We were both careful to have only salads for lunch after hearing about the feast that awaited us for dinner, but the bread was so wonderful I couldn't stop eating.

"We'll walk more now," she told me. "We both need it."

We did, and she surprised me again with how much she knew about the buildings, the museums, and the fine restaurants.

"Really. How many times have you been here?" I asked.

"Maybe a few more than I said," she confessed. "I was with someone for a while who had a private jet that could get to Paris from New York."

When we reached Saint-Germain again, she found the café she said was Mama's favorite. We had some *café au lait* and sat looking at the Seine, the boats, the never-ending lines of tourists from all over the world streaming past us, all filled with the awe and excitement that came from being in Paris.

Maybe it was the magic of the city or just the magic

that came from being away from where we lived, a magic that blossomed out of the sense of freedom and adventure, but I felt as though Roxy and I had never been apart. We were the sisters we were meant to be. We shared thoughts and feelings, laughed at the same things, wondered about the same things. It was truly as though we had been brought up in the same home and not apart so many years. Was blood so strong that it could quickly mend the split we had endured, fill the chasm between us with an avalanche of the love we both shared and desperately needed? I hoped so.

"Weren't there many times when you had to be with someone you couldn't stand, someone like that man who hit you?" I felt brave enough to ask her now.

"You close your eyes," she said.

She knew that flippant response wasn't much of an answer.

"Look, M, it's really better that you don't hear about the ugly part of my life, and I don't relive it by telling you about it, okay?"

"Okay," I said, and then I added, "I wish you never have to live any of it again."

She was silent. "We'd better get back. We need to rest up for tonight. I think they're planning a big evening for us."

I nodded. She paid the bill, and we walked all the way back to the apartment, neither of us very talkative. When we arrived at the apartment, we decided to dress up. Roxy helped me with my hair and makeup. We wore the beautiful new dresses she had bought for us, with the matching high-heeled shoes.

When we emerged, Uncle Alain looked as if he was bursting with excitement.

"I can't wait to enter the restaurant with the two of you on my arms," he said.

It was a beautiful restaurant and already nearly at capacity when we arrived. Our table put us in full view of everyone, and from the way the waiters fawned over us, anyone would have thought we were celebrities. The feast began, and it was truly a feast. Maurice came out himself twice to explain the courses. The waiters spent time explaining the wines and why they were right for each preparation.

Many of Uncle Alain's and Maurice's friends stopped by our table and were introduced to us. Not all of them were gay. There were couples of all ages. They seemed to know so many people.

Later, after most people had left and the restaurant was calming down, Maurice came out to join us and told us more about the food, the places he had gone for recipes, and more about his own life.

Everything was dazzling, whether it was the stylish women and men who were there, the conversations, the music and the wine, or just being with Mama's brother and feeling that I had family again. Sometimes, maybe because of the wine, I burst out with things that made everyone laugh.

"Everyone is so friendly," I said. "It's like being in a small town and not one of the world's most famous cities."

"You'll see some small towns, too," Uncle Alain promised. "We have to visit my sisters soon. But somehow I think you're made more for Paris," he added, and winked.

Later, when we were home and getting ready for bed, I went in to see Roxy. She had just slipped under her blanket.

"Aren't you exhausted?" she asked.

"Still too excited. You want me to let you sleep?"

"No, it's all right." She patted her bed, and I sat beside her.

"Thank you for doing this for me, Roxy. I love them."

"They are sweet."

"How long has Uncle Alain been with Maurice?"

"I'm not sure how long, exactly, but more than ten years."

"Papa didn't like having a gay brother-in-law."

"Maybe he was threatened."

"What's that mean?"

"I don't know. I shouldn't say anything about him. I never got to know him. It wasn't all his fault, either. He was brought up in a very cold home. The military life his father imposed on his own family made it difficult to show emotion. Except for anger, which I was able to bring out of him like no one could. I wanted to hate him, M. It was easier for me," she admitted.

"I don't think he hated you, Roxy."

"I know. One of these days, I'll go to the cemetery and ask them both to forgive me."

"They will."

"Maybe they already have, through you," she said.

We hugged, and then she turned over to go to sleep. I sat for a moment before rising to go to bed myself.

I never felt as sorry for her as I did that night, but I never loved her as much, either.

Epilogue

The next few days became a whirlwind of touring. Uncle Alain was away on business for three days, and Maurice was very busy with the restaurant. Roxy and I did get up the Eiffel Tower, and Maurice, through someone he knew, got us reservations for dinner at the Jules Verne so we could see all of Paris lit up at night.

The following day, we went to the Louvre, where I could show off my knowledge of art, and we spent a day in Montmartre shopping for a painting Roxy thought would please Uncle Alain and Maurice, and of course, we visited Sacre Coeur. We had trouble finding a painting we thought was unique until we came upon one street artist who had done an oil painting of a man looking down into the Seine. The water reflected images above him that seemed to weave in and out of one another. It was one of the most special paintings I had seen. Roxy thought so, too, and we bought it. We kept it wrapped until Uncle Alain returned.

When they were both home, we presented it, and they both loved it. We had another special dinner at the apartment. The next day, Roxy and I took a tour of Versailles and saw the opulence and the great gardens. We listened to the lectures but broke for another wonderful lunch and later enjoyed another delicious dinner in Saint-Germain. We complained that we were going to have trouble fitting into our clothes, but neither of us gained a pound.

It wasn't the food I was excited about as much as our conversation, anyway. I let her talk as much as she would about other places she had gone and things she had done. She asked me lots of questions about Mama and Papa. Sometimes it felt as if she had been in a strange prison all these years and had just been released. If either of us got too maudlin, the other would change the subject.

One night, Uncle Alain took us to the famous Moulin Rouge. It was a wonderful show, and I saw the famous can-can dance. Afterward, Maurice joined us at a café near their apartment. The four of us talked into the early hours, but I never felt tired. I thought I could go on all night. Of course, Roxy and I had the privilege of sleeping late into the morning and then laughing about how decadent we were becoming.

Two days later, she wanted me to see the Latin Quarter, the fifth district of Paris, also on the Left Bank. It was named not for Latin people who lived there but because educated people once spoke in Latin. Here was the famous Sorbonne university.

"What a wonderful thing it would be to go to school in Paris," Roxy said. "That's one regret I'll readily admit to, M. My lack of formal education."

"It's not too late," I told her, and she laughed.

"Who knows?" she said. It was the first time she had ever suggested that she might somehow change her life.

That evening, Roxy finally admitted to being exhausted and was eager to say yes when Uncle Alain offered to take me to dinner at one of his favorite small restaurants. I didn't want to go without her, but she insisted.

"Aren't you feeling well?" I asked.

"I'm fine, M. Just enjoy a night with Uncle Alain. You really should get to know him better, too."

Reluctantly, I gave in and left her behind, but Uncle Alain was too interesting and entertaining for me to worry. He was almost as knowledgeable about food as Maurice. He told me how they had met and how much they meant to each other now.

"I hope it doesn't make you uncomfortable," he began.

"Oh, no, no. Not a bit," I said. I thought about how Papa would react, but I also thought about Mama and how she would get him to be more open-minded.

After dinner, he showed me one of his favorite places on the Left Bank, and we continued to talk about our family, our plans for me to meet the others, and how much he looked forward to showing me more of France. I thanked him and told him I was looking forward to all of that, too. We walked back to the apartment, and I listened and learned more about Mama, her sisters, and their early lives. He told me things about my great-grandparents that I never knew, especially how they had coped with the German occupation during the Second World War.

I realized I hadn't thought about Roxy all night until we entered the apartment, and I thought I would look in on her to see how she was, even though it was late. I tiptoed to her room and opened the door slightly, expecting to find her asleep, but to my surprise, her bed was empty. It didn't even look slept in.

Uncle Alain was in the living room talking softly with Maurice, who had just returned from the restaurant. They both looked up when I came hurrying in.

"Roxy's not here. She must have gone out," I said.

Neither spoke.

Then Uncle Alain picked up an envelope that was on the coffee table and held it up. "She left this for you, Emmie."

"What is it?"

I took it from him, looked at them, then opened it and read the letter.

Dear M,

By the time you read this, I will have left France. I am not running away from you. It's actually because of you that I'm doing what I'm doing.

Having had you with me, even for this short time, has woken me up. Perhaps it's ironic, but you were able to do what Papa wasn't, and that was to get me to take a long and serious look at myself.

I have never enjoyed my family or seen why so much of the world is beautiful as much as I have with you and because of you. In a real way, you have given me reason to hope and, probably more important, care about myself.

I am returning to New York to settle my account with Mrs. Brittany. You once asked me if there was someone with whom I could see myself spending my life. There is, but until now, he wasn't free. I received a message from him while we were in Paris, and he told me he was free and wanted me to be with him.

I realized after the bad incident we experienced at the hotel and by Mrs. Brittany's actions that you are simply not safe with me right now. On the other hand, I didn't want to send you to live with Uncle Orman and Aunt Lucy. I brought you to Paris because I wanted you to get to know Uncle Alain and Maurice, who both want very much for you to stay with them. At least, until you're old enough to strike out on your own.

While we were away, I did have most of what was required done. Uncle Alain will have you enrolled in the right school for you, and maybe one day, you'll attend the Sorbonne or another school in the Latin Quarter. I could see how much you love Paris, so I feel confident that you will enjoy being there.

Please forgive me for doing it this way. I

*was afraid you would argue about it, but if
you made me change my mind, you would be
taking away my new chance, too, and I know
you would be sorry forever.*

*I'll see you again someday, I promise, but
for now, think of Mama and Papa and how
happy they would be that you're not in my
world as it is right now.*

*Love,
Roxy*

I lowered the letter and looked at Uncle Alain and Maurice. "You two knew about this all along?"

"*Oui,*" Uncle Alain said. "She wanted it that way."

"This was the plan from the start?"

He nodded. "It was her intention to bring you here. You would make Maurice and me very happy if you would do what she asks and stay with us. For me, it will be like having my sister back, even if only until you are old enough to do whatever you want and go wherever you want."

"But . . . what will happen to her?"

"I think she'll be fine now," Uncle Alain said. "I'm doing what I can, too."

I shook my head. "I should have been told."

"Would you have let her go?" Maurice asked.

I looked at him. Tears were building behind my lids. I took a deep breath. "No," I said.

He nodded.

How I needed my mother now, I thought. I bit

down on my lower lip, and then I turned and walked out of the apartment. There was something about Paris that reminded me of New York. Neither city seemed willing to go to sleep. People were still walking the streets. I could hear music and laughter, and the wonderful lights twinkled like stubborn stars.

I walked and walked, pausing finally when I heard someone singing to an accordion. It seemed to be coming from just below the street on the riverbank. I made my way down to it and saw him on a bench.

He was singing *"La Vie en Rose,"* Mama's favorite. It was as if the city had hired him to entertain. Or maybe he was simply someone who had found his true love and couldn't lock up his joy and go to sleep.

"C'est beau," a man walking with a woman said. They paused, too, to listen.

"It's not just beautiful, it's true," I told him, but I said it in French: *"Ce n'est pas seulement beau. C'est vrai."*

They turned to me and smiled. They walked on, but they paused after they had passed our singer and kissed.

This is Paris, I thought.

I turned to walk back to Uncle Alain.

I would embrace him. I would embrace them both.

It wasn't Roxy who had brought me back here. It was Mama.

I was home.